Marketing and promotion will include a national
media campaign, bookseller/librarian outreach,
digital advertising, targeted newsletters,
social posts, and giveaways.

FOR MORE INFORMATION, CONTACT:
Rachel Fershleiser, Associate Publisher,
Executive Director of Marketing
rachel.fershleiser@counterpointpress.com

AMERICAN CROW

"An ambitious and mysterious novel about love, loss, and community, Ryan Burruss's *American Crow* digs beneath the troubled surface of a town haunted by the dark specters of violence and war. Burruss is a tremendous talent—his prose sings and dances, throws off sparks, flashes out bolts of bright lightning. He skillfully digs into his many characters' hearts and minds with delicacy, insight, and a deep wellspring of empathy. What a terrific debut!"

—Dino Enrique Piacentini, author of *Invasion of the Daffodils*

"From its shocking prologue to its inexorable conclusion, *American Crow* examines an America of veterans and war widows haunted by a violent past bleeding through the present. It is a postwar world in which each character is a riddle seeking to be solved, even if the solution is sometimes savage."

—John Biguenet, author of *Oyster* and *The Torturer's Apprentice*

"With a poet's eye for the darkness of humanity, Burruss has written a stylized noir that delivers on surprise and intrigue. In this layered tableau of postwar suburbia, *American Crow* tells an intricate tale of horror and desire where the townspeople of Brookshire, Maryland are haunted—veterans by the war, wives by their husbands, everyone by the past. Written with passion and intelligence, this debut aims high and exceeds expectations."

—Blake Sanz, author of *The Boundaries of Their Dwelling*

AMERICAN CROW

A NOVEL

Ryan
Burruss

Counterpoint
California

AMERICAN CROW

Copyright © 2026 by Ryan Burruss

First Counterpoint edition: 2026

ISBN: 978-1-64009-782-7

The Library of Congress Cataloging-in-Publication data is available.

Jacket design by Emily Mahon
Jacket image of forest © Peter Polter / Getty Images,
house © Patryce Bak / Getty Images,
soldier © FPG / Getty Images
Book design by Laura Berry

COUNTERPOINT
Los Angeles and San Francisco, CA
www.counterpointpress.com

Printed in the United States of America

10 9 8 7 6 5 4 3 2 1

Dedication TK

American Crow
Corvus brachyrhynchos

Common and widespread; certainly one of the best-
known birds in North America. Feeds on a great
variety of animal and vegetable food . . .

Common call the familiar, full-voiced *caaw* with great
variety of inflection and pitch; also a hollow rattle.

FROM THE *Sibley Backyard Birding Flashcards:
100 Common Birds of Eastern and Western North America*

You can never hold back spring.

TOM WAITS

AMERICAN CROW

PROLOGUE

⌣

APRIL 1944

"What in the devil?"

Stan Chandler stood frozen at his front window, steam from his coffee mingling with the smoke from the cigarette precarious between his lips, a tapestry of haze between his gawk and the pale morning outside.

He watched in an engulfing horror as his neighbor—Charlotte Dyson, the easy-on-the-eyes half of the young couple who lived in the squat little white house on its little hill across the street—wrestled with a push mower over her already-manicured lawn. Which in itself was odd, particularly at such an hour, and on Easter morn at that; however, what held him bug-eyed at the window were the even more disparate elements to the scene—how Charlotte wore only her thin nightgown, how she crossed the yard covered in red from about her middle down. Eagle-eyed despite his age, Stan noticed how the blood seemed to have already begun to dry, caking along her naked legs.

The old veteran suddenly snapped to attention, enough to spill a few drops of coffee on his carpet, elicit a muttered curse. Muscle memory from his days in the trenches, the war they called the great one, the war to end all others. Which, of course, it didn't. Probably fast-tracked this one more than anything, another generation of men sent over an ocean to save a world that almost certainly was more than a little mad, but had grown enough into itself to make such madness grievous, all-encompassing. Men refashioned into killers—and all that came with that. Men like Paul Dyson, the bloody woman's husband, just back from the Pacific himself. And maybe a little off-kilter, at that. A little peculiar. Maybe more than a little, if Stan were being wholly honest with himself.

He heard his screen door bang behind him before he realized he was outside. It had been forever since he had occasion to run anywhere, and his breath drew heavy around the bouncing cigarette, his chest instantly on fire as he crossed Tanager Way and up into the Dyson front yard, Charlotte now swinging the mower in loping circles, the blades like some medieval sword too big for her skinny arms. Stan managed to grab her from the side and gently remove the handle from her grasp, the mower falling to the ground with a muted thump.

The woman's face was a kaleidoscope of blossoming pinks and lilacs, even some blue green, the topography unsure, the corresponding swells and valleys just beginning to take shape; the eyes were tear streaked but empty. She murmured non sequiturs not quite at Stan—he wasn't even sure if she knew he was there. Warbly assertions that he wouldn't stop smiling, that he just did it, whatever it was. She shook in Stan's ropy arms, the ridges of her goose bumps betraying her chill; he realized she was freezing, so whispering his own non sequiturs, things about it being all right, how she'd feel better inside, he guided her back toward the house.

Once he crossed the threshold, though, he realized just how poor a strategy that had been. He pressed the already-open door with his foot, and his stomach sank as they entered.

The table by the door was overturned, the entire scene streaked with crimson, concentrated in two spots: one thick splatter of blood just inside a den off the main living room and another just outside the kitchen and almost at twelve o'clock from where they huddled, past the dining table. And beneath that final spray of wet red rested the mortal remnants of Paul Dyson.

Stan turned to Charlotte staring at whatever narrowing reality she could yet endure. He scanned her up and down, even patted at her, pawed—she didn't flinch. The wet blood on her nightgown didn't seem to be hers, or at least wasn't stemming from her. The red on her legs, he wasn't so sure—but he didn't find any wounds to which he could attend.

Stan bent and put out his smoke in a toppled ashtray that had landed right side up on the floor, then rose. "What happened?" he asked, and Charlotte just gazed back dumb. He shook her a little, then hesitated. "What hurts?" he called out, almost hollering, as though she were a million miles away. Still nothing.

Behind her—maybe beside her, he couldn't tell—he thought he saw something move. Like a shadow. Or—and this made no sense to him then or for years to come—like the wall itself had rippled. He looked away, then back. Nothing. Then he remembered something. "Where's the boy?"

This, somehow, resonated, rousing Charlotte, if only a little, from her zombie state. She blinked, and Stan could see how much worse the bruises appeared already, darker and meaner. Lumps like she, too, were rippling over bleak currents. "Boy?"

Stan nodded her along. "The kid."

Charlotte stared down toward her own middle, ran her small hand over it. "I didn't know it was a boy," she answered, her voice a kind of metronome. "It's gone. I know that."

Stan's lips pulled back in a tight grimace, the gravity of the situation, and his incapacity to handle it, quickly dawning. He patted Charlotte's shoulder and steered her to the bedroom, using himself as a sort of shield blocking her from the open gape of her husband's near-headless body. "I'm going to call the police," he announced slowly, as if speaking to a child. He had no idea whether that was actually how one spoke to children—he never had occasion to learn, he and his wife never having been so blessed before she passed. "Charlotte, I need you to get yourself decent." He nudged her toward the open closet carved into the far wall. "I need you to put some clothes on, okay?" She didn't answer, but he figured it was worth a shot to give her some privacy, at least while he went to look for the house phone.

Of course, it was likely in the kitchen, and he would need to pass Paul to get to it. A quick closer inspection confirmed the obvious—the man was deader than dead, and looking down, Stan could see straight into the skull's cavern, an empty bowl where the brains were supposed to be. A .45 was still locked in the corpse's grip. Stan's gaze searched the wall, the splatter pattern, and his jaw fell—he swore he watched blood run *up* into the stain's center. He ran his hand over his face and looked again, seeing no such thing. Maybe some of it was seeping into the drywall. Maybe that was all it was.

Either way, he was out of his league. He doubted the Appleton police the next town over wouldn't be, too, but he was also short on other ideas.

He could hear Charlotte crying softly from the other room. He remembered how she had held her stomach, what she had said: *It's gone.* His mouth was so dry he couldn't even swallow. Stan Chandler would call the law, just like he said. He had been around the block a time or two, though, and knew well enough that the law and justice didn't necessarily intertwine, at least not as much or as often as one would reasonably assume. He looked about the broken room, listened to his neighbor's muffled weep on the other side of a thin wall, and sensed he was being recruited to bear witness to some approximation of the latter.

1

The first anyone could recall of the bookbinder was when Miriam Hollanger spied him coming down the hill where Meadowlark Avenue met Sparrow Lane the day after the spring parade, the one where Sam St. Pierre got drunk, stumbled out of a car in the procession, and started cursing in front of the children. In that spring of 1952, Sparrow was still less road and more river of mud—an unpleasant, rusty sort of clay that stunk of gunpowder and rot. Miriam watched from the picture window that centered her living room, drying off a plate; she recognized the man's boots, ankle deep in filth, as military issue, same as the large rucksack he carried over one broad shoulder. He wore his hair and beard long, something primeval in the roots, a match strike in an otherwise muted palette, and he elicited a hitch in her, a flutter, a push, a pull.

In the wet, overcast days that followed, her neighbors spoke of the stranger walking the streets and streets-to-be of Brookshire, always looking square ahead, rucksack in tow.

Word spread that he might be a vagrant, but no one had any notion where he rested his head.

A week after that first sighting, Miriam ran upon the man once more, standing stoically before Stan Chandler at the register of Chandler's Hardware. The door's bell clanged above her, and she winced; the man looked up, his baby blues cold and flat, then back down at the change Stan was placing in his palm. He collected his purchase and silently slid past Miriam, leaving only a quiet growl of an apology and a hint of pipe tobacco, old burned forests, in his wake. The bell rang again, the door slammed behind him, and Miriam stood there in the front of the store, dripping from two straight months of rain. March had come in a drenched lion and left a sopping, choking lamb. April had kept the fashion.

Stan Chandler turned back to his day's paper, one hand gripping the counter, a long-ashed cigarette dangling precariously between his index and middle fingers. He sniffed and adjusted thick reading glasses with his free hand. "Madam Hollanger," he declared, not so much in greeting as stating a fact.

"Stan." Miriam pulled out a handkerchief hidden in her sleeve, wiped her face and neck. "This rain has been wearing my umbrella out," she complained. The store owner buried his assent in another sniff.

"I just stopped over at Roy Dickerson's office," she continued. "You know, business is still booming over there. He says the last of the lots will be sold by winter at the latest, probably fall. All this god-awful construction will probably be done by next summer."

"That's good."

"Indeed. It's been ten years." She paused. Her voice dropped a register. "I'd even venture to say it's gotten a bit crowded around here."

"Yep."

Miriam considered the store. "Lot of folks will be needing your wares, though, Stan. A man's castle and all that."

Stan looked up at this, his shrewd eyes mirroring Miriam's. "Sure hope so."

"Roy mentioned your customer. The gentleman that just left."

Stan's gaze tightened, the wrinkles around his eyes closing in like a long night's sky. "He just mentioned him, eh? Just like that?"

Miriam smiled demurely. "It's worth noticing, Stan. Stranger comes to town, nothing but the dirty clothes on his back and an old army bag, walking the streets, casing the neighborhood and God knows what else." Miriam slipped the handkerchief back in her sleeve. "It's queer, don't you think?"

Stan pulled a drag from his cigarette, saying nothing but peering out through the front window of his store, out past the parking lot and the sidewalk, the highway beyond. He gravitated back to his newspaper.

Miriam ran her finger across the edge of a can of turpentine on display, sighed, furrowed her brow as if she were looking into the face of some great and complex clockwork. "Roy just told me the stranger bought Doc Magruder's old place on Kestrel outright. In cash."

This revelation made Stan rise from his paper again, steal another look through his painted glass. Of course, his customer was long gone. He stubbed out his cigarette. "You don't say."

Doc Magruder's house sat on a corner lot a little more than halfway down a gently sloping hill near the eastern edge of town, where the forest held its line. The Cape Cod had served a dual purpose in its time, the top two floors as the middle-aged bachelor's home, the bottom—cut against the rise of the hill—as the office for his popular dental practice. Built into the slope as it was, patients could walk around back to the office's screened-in entrance without having to trespass on the doctor's personal space.

Almost a year ago to the day, though, just after the migrating birds had begun making their way back north, back to singing along the streets named for them, Doc Magruder had suffered a massive heart attack in the middle of delivering a root canal. He was not a large man, but it still took his assistant and Miriam, shocked out of her *Ellery Queen* in the waiting room, to pull Doc's slack body off Miriam's eldest child, Tess, the screaming, hysterical eighth grader on whom he had collapsed.

The house with a dentist's office tucked into the basement had sat vacant since that catastrophe, despite the efforts of both the good doctor's out-of-state family and Roy Dickerson—each on occasion pressured by one J. M. Brooks, a local developer and entrepreneur whom few in Brookshire proper had any occasion to know personally, but whom most unknowingly dealt with from afar. Nobody wanted another Dyson albatross—that little square of a house on Tanager had held vacant for years now, marred by a more salacious death inside its walls and what Roy had taken to calling "strangeties." The stories about the two bloodstains, of course, but other occurrences, too—like how the structure could appear bigger than its size in a way most folks couldn't equate, shifting one way or the other just out of the corner of an eye. And how some folks were struck with black thoughts, or even nausea, if they strayed too close. The affected would describe something like a pulse, a sort of baritone tinnitus.

But that second-albatross fear became moot when a tall, bearded stranger slid the Magruder place's full asking price in wrapped bills across the pockmarked desk of the third-ranked real estate agent in the county.

"I guess he's fixing to stay," Stan said, folding his paper closed.

"We'll see," Miriam shot back, her own baby blues cold and flat.

2

There was a time, and not too long ago, when Joe Hollanger was sure he would follow his big sister, Tess, over a burning cliff into a bed of salty razor blades if she asked—even now, he had followed her to the creepy Dyson house, albeit uninvited and holding back, hidden in the farthest corner of the yard. He watched her edge closer in the rain, hedge to hedge, his stomach dropping when she broke into a sprint across the yard and then down into the chasm of the basement entrance and out of sight.

His loyalty was not born of some romantic sense of sibling fidelity or chivalry, but from the basic nature of their existence—Tess was two years older, so she was the lead. This was the arrangement he was born into, and for the last twelve years and change, it had worked out pretty all right for everyone, all things considered.

But things were starting to change. Tess was changing. Joe was old enough that, if he could distance himself from the situation (he would sometimes, when no one was around, close his eyes and imagine a Ghost Joe stepping out of his body, and this Ghost Joe would observe real Joe and tell him what was what, especially when no one else would), he could accept that this change was inevitable, that both he and Tess were growing up, that childhood was beginning to loosen its grip, and they were becoming untethered in the way everyone does.

But mostly Joe just blamed her tits. It was Tess's tits that were making her crazy. Once those two mounds first pushed against her blouse, and then, seemingly overnight, sprouted into obnoxiousness, the weather inside the Hollanger house had shifted forevermore. Just as he trailed Tess, it were as if she trailed them, a zombie enslaved by two alien overlords embedded inside her skin. Their mother toggled between dramatic exasperation toward her eldest child and purposeful obtuseness, doubling down both on Brookshire chatter—the comings and goings of others' offspring, spouses, grievances big and small—and her own heroic, one-woman battle against dust and fingerprints. Against disorder. Chaos was eternally just around the corner, according to Miriam Hollanger, a scourge requiring constant vigilance.

Whether his current circumstances were inevitable, or the product of tits, or the inevitability of tits, Joe found himself alone more often than not these days. After their father died, he and Tess had grown close in a way others couldn't always see, the borders of brother and sister blurring into teacher, mender, nagger, protector, instigator, accomplice, confessor, punisher.

And now: stranger. Mystery. Alien. It was not a turn of events Joe particularly relished, but he had been around enough to know that his stance on an issue generally didn't affect its outcome. He would just have to deal with it. So he'd dealt with it the way he dealt with most unpleasant things these days—he'd gone for a long walk.

The Hollangers, or what was left of them, had been a staple of the neighborhood for most of Joe's life. Time being a relative player, a lot had changed in his young span, and he walked the streets and almost-streets with something verging on nostalgia, though if he allowed himself to think of it for too long, Ghost Joe would chastise real Joe for being foolish. Boys like him had their whole lives ahead, and there was no use looking back; he was a tadpole, and there was nothing interesting about a tadpole beyond its singular mission to become a frog.

The rain held, of course; it had rained for two months, steady if not always hard. The world was beginning to sprout, but a shade darker than most years, a soaked sort of hunter green. Grass grew too quickly and drooped, shaggy in even the best-kept lawns. Brookshire being a town still under construction, at least in pockets, the mud was not just unavoidable, but intrinsic; it was a part of life, seeping through clothes and into skin, its detritus scent invading noses, brains, dreams. It overran curbs where there were proper curbs, and ran like crime scene blood across every paved surface of the town, starting at the top of the hill where they had finally broken ground for the church and running all the way down to the lowest part of the valley, the southernmost border. Joe had overheard a neighbor couple after Mass—Father Jim held two on Sunday in the school gym, folding chairs for pews—complaining to his mother about water seeping into their basement. Joe turned from the conversation, from Miriam Hollanger's empathetic headshake and tongue clicks.

It all made him think of Noah, made something inside him crumple along well-worn lines. Noah was a dad, one of the more famous dads, in fact; Joe had no dad anymore, famous or not, and everything, even the *stinking* rain, reminded him of that hurt, made him sore. He kicked a rock and took a deep, hitched breath. He hadn't cried in a long, long time; he almost cried almost all the time.

Sergeant Joseph T. Hollanger (Joe was technically a junior, but since there was no senior anymore, he had quietly dropped it from his school papers, and nobody had stopped him) had something of the matinee idol about him. Handsome in a hard way, all sharp angles and straight lines, he had been career military. He had not been conscripted into the war, or a volunteer in the strictest sense—it was his calling, what he seemed built to do. Officers and subordinates both noted a serenity in battle that bordered on indifference, a courage that bordered on folly. The night before landing on Normandy's beachhead, he walked among his troops like Henry V in khakis, and reminded them that to be afraid of death was to be afraid of life, that one did not dance except with the other. Whether eighteen-year-old seasick kids bought into Sergeant Hollanger's makeshift Zen or not, they appreciated the effort and made peace with the possibility of dying for a man who was willing to die for them.

Sergeant Hollanger survived the initial landing, the long, hellish walk-run up the coast. The beach was a lottery, life or death a random matter of space and time, a universe in microcosm. Futures ended, timelines shifted, populations diversified, right there in the cold French sand. The sound of each fired shot, each gargled scream, would echo for decades and generations across oceans of guilt and silence.

But Sergeant Hollanger's end came after the beach, after the microcosm, in a quieter corner of battle. He and three privates (two his, one inherited in the melee) swept a blown-out gunnery at the top of a hill a few hundred yards from the main landing site. One of the surviving Germans— legs shredded, leaning against a blasted wall, his face pulled tight into a horrific grin, his cheeks gone—drew a Luger from his belt with his one good hand. Hollanger jumped in front of the three troops and fired; the Luger's bullet struck him through the bridge of his nose, and he was dead before his body hit the ground. The German likewise died *immediatement*, his brains left to drip down cinder block. When another officer came upon the three shivering, chain-smoking boys, all they could emit were variations on a theme: "Fucking Kraut. Fucking fuck. Fucking Kraut motherfucker."

Sergeant Hollanger saved three privates that day. He left behind a wife and two children. Had he lived, he would have deemed it symmetry.

Joe pursed his lips, kept trudging the streets of Brookshire. The rain had tapered off to a mist. Passing Doc Magruder's old place, he almost didn't notice the man perched on the rear slant of the roof, smoking a pipe and staring out over the bird-christened boulevards below.

3

Father Jim swirled the whiskey in his glass, struggling to pace himself. He sat alone at a small corner table, his favored spot in Wilson's bar, where he could almost disappear yet still keep tabs on the other patrons, their own lined faces veiled by rolling waves of cigarette smoke.

He tilted his glass, letting the liquor rest on his upper lip, letting it burn, then leaned into a healthy swig.

A reed voice cut through hushed, duskier tones: "You're going to tell me there's not something fishy about the whole thing?"

"Maybe it is, maybe it ain't."

The bell over the bar's front door tinkled; Father Jim and the other drinkers turned together, well-trained dogs.

"Well, speak of the devil," someone announced.

"Devil, hell!" Roy Dickerson barked back, and the room erupted. He wore a gray houndstooth suit, and his dirty-blond pencil mustache was severely trimmed at the edges, two shanks above his pearl grin. He strode up to the mahogany edge of the bar. "What's the matter, Wilson—can't pay your electric bill?"

"What are you yammering about now, Roy?" The owner's bark was gruff but good-natured. Big jaw and brow, Wilson looked tough enough to not need to be.

"It's always so damn dark in here."

"You think I want to see all these ugly mugs?" The room laughed again. Wilson poured a beer and set it before Roy.

"And a bourbon, too, please. Long day."

"You got it."

Roy waved to a recent client at the far end of the bar, then turned, caught sight of the priest, and nodded. Father Jim hovered his glass in a toast, then stole another drink.

Roy threw a peanut into his mouth, leaning over to the drinker beside him at the bar. "Should my ears be ringing?"

The man grinned under his cap. "Nah . . . we was just discussing one of your buyers, that stranger done come to town."

Roy's face darkened to match the room—just a shade, but enough for Father Jim to register, watching the Realtor's profile from his corner. "I see," Roy replied, the words quick but careful out of his mouth.

"There's tell he paid full price. In *cash*."

Roy demurred and, turning to face the patrons of Wilson's, leaned back, one foot pressed against the bar—a welcoming, graceful salesman pose. "Ah, boys, you know I can't kiss and tell."

"Did you pop a woody when he tossed all those greenbacks on your desk?" someone hollered. More laughter.

Roy smiled, but the cautious thing still held behind it, thick and smooth and hard to get around. "I've had worse days," he murmured after some thought.

"So what's he like?"

"Regular," Roy lied, taking a long drink from his bourbon, chasing it with his beer. "Quiet."

"He sure don't look regular. What's his angle?"

"Angle?"

"With all that stuff he's doing. Hammering all day, every day. My sister-in-law said four guys lugged in a giant rolling pin yesterday, big as a tree trunk. A rolling pin!" A pause. "He's building something in Doc's house—you know what it is?"

"I don't."

"You don't?"

"No. Honest."

Father Jim noticed the Realtor's hand tighten around his glass. His own mimicked the motion; he wasn't sure why, save that his years in the church had honed his empathy into a physical thing. Sometimes he imagined himself something of a radio for human strain, its peculiar wavelength. It was not a quality he often cherished.

The priest had heard tell of the man's appearance, of course, and was as curious as anyone about this new neighbor's perceived eccentricities. He himself, though—he admitted with the cumbersome bemusement of one who doesn't blink in the mirror—had dedicated his entire life to a figure who, for all intents and purposes, fit exactly the description of this very stranger. The layers of truths and hypocrisies chattering in his wake were not lost on Father Jim's mind in this slackened hour.

Roy cleared his throat to shoot back the rest of his whiskey, then placed its empty vessel softly back on the bar behind him. He had perhaps shared a little too much chatting on the sidewalk with Miriam Hollanger, but she had that way about her of talking like the tides, pulling you along until you heard yourself saying things you never intended to share. Here he would draw a line. "Guys, I hate to disappoint you. A man bought a house from me, and yes, he paid for it. I'm sorry, but that ends my concern in the matter."

"I call horseshit!" The commotion of the barroom rose, shifted, like static building. And then another kind of roar manifested a little farther off, something disconnected from this local shouting: Father Jim noticed Wilson's big box of a radio on a shelf over the bar, the huddled cohort of men leaning toward it, ears perked.

He called to Wilson from across the room. "What happened?"

The barkeep hitched his thumb back at the contraption. "Mele just hit a pair in. Three–zilch."

"What inning?" Father Jim hollered back.

"Bottom of the third."

"Plenty of time, either way," the priest muttered, looking around at the crowd now looking at him. He shot a glance at Roy Dickerson, ramrod straight, then quickly away. "Say," the priest offered, louder than he needed to be, "I heard we were looking to trade him."

The bar's collective jaw dropped. The commotion landed as an uproar, the patrons of Wilson's—their insight and expertise regarding the inner workings of the national pastime fortified by cheap beer and whiskey—off to the races, their arguments and agreements colliding against each other like so many mindless atoms. Roy Dickerson and his mysterious buyer, for the moment, were blessedly forgotten.

Roy stared at the priest, who made a point not to look back but offered a small, vague nod that Roy supposed was meant for him. The number-three real estate agent in the county discreetly bought the collar's next drink, a double.

⌄

Over the past week the rain had not so much ended as surrendered, seeming to call an armistice with the sun, and Roy Dickerson's evening walk from Wilson's was chilly but dry. The lot where the new Saint Anne's was being raised stood large before him, and he could almost make out the outline of what it would become; he had been privy to the blueprints. Father Jim hoped to celebrate this year's Christmas Vigil inside, and J. M. Brooks intended on being featured in the freshly polished front pew, clean as a whistle, or a New Year's babe. *Nothing to see here, folks.* In the meantime, the priest continued to say Mass from underneath a basketball hoop in the school's gym on the far side of the parking lot, abutting the highway.

Roy took a left into Brookshire proper, into the quiet blue black that overtook the big road's lights and engine coughs as one traveled deeper. He mulled why Father Jim had conspired to distract his inquisitors. Maybe it was just one decent guy looking out for another. Maybe something else entirely—he was not beholden to understanding the ways of the cloth.

Whatever it was, it had worked. Roy was relieved, because he had made a promise, and he was the kind of man who aimed to keep his promises—his bond was his word, he would tell prospects—not just because it was good for business, but because it was good for him. He liked that he could look a man square in the eye and not be ashamed of who he was, how he spent his days and made his living. He would disarm prospects with that big white smile; he wasn't noble—no sir, no ma'am—he was selfish. Being a straight shooter felt good, and he wanted to feel good all the time. They always bought it.

The man of the hour, though—the stranger everyone

seemed so fascinated by—required no such casting, no such bait. In fact, he had already been sitting statue still in one of the two folding chairs right inside the glass front door of the office when Roy arrived at work one wet morning. The uninvited guest had two walnut-size metal balls in his hand, rolling them in his palm, the rest of him unmoving, as if bronzed. Roy almost had a heart attack when he caught sight of him, assuming it an ambush.

"How did you get in here?"

The man had shrugged, disinterested. "I've been circling a house," he rumbled low, those balls just spinning, little chimes inside softly ringing, as if their song were being played from far away and Roy was just hearing it off the wind.

He handed Roy a stack that counted out to $30,000—five thousand more than the asking price for 600 Kestrel Street—the extra five earmarked for the Realtor himself to cover certain ethical inconsistencies with the sale. First, any corner that could be cut needed to be cut. Second, the man had no official identification and no real desire to supply a name; Roy registered the deed under a false one, a woman's he didn't recognize. It was fishy—practically Brooksian—but it was also five thousand tax-free dollars.

Lastly, the man asked that the details of their arrangement not be discussed with anyone. Roy, not just out of magnanimity, quickly agreed. Business was flourishing, but Brooks was always a bear, with his own skims and pecks, and there was always the burden of the house on Tanager to deal with—not just the rumors and tall tales run amok, but the unsettling episodes that sat barely hidden behind them. Technically, the bank owned the structure now, but the bank did whatever Brooks told it to do, so when Roy would beg up and down for someone to raze the godforsaken place and start over, it always fell on deaf ears deep in the pocket of other, deafer ears.

Even so, Roy's most immediate concern was how close he was getting to the end of the Brookshire pipeline, the sweetheart deals he could cut on the dwindling empty lots and new constructions. Ten years of shooting fish in a barrel were coming to an end, the town nearly complete. He would have to start hunting for his own food once more. And soon.

Left or right? Right, Roy would pass the rectory, which would stand empty for a few more hours, Father Jim just now beginning to feel the click, the loosening of the grips that seemed to multiply inside him. He'd pass it, the little adjoining church office, too, the landscape beginning its quick descent. He'd cut down Falcon Street, take it all the way down to Warbler. Or he could go left instead, take a more looping route along the retaining wall that guarded the high-ground houses on Robin Road, follow the trajectory of a nasty lefty inside curve, down to where the hill would meet the asphalt, where the houses would drop back to his level, the whole caboodle *then* taking its steep dive. He veered left.

Roy didn't want to discuss his newest client, because he felt the stranger was a slippery slope. He had not told his wife, Rachel, about the money yet. He did not know whether he would. He thought he might surprise her with something nice or, hell, a bunch of nice things. A new car? Airplane trips? Or perhaps he would sock it away, something to keep them afloat in lean times, keep them comfortable. Maybe he would invest it. Or put it toward the children's schooling. Roy had options. Because of this one massive and odd-looking fellow, he had options precisely when he needed them, and he was protective of those—and of the man who had provided them.

Before he knew it, Roy emerged on Warbler Avenue. He walked the few blocks to 1402, scratched at his hairline and stole a look at his plodding shoes as another figure passed in something of a rush.

He made his way up the concrete steps to the porch and slapped the big brass knocker against the door. He could feel the eye on the other side of the peephole, like on the back of a dollar. He tried to keep from smiling, his natural nervous reaction when he was being watched.

A tall redhead with the slightest hint of South Texas in her voice opened the door, feigning annoyance. "You're late."

"I didn't know I was on the clock."

The redhead let go of the robe lapels she was clutching over her chest. The whole thing loosened around her, revealing black lace panties, garters. Two other girls, younger than the redhead by half, were in the parlor, half naked and arguing over a Charlie Parker record.

"You come the same time on the same night looking for the same woman for two months straight, it becomes an appointment. Common law and all that, hon."

"I'm sorry," Roy said, not sorry at all.

The redhead's smirk was perfect in its crook, a spicy crescent. "I'll think of something you can do to make up for it," she said, grabbing Roy Dickerson's tie, pulling him in, closing the door.

Six blocks up the other side of the hill the real estate agent had just walked down, the strange man who now owned the house once belonging to Doc Magruder perched on his slanted roof, watching the comings and goings of the brothel with something like a naked eye.

4

⌣

The first volume appeared on a Thursday, its cover two-toned—an elegant jade against a buttery cream—in a material like silk, and it contained a collection of classic Norwegian recipes typed in their native tongue. It leaned against the concrete porch of 1402 Warbler Avenue to be discovered by an immigrant prostitute, all milky skin and abrupt angles. The young woman crouched to open the book where it lay, as if it were too heavy, or too precious, to lift. Mae came up behind her, could see the heave of her back betraying choked sobs, and thought it another goddamn man's mess she would have to clean up herself, until the woman turned, the tears shaking from a smile almost bigger than her face. Not knowing quite what she was dealing with, nor where it might lead, Mae did the only thing she could, leading the skinny blond to her Studebaker and driving her to the supermarket for ingredients.

The Norwegian made supper for the other girls, a delicate *rommegrot* with smoked salmon. They cleaned up just in time for nightfall and their first rush of customers. The men were tentative at first, uneasy with the smells of home cooking, of family, but the prostitutes fucked them like feral animals, fucked beyond caring about the money, and every single john who came that night was ruined forever, doomed to chase an elusive craving he would never quite be able to slake again. Such is the price of heaven.

The tomes blossomed around town with little obvious rhyme or reason. A series of Gothic architecture prints bound with golden thread and swaddled in layers of thin russet cloth was propped against Joe Hollanger's bedroom window. Farther up Sparrow, where the land swelled toward the Catholic school, the church to be, an old widower found a copy of *Troilus and Cressida* in his rose garden, scrawled on a scroll in a looping longhand. His neighbor across the dirt-streaked street discovered in her mailbox a perfect square of a book bearing detailed instructions on clock-making.

Returning from a long, wet lunch at Wilson's, Roy Dickerson discovered on his desk an illustrated collection of Victorian-era sea adventures . Before opening said bar one morning, Frank Wilson noticed something unfamiliar on the table nearest the door, a table he swore he had wiped down the previous night. It was a book of haiku, and the front cover, wrapped in a rough canvas, depicted Saint Francis and a small holy menagerie in seven black strokes. Wilson flipped a rag over his shoulder and sat down; the bar opened an hour late that day, but no one noticed.

Inside his store, Stan Chandler found a French translation of *A Tale of Two Cities* where a hacksaw should have been, a five-dollar bill pinned to its *table des matières*.

As the days came and went, the tomes kept materializing in unexpected places, distributed with an emerging logic that the town's residents could almost, but not quite, decipher.

⌄

Rebecca St. Pierre walked her little yard, looking for the morning's *Post*—the boy never seemed able to get it anywhere near the front door. She was exhausted; Ava had been up until nearly dawn, slamming dishes against the kitchen floor, seemingly to delight in their crash. She would break free from her mother's embrace and run to find the first breakable object she could, a banshee all the way, and smash it to sharp, useless pieces.

Her husband, Sam, had hidden first in a bottle of rye, then the basement, then out of their reach, the back door slamming behind him. He had still not returned home. His vanishings had been snowballing lately, both in frequency and duration, and Rebecca supposed she and Ava were probably the better for it; she could not fathom juggling both grenades at once— her broken daughter's and indignant husband's competing hysterics. She absently touched the small welt under her eye and held her fingers there, pressing until it hurt. Sam could be smart in the way snakes were, most of the damage blossoming around her ribs, but occasionally he slipped in his own eruption, an errant note, a lavender-tinged breadcrumb. There was relief in his exits, his flights into the night, but there was also almost always a receipt.

How could a man who had survived the forests of Germany, forced to watch Nazis crow across victorious battlefields, shooting his moaning buddies like children pop balloons— who saw firsthand the darkest underside of breathing, *endured*, and now enjoyed the security and privileges of a grateful home front—how could that man, safe in Brookshire and comfortable shoes, become so afraid of living? Of a little girl?

Rebecca had married a whole person, she was sure, but now whole pieces seemed to be falling away, leaving gaps where a man used to be. There was something rancid to Sam now, spoiled, and though she was uneasy with such a harsh verdict—thought herself even a little cruel for it—she knew it was not inaccurate. Rebecca tried to skirt resentment, not for Sam's benefit, but for her own and Ava's. She knew that her daughter needed a protector, and if it wasn't going to be Sam, she would have to don the armor and face whatever came their way with her own skinny arms. Her own bared teeth.

She was not a naive woman and accepted the future as it came, nothing more than an imperfect promise. She still couldn't help feeling tricked, though—she had married a warrior, she thought, but found herself surviving the shadow of one, a tape of a tape.

Rebecca recovered the newspaper resting on top of a tulip trying to burst through; she was turning back when she caught sight of a small black rectangle in the grass. She knelt and picked it up, dropping the *Post* to open the tiny thing, which turned out to be a delicately contrived prayer book full of incantations and pleas from untold faiths, in untold languages. Something inside her fluttered, recognized the most exotic of them as familiar, her own unwritten song, words she couldn't even read scratching against a raw wound she could barely acknowledge. *Someone saw*, the little black book announced, silent as it was. Rebecca could feel a cocktail of emotions rising, burning through, exacerbated by a profuse lack of sleep, shame dancing with relief only to have sorrow cut in.

She fell against her little dogwood tree, bone-tired, and slid the length of its trunk, the bark scraping her back. Rebecca didn't care; she balled her hands into shaking fists and let loose the tears that seemed to pound from inside her head, little fists themselves; she wept in long, looping convulsions.

When she finally heaved herself back up, Rebecca wiped her eyes and flattened her hair as much as she could. She looked around and started: A tall figure stood in the middle of Phoebe Street, man shaped, his jacket collar up and hands at his sides. The stranger's hair and beard were long, and she was surprised he seemed familiar to her, though she knew she had never seen his face before. Something about his shape, though: The man was well built, she could tell, and sturdy, the battered canvas jacket hanging from the broadest of shoulders, something like wings. Like a dream she could almost but not quite remember. As spent as she was, streaked with her night's toil, she still found herself carried by a surge, not just inside her but around her, in the space between the tiny, pale hairs on her arms and this man in the street, a drop in pressure, the trace of ozone before a storm. He stood still, staring not just at her but through her—into her little home, where her daughter—just turned eight, but nothing like any eight-year-old Rebecca had ever known—finally slept. Rebecca thought she saw some small twitch in his squared-off jaw, some tell of concern or strain. She had the sense, as unexplainable as anything else that morning, that he had not appeared for her at all. More raised hairs. The taste of pennies in her throat. She felt her lips part, but no words lent themselves to her tongue.

The little prayer book began to throb, and Rebecca dropped her gaze; she had pressed it so tight against her chest that it had dug into her breastbone. When she lifted her eyes again, the familiar stranger was gone.

5

~

"There must be better ways to introduce yourself, kid."

At the sound of the man's voice, cattails against the breeze, a low *caw* against the twilight, everything inside Joe Hollanger braked—his organs, his place in time and space. He knew he was finished. *Kaput.* Then, just as out of his control, the engines started to turn again, pistons fired, and the works sped back up, overshooting a resting rate, his heart off the rails, breath hitched and jackrabbit quick, thoughts crowding out other thoughts, a fire sale.

The man, cast in drapes of shadow that played heavily against the bursts of color ignited by the daylight's last stand, waited outside the bushes in which the boy purported to hide. He spoke through his pipe, both hands shoved into the pockets of his jacket. "Why don't you step out from there."

Joe stalled to buy the time he needed to regain control of his body. He shivered and then, resigned to his fate, stood and stepped out from the hiding spot, rubbing his scratched arms as he pushed the branches aside.

"How long have you been watching me?"

Joe guessed he could break for it if he needed to, but the man looked pretty fast and pretty strong. Joe wasn't sure he wanted to test him that way. Not yet.

"How long have you been watching everyone else?"

The man exhaled a plume of smoke, looking south where the sky was stuck between day and night. It tossed a strange, bittersweet hue on the land. "Depends on what exactly you mean," he said, "but I imagine the simplest answer is a long, long time." He pulled a last drag from his pipe and tapped it out against his heel, smashed the embers into the grass.

"I see you on your roof."

The man scratched at his thick beard. "Well, it's not exactly stealthy when you're on the roof." He studied Joe, the boy's bird chest jutting slightly forward. "It's not like hiding in the bushes or something."

Joe swallowed air. "I know who you are." He wondered whether you could call it bravery if it was beyond your control. He had run hot and cold with authority ever since his father passed. Joe Sr. was a decorated officer, and died so three grunts could live. At a certain point, rank didn't matter a shit. The junior felt a small blush at his own unsaid curse.

To be fair, the Joe Hollanger still kicking topside was a good soldier, would willingly submit, but he was finding more and more that the grown-ups around him had to earn the right to order him around. He did everything his teachers asked of him, no questions asked, but if the fat paper pusher of a principal so much as looked at him cross-eyed, he'd tell that man to go pound sand, he knew he would. He could see he was yellow, the kind of phony who demanded little kids call him "sir" because they were the only ones who ever would.

This man, though, streaked by sunset—almost part of it, in a way Joe knew he couldn't quite account for or wrap his head around—appeared only bemused, his eyes back on Joe, his mouth a crooked slit. "You don't say."

"You're the one leaving all those books around town."

"You figure that out all by yourself?"

"There's a lot of gossip."

"Again—you don't say."

"If you don't like it, you're welcome to leave." Joe couldn't believe the words coming out of his own mouth. The man, for his part, seemed untouched either way.

"I never said I didn't like it. It's good for business."

"What's your business?"

"C'mon, kid, you can do better than that."

Joe shifted his weight from one leg to the other. He thought of the hardback on his windowsill; he had digested it cover to cover in one sitting. "Books."

"*Ai.*"

"What?"

"Right."

Joe pinched his face. "But what kind of business just gives them away?"

"I don't give them *all* away," the man said.

Joe eyed the pipe in the man's dusky hand. "Can I see that?"

The man looked up to the sky. The first stars, pinholes in the universe, were appearing. "It's getting dark, kid. You can see it better inside."

Joe knew going inside this strange man's strange house was

about the worst idea he could have—his mother would pitch a fit at even the consideration of such a thing—but he nodded and marched up the hill anyway. For a split second he pictured his sister bolting across the rain-soaked Dyson yard and figured perhaps a propensity for walking into trouble was a family trait. This led to a darker, sadder picture infiltrating his brain, one completely of his own imagination—having never been to France, let alone its beachhead—and he shook the horror off, shut it down.

A sidewalk meandered from the front of the house around its flank and to a door cut into the screened porch that spanned the entire back length. A shingle hung next to that door, *Bookbinding* burned into the pine. Joe pulled it open, held it for the man.

The only light in the room came from a single kerosene lantern resting on an old worktable. "Wait here," the bookbinder instructed. He smelled of incense mingled with the tobacco—of old, operose things—as he passed. He lit a second lantern, and then another. The room became a flickering.

"You don't have electricity?"

"*Ai*," the bookbinder replied.

"Huh?"

The man shook his head. "Yes—but I prefer to work by firelight. Here." He shoved the pipe toward Joe, startling the boy.

"What?"

"You wanted to see it."

"Oh, yeah." Joe nodded. "Right." He balanced the device in his palm. It sat weightier than he expected, with circular ridges just above the base and just below the mouthpiece, and it drooped at a sharper angle than other tobacco pipes Joe had

seen men smoke. It looked like a music note or a jazz saxo-
phone. He handed it back to the bookbinder.

Joe roamed the room, tongues of light lapping against the
metal of the instruments, the stained wooden walls. Paper and
thin cloth hung from lines like pelts. "What is all this stuff?"

The bookbinder leaned against a table, watching the boy
examine his shop. "This is where I work," he said. "These are
my tools. Over there—that big thing in the middle—that's my
library press." The man pointed toward what looked to Joe to
be a medieval torture device, with a massive ink-stained cylin-
der set precisely over its center.

"It's huge." Joe ran his hand over a table, and the bookbinder's loose tools, the needles and spindles of thread, straight-
edges, assortments of razors, blades, knives. "What do you do
with these?"

"I cut things."

"You talk queer."

The bookbinder shrugged.

"You make all your books here?"

"*Ai.* Yes."

"One at a time? By yourself?"

"Yes."

"Neat," Joe confirmed. "How long does it take?"

"Each one is different."

Joe pointed deeper into the basement, where the kitchenette was situated. "What's back there?"

"That's where I make paper."

"You *make* the *paper?*"

"Sometimes."

"Will you show me?"

"Maybe. It takes a while." The bookbinder noticed he had

not yet drawn the blinds. The night was black against the fire-light. "It's getting late," he said. "Somebody expecting you home?"

The boy fingered a large cut of hanging paper. He brushed a corner back, the underside covered in drawings of naked nymphs stretched in every direction, some right side up, others upside down. He was enthralled.

"You fold the pages over," the bookbinder said. "And then back over themselves again. Sometimes more. You have to think ahead when you lay out a book. That's why things look backward sometimes. Upside down. When it's finished, it will all be right."

Joe nodded. He let the paper fall off his finger and looked about the room again; by the flicker of the kerosene, it felt as if he stood at the center of a giant pyre, something both completely wild and completely contained. "Yeah, I better be going," he murmured, as if an afterthought to some truth he couldn't quite grasp yet. He pulled his baseball cap down tight.

The bookbinder nodded.

"Is it okay if I come back?"

"That's fine."

Joe bit the inside of his cheek. "My name is Joe—Joe Hollanger," he announced in a flurry, his names stepping on each other, and just as quickly hustled out through the workshop door.

With the boy's departure, the room defaulted once again into a lonesome outpost, quiet save for the almost impercep-tible hiss of the kerosene. The bookbinder stood beside the press, held his fingers to it, and listened, not with his ears and not for a sound; there was a disturbance, he sensed, and not too far away—though not exactly where he expected. Something different from the low pulse that scratched at his thoughts. Troubled, he passed though the workshop to the little sink and counter tucked behind it, and by only the meager light cast from the front room poured himself a tumbler of milky sake. Unfiltered, like river water.

He took a long sip and drifted to his chair in the corner of the workshop. He pulled off his jacket and tossed it on a table, then pulled out his Baoding balls. He worked the little iron orbs in his free hand, allowing the amber of the room to dance against the illustrations of reveries and nightmares carved into his mighty arms.

6

By the time Joe returned home, the clock over the mantel betrayed quarter past nine. Tess stretched across the sofa, long strands of hair edging her frown. His mother flew in from the kitchen.

"Where have you been?" she demanded of her son, breezing by, not waiting for an answer. "Don't get comfortable. That Ava girl's flown the coop again."

"Who?"

Miriam halted, taking Joe in for the first time. "What's the matter with you? Ava St. Pierre, lives down on Phoebe Street. Little simple girl." Tess shrugged behind her mother and stood up. Joe caught a quick, pained grimace, a tucked-away hitch in his sister's step. Joe started to open his mouth, and Tess's instant furrowed brow stopped him quick.

Miriam continued: "She's been missing a couple hours now. Everyone's aflutter." She punched her arms through the sleeves of her topper. Her beauty was of the flinty kind and had very little time for itself; with sparkling eyes and cheekbones even Rita Hayworth would kill for, she knew how the men in this town looked at her. It was just a thing that happened, though, like the sunrise, and there was little space in her schedule for its further consideration. Besides her job at the rectory—which was becoming an increasingly laudable matter of keeping Father Jim's demons and creditors at bay, not necessarily in that order—there was the Rotary Club, the VA work, the newly formed Brookshire Women's League, the board of Volunteer Fire Company 28, the sewing and book clubs—and Tess and Joe Jr., of course.

Her husband died, so she married a town.

"We're going to the St. Pierre house," she commanded. "Hurry up, both of you." Miriam Hollanger wouldn't be late for a search party. They double-timed across Brookshire—Joe noticed his sister's concealed limp, even if their mother didn't. "What's wrong with your foot?" he whispered.

Tess screwed her face tight in the dark. "Nothing."

"Bull."

"I twisted my ankle at recess."

"You don't *have* recess."

They pressed on, catching up with, and then overtaking, a handful of neighborhood men heading in the same direction. Thunder rumbled, and Joe felt a few drops pelt his head.

Thirty or so townspeople stood outside the St. Pierre house, including Sam and Rebecca St. Pierre themselves, looking as lost as anyone. Sam's face loosened around his pink-tinged eyes when Miriam and her small cavalry came marching over the hill. Rebecca clasped hands with her; Miriam pulled the younger mother in for a quick hug, then motioned for everyone to come closer, huddle together. Sam lit a cigarette, nodded as some small words of encouragement were offered, then faded to the edge of the crowd, hotboxing his smoke as if the only breathable air left for him could be pulled from a quarter-inch hole in the fabric of space.

Miriam separated the party into four groups, one for each cardinal direction; this wasn't her first rodeo with the St. Pierre girl. Despite the auspicious sign of having been born on Easter Sunday, she had never been right, as far as Miriam could figure. Those eyes like mirror balls, the way they could cut right into you—sometimes it made Miriam shiver, even just passing in the street, the grocery store aisle.

They were to push toward the borders of town, flanking out when necessary. If they couldn't find young Ava in one pass, they would have to call in the Appleton police. Miriam anticipated Chief Hillary would be less than thrilled. *I can't have my men running around your little hamlet chasing the village idiot every other week*, he told her after a few drinks at the Rotary's last Christmas potluck. *I have a real town to govern, with real problems.* She had almost snorted at the word *govern*, but caught herself, bit her tongue, and smiled as sweetly as she could, profusely thanking the man for suffering both little old her and the work he was overpaid to do. She'd sighed, defeated, later that evening, when he'd grabbed a handful of her ass on the way to the men's room.

Just as the search parties scuffled to embark, a figure ambled down Phoebe Street. Miriam could make out the outline of an upturned collar, a long beard. A murmur rose from the crowd.

Miriam took a step toward the stranger, but Rebecca held her arm, stepped forward herself. Sam sucked a long drag from his cigarette, witnessing a lingering moment that could neither be seen nor unseen, a humiliating tension mounting between this drifter and his wife, a standoff, until Rebecca clipped it, motioned to the right. "You go with the men heading east, toward Robin Road. Over there."

The bookbinder nodded and slid in with a small collection of stone-faced, smoking townsmen. Father Jim alone offered his hand. "Welcome," the priest said, and the new arrival nodded again, locking eyes.

The rain surged as they walked the suburb, having to that point held itself back, bearing hitched tears. Before splitting up, Rebecca had pressed a photograph of Ava into the bookbinder's hand; he held it as he walked, the child staring fierce electricity into the lens, and now up at him, the human equivalent of a blown fuse. Her rounded eyes were oceans framed in long spiderweb lashes, her straight ice-blond hair almost matching her pallid skin. The bookbinder recalled what he knew of color, how black was the absolute absence of light, white all light combined. Most everything you could see fell between those extremes. *Most*.

"We're wasting our time," someone in the search party muttered. The bookbinder cocked his head but said nothing, didn't slow his pace.

"What d'ya mean?" someone else from the rear answered.

"Kid goes missing, shouldn't we look in the obvious place?"

"What's that?"

"The place on Tanager. That haunted one."

A silence overtook the men, but they kept marching in their assigned direction. "She wouldn't know about that, I'm sure," Father Jim offered. "Besides, there's another group heading that way. If they don't find her closer"—his voice broke against a gust of wind—"they'll get there eventually."

The party reached Robin Road, which ran up the hill that

made up the bulk of the landscape of this side of Brookshire. The town sloped down from high ground along its northern edge, as well as another ridge on its southwestern corner, where the public elementary school construction was near completion; if one were to fly over, Brookshire had the look of an imperfect, jaggedly cut slice of pie. Robin Road served as the eastern border of town, beyond it the surviving deep wood. Father Jim tugged his hat down and his coat collar up, starting uphill to take the cross streets one by one. The bookbinder paused before the sea of trees. The priest stopped, called out over his shoulder: "She would be too frightened to go in there."

The bookbinder held still. The rain continued to ratchet itself up, now whipping about his face and shoulders. Something close to a gale. He turned to Father Jim and the others. "I'll catch up."

The priest regarded him for a long beat, squinting for the rain, then nodded, and the assemblage carried on up the hill. The bookbinder stepped into the shadows of great oaks, maples, birch. The rain was strained under the canopy, but he could hear the drops slap against the branches and leaves knotted above, mimicking the crackle of his step. The temperature changed, too, plunging after his first steps into the thicket.

Just twenty yards deep and he was somewhere wise and unkempt, the world as it was intended, flanked by trees that had stood for a hundred years or more. All the rain of the previous month had charged the growth, and the near-full complement of foliage created a tangible threshold, muted both the concerns of the outside world and the light of the half-moon above.

The hairs along the bookbinder's arms and neck tingled,

tiny feathers catching air; he had traveled woods like these before, the symphony of rain a constant, his breath's fog betraying him to those who wanted—*needed*—him dead. He remembered sprinting, tripping in loose fatigues. He had scrambled to his feet, feeling through underbrush for what had taken him down. He'd found a hand, followed the arm to a torso and then a face so mangled he couldn't tell whether the corpse was one of his or theirs. He could have figured it out from the soldier's weapon, but some other scavenger had already picked the body clean.

There was the *there* of then and the *here* of now, and a labyrinth of long, dank tunnels, sinewy and twisting like hollow tentacles, stitched the two together. This black network ran across time and space and pinned through the very hearts of men like specimens who could no longer recognize their callus-covered and mud-caked wings for what they were, for what they were once intended to be. The bookbinder had known these tunnels firsthand, crawled through them in battle and his bleakest dreams, and he understood how they served both as the vehicle for a perpetual Emptiness and as the Emptiness itself: Just like a word of ink pressed fast into a page of paper, the tentacles were both the road map and the terrible fortune.

In one life, the enemy had mastered the tunnels, but in another, the enemy *was* the tunnel, burrowing itself just beneath the asphalt, the beds of perennials, the parade routes. There were armies of men buried beneath the armies of men still topside, still armed, still virile and shell-shocked. There was a town beneath this town, the shared terror, the lingering taste, each a thread connected to another, shifting, tightening, fashioning currents through a pitch river just beyond sight, all of which seemed to culminate in an abandoned house that otherwise sat idle, but anything but, on the other side of town. The book-binder knew he was not the only soldier who'd brought something back with him that slept and readied itself in the wounds. There was an explosion, or a memory. Thunder boomed—close, even through the trees. There shouldn't be such racket in such a town. It was 1952, unless it was still '45. Or after, in between: He appeared in forests and bars and jungles and parlor rooms; each breath was a bird attempting to land on a different surface with no purchase, then flitting away again.

Another *boom* shouted a jagged shiver down his spine. He couldn't make out what the voices were screaming; they were riddles who shot at him, who slit his brothers' throats from ear to ear. He couldn't tell whether they were cursing him or trying to sing him to a perpetual sleep.

Where was he? Okinawa? No, that was the *then* and *there*; this was the *here* and *now*, a different dark wood. And there were the tunnels, he dreamed of them—could never stop dreaming of them—the chomping sound of their burrow; but now, in this little hamlet, both so very different and so very the same from every other he blew across, there was a wrinkle—a little flicker who, like him, didn't belong. *A girl.* The girl was electric and she was somewhere in here with him. He didn't understand why yet, but he sensed that she mattered, had felt it charge through him that very morning outside her house, her pretty mother weeping in the yard. She had watched him through the walls, the electric girl—and not just him, the "him" whom others could see and touch, but inside, beyond. He felt the thing shift under her gaze. It made the bookbinder shudder, both then and now, here, in these woods, that she, too, was perhaps bigger than her size, a crowned queen carved into the shape of a pawn.

He needed to focus on the mission at hand and find her—though in this moment, and in these dripping woods, he could not be sure that was the case, or the other way around. A coaxing. A pull.

He rubbed his hands together, blew on them. He had slept in mire-infested forests like this more times than he could count: warm mud and cold, thick like old coffee, and clay-red rivulets, pure earth and deltas gelatinous with the rotting things that seep from men. He remembered waking bewildered in a cocoon of filth, blood, gnats, sweat—something buried almost alive, straddling two realms. There'd been a clutching in the center of him, his chest ribbons of khaki rag and skin, and dripping wings snuffing out the stars; a weight, heavy and black, held him down, a shadow fed on him, tightening everything, rendering him a creature both newborn and ancient.

He turned, embarrassed by his sweating, his noticeable shake, but found no one to bear witness. The symphony, the thunder, was overwhelming. It was May 1945, and the book-binder was stretched out in tarns of putrid muck, suffering a fitful sleep in Okinawa; it was May 1952, and he was searching in the rain for a little firecracker of a girl he had never properly met.

The memories and the nightmares turned back on themselves, like serpents in heat. Like infinity. Like coming home.

The mangled grunt's face was a twisted flash plate of shock and rage, one loose eyeball staring dead at the moon; heaven was a lie told by magicians who used hope to sell their wars. The bookbinder leaned against the nearest tree, unsure whether he was tired or already asleep, where one trick ended and another began. He closed his eyes and listened through the earth's melody playing on around him.

Soon he heard a voice sing-speaking to itself, though he couldn't make out the words.

⌄

The girl was shivering at the base of a tall oak, her print pajamas streaked with sludge. Her song was gibberish punctuated with squeaks and barks, her little voice huskier than the bookbinder expected, as if she were pulling it from the bottom of a well fathoms below anything else in Brookshire.

Ava grew agitated as he approached. Her eyes darted about, an azure flash in the wet streaks of moonlight cutting through the canopy, and her sounds grew harder, thicker, clatters she couldn't quite chew or swallow.

The bookbinder took another step, and she scurried up on her haunches, ready to bolt or charge. He retreated a step, two, and the girl stilled, hissing and barking. To the right, he spotted a felled tree and slowly wandered over to it, away from Ava, to sit down alone.

He closed his eyelids, turned his focus to his breathing, and emptied his mind of thoughts, softly dismissed them when they bloomed. He took out his Baoding balls, spun them slowly in his palm, the buried chimes marking time.

It was not 1945. It was not Okinawa. It was here, whatever that was. It was now, whatever that was.

The girl was here, whatever she was.

The chimes became a part of his stillness, his breathing. The rain blended in as well. The brook's babble farther down the slope became the stillness. The whistle of the trees. The crickets. The night birds. The careful, unsure steps approaching. All here, all now, each accepted as part of the stillness, everything made nothing, the steady hum of eternity.

He opened his eyes, and there was Ava, her face inches from his, her sweet and earthy smell in his nostrils. Unblinking. Neither moved, except for the steady orbit of the meditation balls.

A vision drove itself into the bookbinder's otherwise calmed mind, a railroad spike of a memory, or dream, something between: He was hurtling from a speeding airplane in the middle of a tempest, his heart in his throat, everything alive and pressed tightly against death, and he felt—a thousand times over in the space between breaths—the gnaw of those first seconds before the chute opened, when the world was a sputtering, skipping record of a nightmare, too fast to grasp, the air itself tearing at you, mocking your screams with its own. He glimpsed what it was like to live in that moment over and over, to never be wholly free, and realized in the flash before it all snapped away that it was both a thing that had happened and a conjured vision, his own memories twisted into the building blocks of an analogy, a node between him and this pale shock of white, the closest she could come to explaining what she felt, what the world meant to her. Her to it.

He unfurled his eyes and sucked in a desperate, whistling breath. He opened his hand, and Ava plucked out the two small orbs. Without another sound, she began to turn them over in her own little palm, slowly at first, clinking against each other, and then faster, as if they had been hers all along.

She let the bookbinder wrap his jacket around her and traced the tattoos on his arms with the index finger of her free hand. "The rain's stopped," he acknowledged, a rasp, as much to himself as to her. Either way, the girl didn't seem to notice. When the pair appeared on Phoebe Street, Ava was still working the Baoding balls and continued to through the gasp of the regathered crowd, her mother's trembling embrace, and young Joe Hollanger running inside the St. Pierre house to stop his mother from calling Chief Hillary, hollering that the bookbinder had found the girl, that she was safe.

7

Miriam Hollanger drank whiskey when no one was looking. It was not furtive per se; a pattern just petrified over time. She didn't drink socially because there was always so much to do, and if she ever did grab a cocktail on occasion, it inevitably found itself set aside, forgotten in deference to whatever crisis or chore needed to be handled in that moment.

It was only late at night, the children asleep and the town grown quiet, when Miriam would grab a bottle and a glass from the cabinet above the stove and sit at the dining room table or, when the weather was mild, on the little iron porch attached to the side of her house. She drank her whiskey neat, listening to the breeze blow through the magnolia tree that technically belonged to her neighbor, but which she liked to think her own.

Appleton High's school year had ended that afternoon, and after supper Miriam had begrudgingly allowed Tess to go to a bowling party in the neighboring town. It was now almost eleven o'clock, though, an hour past her curfew, and Tess had still not returned home.

Miriam wanted to blame the unwelcome crowd she had noticed Tess running with lately, the matching hound-like stare they all kept, the counterfeit teenage smiles. Tess's problems, though—the rocket temper, her insecurities, her rabbit holes—Miriam had to admit, ran so much deeper than the influence of some stupid pack of greaser peacock boys and dead-end girls who wore too much makeup to cover the bruises left by their drunken fathers and boyfriends trying to catch up, to become men.

Tess, Miriam knew, had taken it hard when her father died, perhaps even hardest of them all. And more to the point, she'd taken it all *in*. Joe—Joe *Jr.*—had at least cried and talked about missing Daddy at first. Tess broke the other, more arduous way, upward and onward like there was nothing strange about the sun not rising, the world in perpetual eclipse. Miriam knew that her daughter kept entire planets, universes, inside her skin, and would sleep all weekend not because she was lazy, but because it was so goddamned exhausting to keep all that at bay.

Miriam heard unsure, asymmetrical steps wrestle with the sidewalk. She stilled herself, listening past the magnolia leaves, tightening her grip around her glass. She spied a figure wobble past hedges lining the front yards, and then lost sight. The steps paused in front of her own front gate, which creaked open. She set her drink under her chair and walked into the house to meet her daughter in the living room.

When Tess tiptoed in, her mother was leaning against the doorjamb of the dining room, a *Home Is Where the Heart Is* needlepoint hanging framed on the wall, over her shoulder. "Shit," the daughter hissed under her breath.

"Excuse me?"

"Nothing, Mother," Tess muttered, the second word a snarl. Her hair hung flat over her shoulders. Miriam had wanted to take her to the beauty parlor for weeks. There had never been time, or the particular urge to fight over it.

"Where have you been?" Tanned arms from weekend yardwork crossed under her chest, still in her day's dress; Miriam suspected she herself looked pamphlet perfect, the last defense for wayward girls against a life of ill repute. It was all bullshit, Miriam knew, but important, necessary bullshit, the subtleties of which she would never be able to translate to her daughter, just on the cusp of fifteen. "I've been worried sick."

"I already told you—the bowling alley."

"The alley closes at ten."

"It's a mile away."

"So you walked home?"

"No."

"Who drove you?"

"My friends."

"Your *friends*?"

"Yes."

"Which friends?"

As Tess made for the hallway, her bedroom, Miriam noticed that her daughter's limp was gone. She realized she had never asked after it, though she had meant to on several occasions. "Where do you think you're going?"

"To bed."

"Come here."

"You're being *impossible*." Tess's tongue fumbled the last word.

"I asked you to come here, young lady."

Tess stepped toward her mother, into the light of the lamp

next to the high-back. Even with the girl looking away, Miriam could see the faint rose spiderwebs straining across the whites of her daughter's eyes.

"Oh, for heaven's sake," Miriam sneered, surprised at her surprise, having heard the girl stumble up the front steps. "You're drunk."

"I am *not*," Tess mumbled. She tucked her hair behind her ear and stared at her saddle shoes, clicking the heels once, halfway hoping it would make her disappear.

Miriam cocked her head. "What is on your neck?" Tess's mouth opened in a slow, shocked *O*. She instinctively covered the fresh hickey—a parting gift from a boy whose name she didn't even remember, delivered in the back seat of his dad's Victoria.

Miriam's mouth twisted in recognition and disgust, and she tried to level some apt, wise response. The words, though, didn't come—or came too fast, one on top of another, and all that escaped her lips was a feeble groan, more of a scrape against the room than anything. She gathered herself enough to play the only card she could see. "What would your father say?" The words jumped the fence faster than she could tackle them, snuff them out.

The girl's pink eyes flickered into glisten. "My father's dead."

Miriam felt the switch flip, the one that hardened her into cobalt. She grabbed a cigarette from her case on the bookshelf, lit it, and took a long, deep drag. "You are not to see whomever that belongs to again, do you understand?" she ordered, wagging her cigarette in the general direction of the kiss-shaped welt.

Tess balled her hands, relaxed them, her arms taut cords at her sides. Head leaning forward, shoulders abrupt, she looked cubist, like something Picasso would paint, all naked angles, every card on the table. "That's not fair!" she barked back, though she cared nothing for the author of that particular mark: It was her neck, after all, and she would stick it out wherever she wanted. Maybe someday someone would take the hint and take a chopping swing. A defiance that burned clean caught fire, making Tess's upper lip curl.

"You've been on summer vacation for about eight hours and you've already shown up at this house past curfew like some floozy."

Tess's ignited eyes widened. "*Floozy?*"

"Don't argue with me, young lady." Miriam registered the jut of her daughter's chin, the meaning of it, set her own jaw.

The girl leaned forward. "Maybe if you got—"

The back of Miriam's hand snapped across Tess's mouth. All the color drained from the daughter's face, which contorted into something desperate, both fathoms older and younger than it was. Tess wanted to scream but could only squeak. Her chest heaved with nothing to grasp. For a moment Miriam thought her child was going to come back at her, dig out her eyes; part of her welcomed it, wanted the whole goddamned room to explode and put them both out of this misery they had been enduring for so long—but instead the girl pinched her face into a tight mask and scrambled down the hall, a startled doe tripping along a polished floor.

From the other side of his bedroom door, Joe had heard it all. He raised his hand against the wood composite to make sure it was still there, this border, however flimsy, that he could keep. To make sure he didn't just pass right through. He listened to his sister's door slam.

Joe wiped his eyes, which were wet but probably not enough

to count for crying. He got down on his knees, reached under his bed, pulled out his father's old cedar box, where Joe kept his valuables: Joe Sr.'s dog tags, his signed Mickey Vernon baseball card, a Saint Michael medallion his grandmother had gifted him at birth, the little book of fortresses, and, underneath all of that, his reserve of Pall Malls swiped from his mother's case. He plucked one and a box of matches, and then, quietly, carefully, climbed out through his bedroom window and five feet up the lattice to the roofline, pulling himself up with a clipped grunt. He lit the cigarette and stretched out on the roof with his arms folded behind his head, watching the stars.

On the little metal landing on the other side of the house, which she thought of as a porch but really wasn't, his mother lit her next one with her last, and retrieved her glass from under the chair. She had brought the bottle out with her and poured a few swigs more, spilling just a little on the skin of her shaking hand. She had never struck her daughter like that before, and she licked the bitter taste from her fingers, found it unpleasant. Licked it again.

8

⌣

"Pull it up slow. It needs to be even."

"I *am*."

Joe shook over the vat, his thin, sparrow frame straining with care. The bookbinder crouched beside him, eyed the deckle, guided Joe without touching the mount. He nodded at the boy's work.

"What now?"

"Now? Now you let it drip."

"For how long?"

The man regarded Joe, little veins beginning to pop out of his little neck. "Until it stops."

Joe sighed. His eyes flared with disgust, but he held his pose. The bookbinder knew this was not the most efficient technique for drying paper, but ease was not his purpose today.

There was a knock at the shop's door. "*Ai*," he exhaled, running his hand down the length of his beard. "I better get that."

"What about me?"

"What about you?" The bookbinder stood. He wore only a stained pair of khakis and his standard-issue boots, and his taut muscles stirred slow as lava, curling around his shifts in languid waves. His long hair was tied back tight, his mouth hidden in bristles. The most striking features of his peculiar form, though, were the numerous black tattoos obscuring every inch of his torso and arms.

His bronzed skin was an amalgam of images and typefaces, in every language: A tea rose bled into Whitman, a line from an Arabic prayer became a flock of black birds, rising from his heart to disappear at his neck. Chinese pictographs (Joe had asked him what those carved along his right forearm meant, and the bookbinder had replied only by walking away) became a woman's portrait, became a swell, became clouds, became a ship, or a crucifix, or a treasure map, all lost in a sea of words, of French, Italian, Russian, Tibetan. Koi, their shimmer, tattooed in Egyptian hieroglyphs, morphed into kisses whispering butterflies. Chrysanthemums consumed nightingales captured by stanzas, by musical notes with poisoned tips. The Sudanese word for *love* was inked directly over the Portuguese word for *work*, over the Turkish word for *blood*, creating an abstraction that ran along the fault of an abdominal muscle. The Virgin Mary appeared, as did Muhammad, Buddha, Ganesh. Three sirens crawled over jagged cliffs, and Leviathan guarded his rib cage, haunted evermore by the words of Job: "The price of wisdom is above rubies." There were more. There were always more. One could stare at the bookbinder for days and not come away with all that had been cut into him.

He wiped his hands with the rag he kept in his waistband, a thing as stained as his surface, and opened the door. The sunlight stabbed in; both he and Joe winced. They had neglected the blinds when Joe arrived that morning, working only by the kerosene the bookbinder had burned through the night. "Jesus," Joe croaked.

Rebecca St. Pierre stood at the workshop's threshold, her daughter in tow. Ava worked the bookbinder's Baoding balls, her large eyes still and clear. Anything but.

Rebecca seemed as stunned by the darkness as Joe and the bookbinder were by the light. "I'm sorry," she stammered, squinting. "This is a bad time?" As her eyes adjusted, the intricate lines across the bookbinder's chest took shape, developed like photographs. She gasped, then tried to couch the gasp in the rhythm of her breathing, failed, swallowed it, blushed.

"No," the bookbinder answered, grabbing a dirty shirt draped over a work stool, sliding it over his head, around his thick shoulders. "We're just making paper."

While he dressed, Rebecca looked past him at the red-faced, sweating boy watching sludge drip from wire. "Joe?"

The bookbinder nodded. Rebecca flashed a small wave to the boy, who tried to nod without moving the rest of his body. She turned back to the bookbinder, realizing how her free hand was tightened into a ball. She relaxed it and stole an extra breath. "I wanted to thank you. For the other night. For finding her." She nodded toward Ava. "Also," she persisted, her eyes falling on the orbs her daughter clutched, "we need to return these to you."

The bookbinder slid his hands into the pockets of his khakis. "Neither is necessary." He had turned toward her daughter, without looking straight at the child, as if Ava were a kind of bright star, not an unblinking eight-year-old with wet snot hanging from one nostril.

Rebecca smiled, but it was tight and held little mirth, a flag born of parts of her waging war with other disparate parts. "No, I beg to differ." The Baoding balls spun a tick faster in Ava's grip.

The bookbinder took a half step to the side, still stealing small glances in the girl's direction. "Would you like to come in?"

Rebecca peered into the cave of the shop, the long, dancing shadows cast by the kerosene. "I don't think I should."

Some small spell broke. The bookbinder shrugged, stepping out onto the porch. He called back to Joe: "Put that damn thing on that worktable over there. *Gently.* You'll be there forever doing it that way." The boy moaned as he lifted the frame and carefully laid it on the table. He sighed like exhaust, all black clouds and relief.

The bookbinder pulled out his pipe. "Take one of those rags—no, the blue ones—and carefully set it over the pulp. Carefully, or you'll push right through it. Then take a sponge from the sink there and soak up the water through the rag." Joe, wiggling life back into his arms, nodded.

The bookbinder shut the door behind him, pointed Rebecca to a chair on the porch.

"No, thank you. We're not staying."

The bookbinder took the seat himself, pinched a dose of dark tobacco from a pouch, and lit his pipe. He leaned back, breathing smoke.

Rebecca let go of her daughter's hand, and for a moment the bookbinder thought the child might bolt; she stood pat where she was, though, staring at the brickwork of the house—*into* the brickwork of the house. Rebecca, hands on hips, looked about the porch. "You're wasting all this space."

"Excuse me?"

She caught herself, blushed again. "I'm sorry. It's not my place."

"Please."

"Well, I was just thinking, there's plenty of room on this porch. You could set tables out, put your books on display right out here. I mean"—she bit back on a small smile—"you still have your shop in your backyard, but at least it's something."

The bookbinder leaned back behind a plume of smoke. "That's a thought. But most of my work is custom."

Rebecca spun—she opened her mouth, then snapped it shut. She instead took a step back toward the screen, the bright blue beyond. "I understand that," she murmured. She thought for a moment. "Sometimes people don't know what they want until it is laid out right in front of them."

The bookbinder nodded. "True. Definitely something to consider."

Rebecca ran her finger along a wooden ledge. "I don't want to take up too much of your time. We mostly came to return your—"

"They're called Baoding balls. They're common in the East."

Her voice tightened along the same creases as her smile, becoming more staid. She clutched at old-fashioned manners to center herself. "Yes. Well, again, we apologize for the intrusion and would like to return them to you."

"It's no intrusion and, again, I will not accept them." The bookbinder was final on the point. "They belong to her now."

Rebecca spoke to the sky. "I don't need any favors from you."

"I wouldn't presume."

"I think you presume quite a bit."

The bookbinder was silent. He studied Ava, staring through his wall. He wondered whether even her mother knew what she might be, what she might mean. Maybe a splinter's worth, but with a thing like this, that was plenty. A splinter would be scary enough.

"Do you think I need praying for? You think that is my salvation—that I need a book of them to help me get through my silly little life?"

The bookbinder took another pull without taking his stare off the girl. It was better when she wasn't looking right at him. The push and the pull all entangled. He wondered whether she knew what *he* was. What *he* meant. He figured she probably did, in whatever way she came to know things. Maybe even better than he could. "I think there are truths that live behind other truths, inside them, whole worlds infusing other worlds. This little spinning rock."

"God?"

"The old man on Sunday with the half-dead son?" He shook his head. "Deeper. Farther back."

The young mother furrowed her brow. "I'm not sure I follow," she replied softly.

"I think that might be exactly what you need to do. Think of that prayer book as a road map, cobbled together from all over the world, all over time. The whole elephant, translated by a small army of blind men." The bookbinder studied his own decorated arms, then turned back to Ava standing off to the side. "Sometimes magic lives in the least likely places."

"I don't know that I like us being looked into like that."

The bookbinder again pulled on his pipe, otherwise still.

The sunlight caught a glisten in Rebecca's eyes. "I don't know that I don't," she whispered, then reached for her daughter, pulling her toward the porch door. "Thank you," she muttered, not bothering to linger for a reply.

Back inside, the bookbinder looked over Joe's work. He was impressed. "Good," he offered flatly, Joe already having learned this to be high praise. There was another knock, and the bookbinder paused before answering it; this time, a stocky, silver-maned official with a cigarette dangling from his mouth and a badge from his breast pocket filled the doorframe. He was looking back, toward the side of the house.

"That was a pretty little bird that just walked by, huh?"

The bookbinder studied the man in silence.

"Are you the owner of this property, sir?"

"*Ai.*"

The man with the badge narrowed his stare. "Well, pleased to meet you. I'm Police Chief Nathaniel Hillary. May I come in?"

The bookbinder skimmed the runes around the visitor's eyes. He opened the screen, then called back to Joe. "You better head on home now," he announced, clean and sharp.

9

⌣

"So, bookmaking?" The police chief stubbed his cigarette into
an empty ashtray and picked up one of the bookbinder's blades,
twirling it in his fleshy hand. "Where'd that come from?"

"The hardware store."

The chief twisted, an eyebrow arched. He let loose an annoyed chuckle. "No, son. Where'd the urge to make books
come from?"

The bookbinder shrugged. "Just something I picked up
along the way."

Another arch. "And what way might that have been?"

"My travels. Asia. Then back west across Europe after."
The bookbinder recalled the ancient story of Emperor Jimmu,
how the *kami* led him to change direction so he stopped fighting into the sun—instead bursting *from* it.

"Asia and then back again the long way?"

"The war," the bookbinder conceded, perched on a stool.
"And then after." Both men were dancing with an economy of
steps, testing who held the board. "The long way, as you say."

"You a veteran?"

The bookbinder nodded, and Hillary mimicked it, made it his own. He walked the room. "A strapping young man like yourself, with a military background," the chief noted, sizing the bookbinder up. "We're always looking for good candidates on the force."

"I don't think I would be a good fit."

"You wore a uniform once. You could do it again."

The bookbinder smiled, parallel to the dark joviality of his inquisitor.

The chief's ruddy face deepened a shade around his coffee-stained teeth, which maintained their separate wattage. "Be straight—is this a thing a man can make an honest living at?"

"As much as anything else, I imagine."

The chief stroked his mustache, scanning over the books that lined the shadowed workshop walls. He picked one from a shelf, then tucked it back. "How does it work? You make books on demand? Somebody wants something about . . . titmice, for instance . . . you whip up a titmouse book?"

The bookbinder folded his arms, leaning back. "Something like that."

The chief pulled out another book to flip through it. "What is this? Latin?"

"German."

The chief lit a new cigarette. "Is that so?" He wrestled the rectangle back into its spot, then started for another, bigger and weatherworn. The bookbinder braced, scanning his knives now disheveled across the table. The chief ran a pink finger along the gnarled spine, let his hand fall from the shelf. "What about the freebies?"

"Pardon?"

"The ones you've been leaving on people's porches. Right there on their desks in locked rooms. Like some sort of ghost librarian, or holy Jesus man of words or something. What's that about?"

"People have been talking?"

The chief took a long drag, pulled the cigarette from his lips, and examined the filter. He nodded. "Yes, son, people have been talking."

The bookbinder nodded back. "Well, that's good. That's advertising."

"Pardon?"

"The extraordinary grabs attention. Gives them something to think about, and then talk about. And then buy."

The chief grinned appreciatively. "An entrepreneur. Color me impressed." Another long drag. "Looks like you've got it all figured out." He pulled another small book from the shelf. His eyes danced across it, seeing nothing. "You of course have all the proper permits and such?"

The bookbinder tried to look as taken aback as he was expected to be. He played a brief stammer, but the chief held up his hand.

"You see, this is a *residential* community and not zoned for businesses."

"But the dentist—"

"No, no." The chief clucked his tongue. "That was a *medical* practice, not a retail operation. A storefront! Apples and oranges, boy. Apples and oranges." The bookbinder knew Chief Hillary was making up his regulations as he went along; he was of the age-old tribe of men who had thrived for eons by employing such a strategy, simply being more audacious with his bullshit than the next. The old chief blew tobacco

smoke and shook the tome in his hand. "And *this*"—he shook
a page with a Victorian nude—"well, I'm a patron of the arts
myself, but there are some in this town who would frown on
a thing like this. Might even call it obscene. And with an im-
pressionable young boy . . . working? Was the Hollanger boy
working in this unsanctioned shop?"

"Not officially."

The chief clucked his tongue again. "So you are a *single*
man, no one to vouch for you, living here *alone*, with a young
boy 'not officially' working for you, and dirty books just lying
around." He pointed a finger at the bookbinder and drew a
lazy circle in the air. "Do you really need me to connect the
dots here?"

The bookbinder scratched his head. "You know that's
not—"

"What I *know* and what I can *prove* are two different
things." The two men examined each other, both affecting
some variation of blankness. Eventually the bookbinder un-
folded himself from his stool, the chief's body tensing as the
tall shadow crossed, his face managing to hold neutral. The
bookbinder retreated toward the kitchenette in the back, and
the old cop slid his jacket behind his holster.

The bookbinder returned with a bottle and two glasses.
He poured each halfway with sake. Hillary took one with his
gun hand. "You're a strange bird, I'll say that." The pair drank.

The bookbinder grabbed a volume from the table. He blew
a bit of sawdust from the cover. "A gift."

The chief sneered almost imperceptibly, reaching for the
book's bloodred cover. He opened it.

"Poems? What am I going to do with poems?" He chortled.
"I believe you struck out on this one, Mr. Holy Bookman."

The bookbinder took another slow drink, then placed the glass back on the table. He wiped his hands together. "They're mostly for your wife, actually. Only the fifteenth sonnet is meant for you."

The chief frowned and blinked. *Thirteen, fourteen, fifteen*—and ten crisp one-hundred-dollar bills. He whistled. "Now, *that's* poetry." He snickered, lighting up. He tossed the rest of the glass's contents down his throat, sighed with pleasure, and shoved the money in his shirt pocket. "Thanks for the drink." He looked around the room. "Nice little shop you have here."

Hillary grabbed his hat from the worktable, turning back to the bookbinder. "Don't think I won't be keeping a close eye on you."

"Fair enough."

The chief started to leave.

"Chief?"

"Yeah?"

"Who tipped you off?"

The police chief opened the door, squinting at the sun now square in his face. "Well, normally, that would be confidential information." He patted the roll of bills in his pocket. "But I will say she has not been overly thrilled about you spending so much time with her son."

10

⌄

Miriam Hollanger made sure all her groceries could fit in one bag, allowing her to switch arms if one got tired on the mile-long trek back home. She thanked the teenage bagger and made for the door and the blazing three o'clock sun beyond it. She could already feel beads of sweat forming on her legs, beneath her long emerald skirt. Miriam stayed calm and carried on, though, just like *LIFE* magazine said the British had done during the bombings, the blackouts.

She understood her country was still at war, or at war again, with more American men dying over in Korea—but it wasn't *the* war. Somewhere between gods and boys, those called upon in that dark hour saved the world—her husband among them, immortal in a way—just not the way that mattered. Not the way that could keep her warm at night, ignite her. She removed her sunglasses from her forehead and pulled them over her eyes.

The supermarket faced the sun pummeling the sparsely

populated parking lot. A lazy summer Thursday was not a peak business hour, but a gaggle of kids sped by on dirt-encrusted bicycles, almost running her over anyway. "Hey, Mrs. Hollanger!" she thought she heard trailing after the cloud of dust, her would-be assassins minding their manners as they zoomed past. She steadied herself and continued toward the highway.

On Thursdays, the rectory closed early, and Miriam would march over to the supermarket for her weekly pilgrimage. She'd sometimes ask Joe to meet her at work, an extra pair of hands, and—if the pastor was around—Father Jim would struggle toward small talk with the boy. He'd say something about growing like a weed, maybe, or ask after the Senators, or school, or the movies.

Miriam and her son would walk to the store together and split the carrying duties on the way back. Sometimes she'd even buy him a soda or a chocolate bar for the trouble. Today, though, it was just her. Joe was either running around town like a Lost Boy or—worse yet—hanging around that vagabond's shop again. She hoped that had been handled, though. And Tess . . . the Good Lord only knew what Tess was up to. She was so secretive these days, but not in the ways Miriam expected, the normal conspiracies of youth. She was becoming complicated in a way her mother felt ill equipped to read, an enigma with no decoder. Every outburst, every tic or clue Tess offered that Miriam couldn't translate, only showcased her own limitations, and the recent exchanges with her daughter, despite Miriam's best efforts to curb those insecurities, were colored and blurred with a resentment that rattled against the cage she had built for them.

The girl was falling, Miriam feared—but not falling *down*.

Falling *away*. She had finished her freshman year with straight A's and attended church every Sunday, checked all the boxes that needed to be checked. No one, though—except perhaps her long-suffering mother—could appreciate the deep black pool that sat maddeningly still and fathomless behind her eyes. Kids will be kids, folks said, but the salvation of your standard-issue teenage troublemaker was how inept they were at said trouble; most of Tess's classmates got caught at whatever it was they needed to be caught at before they could do any real damage to themselves or anybody else. Tess, though, had something of a cat about her, usually landing square on her paws—or at least appeared to, enough to get by.

That was the danger with falling away, Miriam knew: There was no rock bottom. One day, they were just gone.

A car roared by, honked from the highway. Miriam jumped just as a pastel hand waved out from the driver's window of a shiny black Buick. She bit her lip. It was an old insurance salesman from church, a widower. His wife had died in child-birth, and he'd lost the little girl, who was never truly well, two years later. It was a sad story in a town full of them, like every town, even those across the pond—*keep calm and carry on*. Somebody still had to fetch the groceries; everybody still had to eat; everything marched forward.

The widower had asked her out a few times, usually when a little buzzed. He made a decent living and had no one to spend it on, but he smelled like liverwurst, and the one time he had touched her, in the small of her back at a crab feast the August last, his palm just lightly cupping the curve of her hip, it had sent a squid-like shudder along her bones, leaving her squirmy and repulsed. Walking down the street almost a full year later, the memory forced a similar reaction, a deep-sea echo.

She didn't need it. Or him. Between Joe's officer's pension and the money they had socked away over the years—in addition to the little bit of income from her job at the parish—she and the kids had a roof over their heads and food on the table. Joe, and Tess before him, had even gotten a free private school education at Saint Anne's School, another perk of the job and the benevolence of Father Jim.

Joe Jr. had only eighth grade left, and then he, too, would be off to high school. He would follow his sister on the bus to Appleton unless Miriam bit the bullet and paid for the Catholic boys' school over in Stewartville. It was a strong consideration—Joe could break either way, Miriam thought. He was too serious at the wrong times and too careless when attention was warranted, as if he were mounting a secret rebellion against everything, so subtle no one else could tell, a lifelong silent protest.

After the last car in sight whizzed by, Miriam hustled across the four lanes of Highway 450. She was not sure she would ever entirely be used to automobiles—growing up on the Eastern Shore, they had been infrequent, each one a spectacle. She switched the bag into the crook of her left arm and started walking the long sidewalk that flanked the strip of businesses—the bank, Chandler's Hardware, Wilson's, the fabric warehouse on the end—that served as a sort of gathering spot on the north side of Brookshire. She waved to Stan Chandler sweeping in front of his store, a cigarette dangling from his lip, and he waved back.

"How you doing, Stan?" she called.

"Hot. You?"

"About the same."

Stan nodded, then halted his sweep. He pulled the butt

from his lips, ashed. "Say, the father back at the rectory, you think?"

Miriam wasn't sure how to answer the question. She suspected he was but wasn't sure he would be in the right state for visitors. "Thursdays, he starts on his sermons," she called back, crafting an alibi. "He might not want to be interrupted."

Stan lowered his head into a slow nod. "Fair enough." And then, sounding farther away: "It's not important."

Miriam registered how the last bit didn't ring quite true. "Anything I can help with?"

Stan shook his head and stuck his cigarette back in his mouth. "Nah. Just wanted to talk about some old times, is all. Like I said, not important."

"This unfinished town has old times already?"

Stan almost smirked around the cigarette butt. "Fair enough." Then that far-away voice one last time: "Maybe they aren't so old after all. Maybe you're right."

"The past is the present, Stan."

His face darkened as he muttered something she couldn't quite hear.

"What's that?"

"I said, 'I suppose you're right.'"

Miriam watched two women chatting outside of the fabric shop farther down the strip of stores, and then, once closer, realized they weren't chatting at all, but quarreling through their teeth. One was Rachel Dickerson, she knew, but she couldn't place the other, and the words they were using—she had never heard those curses strained through such polite, measured voices—struck her more with confusion than shock, so much so that she was already half a block up the next road with her arms tight around her shopping bag before she realized she had run away from the confrontation. She blushed at her cowardice and turned to go back, but the women had already separated, stormed off in opposite directions. Miriam blinked at the shop's entrance, unsure of the reality of what she had just seen, wondering whether it could have been some mirage, a trick of the heat. Or maybe it was her all along. Maybe her ears were going, and she hadn't heard what she thought.

Flustered, Miriam carried farther on, passed the site for the new church and the workmen pushing through the sun's blaze. They were moving quickly, the framing mostly up already, enough that you could get a sense of the enormity of the thing. Nestled in an existing curve in the highway, where her young town began, the new Saint Anne's promised to be the jewel in the crown of Brookshire. The whole thing, though, as beautiful as it was auguring to be, left a charcoal taste: "Crooked" Brooks had wedged himself deep into the process—too deep, Miriam surmised, calling shots she felt were not his to call, cutting corners not his to cut.

Father Jim was a kind man, but kindness wasn't always what was needed, even for a servant of God. Maybe especially so. Miriam had the occasional disloyal thought that he was corruptible (and crossed herself with her free hand against the blasphemy). It wasn't that he had a shred of badness, in her estimation—he was moral, considerate, stand-up by nature— but he was a light man, both against gravity and in temperament, and she felt that he could be easily nudged. Pushed. Father Jim was a preacher of the Good Word and was also at its mercy, the tamer steered by the tiger. That was why, Miriam supposed, Brooks had gotten his big, audacious statement church. That was why the Knights of Columbus still got to hold their Sambo Circus every year, the pillars of Brookshire society in blackface on the parish's dime. That was why the drink had taken over Father Jim's nights and started creeping on his days. A few times these last months, he had returned from his clerical visits with eyes a little too wet, a little too pink. One time she found half-pints stowed in the back room of the school's gym, the church's makeshift sacristy. At her most put-upon, she felt she was a boat rocked by the slosh in all directions, that she had another teenager on her hands.

She paused at the rectory only to pick her pace back up, passing the school, now empty until the fall, a square, rust-brick rook guarding the queen to come; she cut left onto Sparrow, her street. She was nearly to the bottom of the hill before she noticed a figure stretched across her front steps. She didn't break stride.

The bookbinder reclined with one arm nestled in the crook of a step, the other holding open a battered volume Miriam didn't bother to identify. He smoked his pipe in even, steady bursts.

Miriam stopped at her front gate. "You're trespassing."

The bookbinder closed his book, his eyes drifting up to hers.

"I could call the police on you."

"You already did."

Miriam tucked her chin into her neck, smirking. "You've met Hillary?"

"Charming man."

"Indeed. And what came of it?"

"I gave him a book. *Gratis.*"

"That's nice. Did he convince you to stay away from my son?"

"We left it open. My interpretation, anyway."

Miriam shook her head, barely surprised. She opened the gate with her free hand. "I swear, that old goat is worthless."

The bookbinder watched a bug crawling along the step. "Actually, I suspect he is very good at what he is very good at."

Acknowledging that the large man was making no effort to move out of her path, Miriam set down her grocery bag. "What do you want with Joe?" she asked, exasperated, as if the wear of the long walk—all her long walks, each one its own little footfall in the journey that had begun the day that some sergeant appeared at her front door to tell her every wish she'd had was already dead, sunken inside the beatless heart of the only man that she had ever asked to touch her—had finally caught up with her all at once. It might have been the heat, or something else shaken loose along the way, but Miriam had no more time for niceties. "Why don't you leave my son alone?"

"He came to me."

"You should have sent him back."

"I apparently never got that order."

"Now you've got it and now you know. I don't want him anywhere around you."

The bookbinder sat up. "Why do you dislike someone you've never met?"

"I don't *dislike* you. I don't *like* you because, yes, I don't *know* you. You blow in here one day, all kinds of money, no one knows where it came from—"

"What do you know of my money?"

Miriam laughed. "You're not that naive, are you? Folks talk. I know you paid cash for Doc Magruder's place."

"Why is it 'Doc Magruder's place'? When does it become my place?"

"Probably never."

"Never?"

Miriam leaned against the iron railing, crossed her arms. "This town didn't start when you showed up. Besides," she said, her pale eyes dancing, "nobody knows your name. What are they supposed to call it?"

The bookbinder puffed a thick cloud of smoke.

Miriam shook her head. "*This* is why I dislike you. I don't need riddles in my life." She twirled her finger at him, conducting the absurdity of what she found sitting before her. "I don't need cryptic tattoos and faces hidden behind big beards. Unexplained money. You know who doesn't give their name and has lots of unexplained money? Gangsters. People up to no good."

"You make a lot of assumptions."

"What most people are afraid to admit is that assumptions often prove true."

The bookbinder allowed himself a small smile. "On that point, we agree."

She regarded him harshly, conceding nothing. "I have eyes and use them."

"Have you asked Joe what he thinks?"

Miriam flushed. "*I* am the parent and *he* is the child. That's how this works."

"Maybe he needs a friend."

Miriam narrowed her eyes, folding her arms. "Joe has lots of friends," she embellished. "*I'm* his friend."

"You're his mother."

"That's right. I *am*. And who is a better friend to a boy than his mother?" Miriam knew she was careening toward a dead end of an argument but couldn't see a way out of it other than to double-down and brace for impact. She could feel her blood pressure rising, spurred by both shame and indignation.

"Sometimes a boy needs—"

"Don't. Don't even go down that road."

"Joe said his father died in the war?"

"I said don't. Don't you dare ask questions about my husband."

"I was there, too. The Pacific, actually."

"Good for you."

The bookbinder leaned forward. He rested his book on the step. "I saw a lot. I learned a lot. Some good, some bad, I imagine." He scratched at his temple, hooking a strand of hair behind his ear. "The point is, I think your son is a good kid, and there are things I can—"

"I think you've enjoyed my steps for long enough, among other liberties," Miriam snarled. "I think you need to go right now." She took a deep breath but didn't flinch from the bookbinder's gaze. "Please," she exhaled.

The bookbinder stood up, pulling a drag from his pipe, rising a few heads above her. He nodded toward the bag.

"Want help with that?"

"No," she replied. Then, through set teeth: "Thank you."

He shrugged. As he passed, he caught the faint flowery scent of Miriam's skin. He paused at her gate. "Do you even know what bookbinding is, Mrs. Hollanger?" Given no answer, he answered himself: "It's fashioning garlands out of the wreckage of the world. A boy could do worse."

11

Only after Miriam placed the grocery bag on the dining room table did she allow herself to shake. It came in rolling waves, starting in her hands and traveling up her arms, over her shoulders, the base of her neck—the secret place she most longed to be kissed. Her whole body shuddered. She put her hand to her lips, released a tiny, almost imperceptible gasp, tasted how desert dry her mouth had become. She grabbed a glass from a cabinet and poured water from the tap, then gulped it down. Its lukewarm ran over the edges of her bottom lip, the corners of her mouth, dribbled down her chin. She poured more, drank again.

When Miriam first spotted the figure on her steps, when she recognized his shape and the strange markings up and down his arms, the hairs on her neck stood and her heart beat double time. She had trained Hillary on him but had no idea what that crooked old bird had done or said: The danger of wielding a weapon like Chief Nathaniel Hillary was one of misunderstood degrees, a machine gun for a hole punch.

She had examined the bookbinder's face as she approached. It was a good face under all that hair, she thought, strong and tanned, with two blue eyes that didn't seem to reflect light, but catch it, best it, throw its husk back at you. They were eyes that had seen things. She didn't need him to tell her that he had once been a soldier; it was printed on his every edge.

There were no fresh markings on the man that she could see, though, no bruises and nothing raw—no evidence that he had been worked over by an old mound of a cop. However, she now understood the unlikelihood of that scenario in a way she hadn't been able to grasp before; with him sprawled across her steps like a lion in the sun, his undershirt stretched and straining, she realized not just the size of the man, but his density. His muscles flexed his tattoos into dancing whenever he bothered to shift his weight.

Any sense of menace Miriam felt emanating from him was tinged with her own anger—at how he had made himself so comfortable with what was by all rights hers, how he stretched, careless and reading, smoking his pipe, as if her doorstep were his den. As if her son were his uncontested apprentice. She felt judged the moment his eyes overran the deckled edge of his book and met hers. She felt herself instantly exposed. And in that wake, it became ever more maddening how he wouldn't speak, wouldn't explain his presence, daring her to object to any of it.

Miriam wiped off her face with a dishcloth. *I was his prey. Naked and defenseless.* What she couldn't let go, what scared her most, long after she had realized that the bookbinder was not there to harm her—at least not in the clumsy, obvious ways she first expected—was how this was not a wholly unpleasant vision.

No. She had been scared—an interloper had blocked her from her door, her heart was racing, and everything under the sun was bent by fear. Her husband had taught her that. Whatever reaction she had in that context couldn't possibly be trusted. She repeated the thought to herself, hoping it would take hold.

But she *had* felt naked before him, it *had* made her angry, *and* she liked it. This made her angrier, because Miriam Hollanger had no room for unexplainable things, except for the Father, Son, and Holy Ghost. This incongruent man stared into her—then and, in some way she couldn't explain, still *now*—and she felt displayed, beads of sweat from her supermarket journey transmuted into some exotic jewelry, the secret diamonds of a queen. Her hand slipped from her heart to her breast, felt the hardness of a nipple through her blouse and bra. Miriam dropped her hand as if it were singed; she pulled groceries from the paper bag and began supper as fast as she could.

⌣

The Hollangers sleepwalked through their meal. Tess kept her head low and her breath small, praying her mother could not smell the medicinal tinge or catch the stupor of her tongue. She had overdone it this time, she knew, the nips picking up speed into sips, and then delving into gulps. She had been able to sleep some of it off, a quick catnap in the woods, but the room still threatened to spin. The voices, the chorus, at least, had stopped.

Miriam, though, was oblivious, wedged in her own thoughts, stuck on the man with pictures carved into his arms. There was a loose thread, something left hanging, and she wanted to pull that thread to an unraveling, feel that naked again. She shuddered and looked up, noticing only that her children were picking at their plates of spaghetti. "Eat," she ordered, not caring if it were heeded.

Behind his blank dinner mask, Joe, too, could not unthink the afternoon, the discoveries he had made. When he was younger, the world had changed gradually, or he had perceived it as such; by the time the ripples reached him, the deed was already done, and he found himself carried along by the momentum, as if waking from a slumber, the familiar as unimportant as a dream, an old testament replaced and rendered obsolete. It had happened when his father died; somewhere, half a world away, a bullet had pierced through a man, stopped him dead. Joe had probably been sleeping, his clock hours behind. He'd woken up, had breakfast, brushed his teeth, and played, still sure that Daddy was coming home, even as flies had begun collecting around his corpse's purplish, gritty mouth. It would be days before an officer would arrive and deliver a telegram to his mother, telling her their world had already ended and begun again. The record skipped and they were somewhere else, a room that looked and felt exactly like where they had been all along but no longer was. Not so much as a potted plant had moved; everything had moved.

It wasn't until his aunt arrived from Pennsylvania, and strange cars filled with men and women—some in uniforms, some in civvies—came and went at all hours, that Joe, almost five at the time, realized something was wrong. His mother sat his sister down, then him beside her, told them the news and asked them to be brave, just like Daddy would have wanted, and *still* it wasn't real for Joe until he saw them put the box in the ground and he grasped that his Daddy wasn't going to army crawl his way out. It was the sound of dirt against metal that announced to him that his family was forever broken.

Now, though, on the cusp of thirteen, the half-life of calamity had shortened considerably, the comfortable lull between truth and realization vanishing as a price of impending manhood. Joe had watched Brookshire evolve and, sometimes more frighteningly, he saw what it had been all along.

Earlier, he and a bunch of the neighborhood kids had been playing baseball on a patch of grass on the far southern edge of town, a typical June day, the summer still new. It was a grand time until a fly ball to deep left soared out past the tree line. Joe waved the others off and ran to get the ball as the batter circled the bases. He heard another shout out behind him, "Man, you'd be some kind of good if you weren't such a four-eyes!" Everybody laughed—and laughed harder when the base runner flipped them all the bird heading into home.

The jeering faded as the underbrush crackled beneath Joe's feet. There was no way he would find the ball in this thicket. He stumbled in farther than he needed to go until he heard twitters past the trees, as if birds were carrying on a conversation in human tones. He stepped forward.

Joe couldn't make out the words, but he could see, deeper and to the left, a row of backyards. Taking another step forward, now careful of the sounds he was making, he grabbed a branch overhead, scrambled up the side of a trunk, and pulled himself high to peer over a tall fence. He could see two figures on the back porch of the house in front of him, a man and a woman. The man had a drink in his hand, and the woman, hair like flames, wore a loose robe and what looked like nothing else. She was laughing, a kind of laugh that punched at the sky around her, echoed against Joe's gooseflesh. She touched the man's arm. They stood up, moved inside, the man slapping the woman's behind as the door shut.

Joe heard his name called. *The ball.* He jumped from the tree and ran back toward the field. Kids were scowling at the ground; one looked up suspiciously. "Where did you go?"

"I was looking for the ball."

"Geez, he didn't hit it *that* far. He's not Kiner."

"It could have rolled."

"It has to be around here somewhere."

The players broke off in different directions. Against all odds, Joe spotted the ball, half buried in leaves. He looked around, making sure the others were distracted; in one swift motion, he swiped the ball and underhanded it deeper into the woods, as far as he could. It split two trees and landed out of sight.

"What was that?"

"I think I kicked a rock," said the four-eyes.

"No way, Magoo. It was a squirrel, back over there. Keep looking."

"I still think I kicked a rock."

"Shut your yap."

They carried on like this for a few more minutes, looking in vain. Joe only made sure he was not the first to throw in the towel.

"Does anybody have another ball?"

A collective headshake. "What now?" another asked.

Joe looked at the sky as if he could decipher the time from the sun. "Might be close to supper. I better be getting back."

The flock groaned and pleaded, mimicking their parents at neighborly dinners and living room cocktail parties, but in the end they were all a little tired, and the mention of food had triggered a chain reaction of hunger. They all followed Joe out to the end of Warbler Avenue, then broke again their separate ways.

When he thought it was clear, Joe doubled back, heart pounding, mouth dry. He didn't know what he was going back to find, but every corner of him fluttered. He turned around full circle, never breaking stride—*be cool, Daddy-o, be cool*—as he tracked any loose shadows or steps, any hint of a witness.

He slouched back to the field, hands in pockets and head down, as small as he could make himself. He thought his chest would calm when he crossed back under the cover of trees, but it only sped until it hurt. *Twelve-year-olds don't have heart attacks*, he admonished himself.

He pictured his father, his namesake, and a shroud like cooling lava poured over his thoughts. His father wasn't scared. Sergeant Joe Hollanger wasn't scared of anything.

But his father was dead. *So what does that tell you?*

That's not what I mean, Joe thought, pinching his face closed. He shook his head and focused; he stood under the cover of a tall oak on the verge of crying. *What had the book-binder taught him?* "Be now," that rolling voice, when Joe had nicked his finger with a straight-edge razor, sizing paper. "Be the pain. Don't run away. Run *to*." Joe braced himself against the tree. He closed his eyes and centered himself with his breath. *Inhale. Exhale . . . one . . . two . . . three. And again. Inhale. Exhale . . . one . . . two . . . three. Be the flutter. Be the heartbeat.*

Joe opened his eyes: Leaves rustled, squirrels scurried. He watched the long late-afternoon sunlight cut through the space the trees allowed; it played against his hand, warming his skin. He returned to the spot behind the row of houses, where he had been not twenty minutes before, and scoped out the best tree for climbing. He quickly found a good candidate—higher branches, better cover.

He was a talented climber, scrambling up in seconds. He adjusted his weight and leaned forward, hugging the base of a thick branch for support. Two windows sat above the porch, one with the blinds pulled, the other framed with sheers billowing in the summer breeze. Joe could hear people—a laugh, softer than the redhead's from before, then a small cry. The sheers wrenched wide, offering Joe an unimpeded view: A man was sitting on the bed in his undershirt, his back to Joe, and a woman before him, her head bobbing over his lap. He couldn't make out what was happening, but he knew it was significant—an explanation, or a confusion, an act tied to his murky dreams, the ones that left him sticky and ashamed. He understood only that it was all there before him, a great book with big, unfamiliar words and common ones arranged in strange ways, a riddle that only time and losing things could solve.

The woman rose and led the man to his feet. They were not the same couple from the porch; this woman was blond and younger. She guided the man behind her, and when he turned, facing the window, Joe was disgusted and intrigued by the size of his member, the bounce of it, like an excited puppy under his belly. He was even more disgusted, more intrigued, when he caught sight of the man's face and recognized Chief Hillary.

The woman, naked, stared straight ahead, out through the wavering sheers. Joe took in all of her, her teardrop breasts with faint, pink nipples, the tuft of blond hair between her legs; the boy's body crashed into itself, Joe mesmerized, sweat spreading across his palms, under his arms, a yawning throb between his own legs.

The blond woman bent over the bed, stretching her torso to the threads of light, bunching the sheets with her hands, hips thrust back, and Hillary entered her from behind, slowly at first, but soon reckless, off any rhythm, his fat belly barely contained by his damp undershirt. Joe's breathing jumped the tracks, too, the boy both attracted and repulsed; he locked in on the woman's face, the only beautiful thing in the frame he could completely understand. He watched each tiny little breath escape, each jostle, each loose strand of hair dance against her high cheek, across the bridge of her small, upturned nose.

She saw him. Her eyes widened in surprise, and for a moment she had the look of a frightened jackrabbit about her, as if she was going to scurry off the bed, out whatever door or window she could muster. That was not an option, though, in her precarious position, and she held her pose, first looking anywhere but at the boy, and then right at him; her green eyes flashed, but her brow locked itself into a severe furrow, and the combination transmitted a clear signal directly into Joe's brain: *Don't move.* It was only then that Joe realized the full extent of the limb he was on, the jeopardy at play, the price that would have to be paid if Chief Hillary caught him peeping. The woman closed her eyes and caught up with the bouncy cadence of Hillary's thrusting, and Joe watched her play it up, moan and bark, and whether the performance was professional courtesy or cover for the boy frozen before her, all Joe could remember of that moment afterward ("*Run to the pain*") were the tears streaking her mascara.

Hillary roared something hoarse, choked, a sick bear; he heaved against the woman's body twice more, then pulled himself out.

There was not much more to see. The chief quickly threw on his pants, buttoned his shirt, and straightened his badge. He returned his gun, set on a little table by the bed, to its holster, tucked everything in. He patted the woman on the head but said nothing Joe could hear as he left. The woman, still undressed, grabbed a cigarette from a pack near where the gun had been, lit it, and ambled to the window. Loose hair framing her cheeks, she pulled down the shade. Too little, too late.

The scene played itself over in the space between the noodles on Joe's dinner plate. He worked through it and then back again, trying to decipher his own entangled notions. His mother, too, was busy accounting for shuddering truths that had been shaken from their base. She did not have room for unexplainable things, and she certainly did not have room for this unexplainable man who seemed to be intent on stalking into her days, first through Joe, and now through her own tortuous urges. He was insidious, Miriam thought. The word *infiltrate* crossed her mind, and she flinched; there was something of the coup about the bookbinder. She remembered him parked on her steps—the only thing missing was a damn flag to plant—and the ladies' dustup she had run away from just before. Miriam shot up from the table and tossed her cloth napkin on top of her cooling food. She could feel how flushed her face was, the heat emerging from just below her skin.

She marched to the bathroom and shut the door, taking three long breaths to steady her hand as she reapplied her lipstick. She stared hard into the mirror, plucked an errant hair from an eyebrow, stared hard into the mirror again, and pursed her lips. She sighed and flicked off the light behind her.

"I'm going out for a spell," she called to her children. "The dishes better be done before I'm back."

The front door slammed, and Tess's entire body seemed to collapse, as if strings had snapped. "Holy Christ, I need a cigarette."

Joe blinked at her, then pushed his chair back from the table. He walked to his bedroom and returned a moment later with two contraband smokes and a match. He sat at the head of the table, lit them both, and handed one to his stunned sister, who took a long, tired drag. They smoked in silence, then cleared the dishes as they were told.

12

~

Running alongside the avenues of Brookshire, the new electric streetlights whirred and awakened before the twilight like clockwork. The days were longer now, so they sat empty vigil, the approaching night never having the opportunity to root in the places they shone. Thus, as such things go, the lights were already being taken for granted, the opaque time before their sentry already fading from collective perception.

That was just fine by the powers that be; the lights were advertised as a perk of the zip code already in the works, but the truth had more to do with J. M. Brooks strong-arming the power company into prioritizing their efforts in the wake of a recent uptick in petty crime throughout town. Nothing too severe, probably the work of idle kids—devils and hands—but a few broken car windows, discarded liquor bottles, and hot-rod tire treads serving as eyesores were enough to get the town's namesake to call in a few favors.

Hells and handbaskets.

Stan Chandler sipped from a can of beer behind his storm

door. His street stood out in its veer toward indigo, and then black; the lights along his block of Tanager were out again, as they had been pretty much since they were installed. He pressed his nose against the door's glass and peeked to his left, then right: They seemed to be working fine just a few doors down in either direction. He wasn't sure how the grid was set up exactly, but this little swath being consistently out didn't make a hell of a lot of sense. Except in the way that it very much did. The fact that the power company had already been out three times with no solution seemed to validate his estimation.

He surveyed the little white house straight across, itself perpetually dark, and tried to imagine a scenario where it didn't have something to do with the electricity, the faulty streetlights. It was a bizarre dot to connect under normal circumstances, he knew, but he had seen a lot of so-called bizarre connections in his years on this spinning rock, and not many of them surprised him anymore. And circumstances were rarely normal. He still thought of them from time to time, the Dysons, wondering whether anyone else really did beyond the mythology that had taken—he supposed not. The town was just stirring back then—the bird-christened streets just being cut in alongside the defense highway there since the twenties, plots being leveled, a few structures rising like toadstools. There weren't all that many folks around, and those who were crossed their gleaming new thresholds with their own baggage in tow. Nobody ever sees what we think they see, Stan figured, enamored as they are with all their own shit. And then time has its way with everything on top of that—twists the story, smooths an edge here or there, planes the door so it'll fit nice and snug. What you're left with is a ghost story by way of telephone game.

The terrors were myriad, tales of purple bloodstains that burst back right after being painted over, same as from the floorboards, through the shag. What folks called the pulsing of the house, how from the outside it could look bigger at times, smaller at others, like the apogees of the moon. Distance being a perspective, of course.

The voices, though no one could make out the words. Something like a moaning cadence song, but in a tongue no one could ever translate. Almost no one.

But Stan had seen with his own eyes—he wasn't sure he would ever be able to unsee the vision of Charlotte Dyson on that little hilltop, all soaked in blood and flinging that mower with a blank, pummeled face like it was the sanest thing to be doing on an Easter morning, half naked and all busted up. Stan shook his head and stole another sip of his beer.

The pair had always seemed different, even before that fateful spring day. Especially Paul, the husband. The man had an easy enough Clark Gable smile, but there was a parlor trick behind it—more like a baring of fangs than any real camaraderie. *Bonhomie*, as the frogs say. They'd small talk every now and again, he and Stan—the usual pleasantries, nonsense about the weather, the Senators, but even in those superficial moments, there was a kind of lingering—an extra, uncomfortable beat. And though Stan could generally account for the glisten in Paul's eyes as a product of the drink—Dyson would not be the first or the last vet to make imbibing a regular part of his peacetime regimen—it seemed as if there were daggers spinning in there, too, around the pupils. Something more. Something worse.

He had heard things, too, troubling things—even before it came out about the horrors Paul beset on his wife, before Stan had collected her up, walked her back into the bloody mess of their living room—from the men who frequented his shop. Late nights at Wilson's, bragging about things nobody in their right mind would brag about, things he did when he was in the Pacific. Trophies he took. Human things.

And now there was the other one. "What are you doing back here, boy?" he whispered against the door's glass, fogging it. "That son of a bitch is long dead." Stan had lived alone for the better part of a quarter century, a widower since his young bride succumbed to the consumption back before the country was allowed to drink again. Even so, he made sure he bit the next part back, not letting it escape his lips: *I know, because I was there. And you were, too—I'm sure of it. Different—a hell of a lot different—but it was you.*

Stan sighed and took a last gulp of his beer, crushing the can in his hand. He also had to decide whether he was going to mention anything to Miriam Hollanger about her daughter. There had always been prowlers messing with the Dyson house over the years, whether testing out their own mettle or some other kind of sick pilgrimage—Roy Dickerson had confirmed as much just a few weeks ago, some new delinquent breaking the locks almost faster than he could fix them. But Stan hadn't seen anyone—maybe save a shadow darting in the night here and there—except for the Hollanger girl rising from the back steps, stumbling around that backyard in broad daylight, so drunk she looked like a foal learning to walk for the very first time.

⌣

Across town, that girl's mother strode down Kestrel, past the stares lobbed from porch rockers and second-floor windows, from men in their garages, beers in hand, the night's ball game droning in the background. A band of chatting neighbors hollered greetings, and Miriam thrust out her hand, a gesture between a hello and a hurried apology. Her eyes remained low on the asphalt before her; if she didn't look up, they might lose interest and not watch where she was going.

Near the end of the street, she made a right turn onto the bookbinder's walkway, down the four steps to the moat of a front yard, then rounded left, down the path to the workshop's entrance. She banged on the door, her heart pounding; night had fallen, inverse to the stakes.

She moved to strike the door again, but it opened before she had the chance. The bookbinder stood, bare chested, broad shouldered, and seemingly of onyx—an eclipse of the kerosene lanterns flickering behind him. He towered over Miriam like a sunspot. She swallowed air.

"Who are you and why are you here?" she demanded, her chin thrust forward.

The bookbinder studied the woman, then past her into the thickening night. "Anyone could ask that of anyone else."

"No," Miriam replied.

"No?"

"No. That's not the answer to my questions."

"And who exactly do you think *you* are?"

Miriam stole a deep breath and curled her shoulders back. She didn't blink and set her jaw at the same hard angle as the man in front of her.

The bookbinder tapped at the frame and turned inside, the door left open behind him. "I'll put on a coffee."

"What do you want to know?" The bookbinder sipped from his mug. He reached for his pipe as Miriam pulled a cigarette case from her purse. He lit hers, his.

"The truth."

The bookbinder leaned back on his stool. "That's not a singular thing."

"Do you think your riddles make you wiser than the rest of us?" Miriam expected a reaction, but the man before her was static, puffing on his pipe in even bursts. She blushed a little. "Fair enough," she ceded, as much to herself as to him. She took a drag. "Start with *your* truth, and we'll go from there."

The bookbinder crossed his legs. "Even that is a more complicated thing than you can possibly imagine."

"Try me. Start with why here. Why now?"

"Here and now?"

She straightened, irritated. "What brought you to Brookshire?"

The bookbinder blew a giant plume of smoke, and in the context of the lanterns and the intricate shapes they cast across the paneled walls, he resembled some sort of primitive idol off the cover of a pulp novel, a talisman with a dangerous treasure encased inside. "I was invited."

"By whom?"

His eyes rested on her, but she could tell he could not see her. He was somewhere else—a different *here*. A different *now*. "That doesn't matter much anymore," he admitted, parsing each word, his voice suddenly hoarse. He cleared his throat, then coughed it out. "The fact is that I'm here now."

"That doesn't answer why."

"Brookshire is a special place."

Miriam pushed her skirt flat. "I know that as well as anyone."

"Maybe," the bookbinder rejoined into his coffee.

Miriam narrowed her eyes at the man, and they sat in silence until she softened and pulled at a new thread. A wild, random one, maybe, but she also understood that the past was the present and the other way around. She only had to take one look at half the men in this town to know that. And this man before her, strange as he was, was perhaps a kind of bridge, a decoder ring, same as Joe used to get in the post. "You said you were in the war."

"*Ai.*"

"In Japan?"

"I landed in Peleliu but was in Okinawa at the end." It seemed both another existence and a wound still raw, the blood yet wet, fighting phantoms, men who had already lost their lives, left to climb into foxholes in the night, stabbing at anything they could, screaming like coyotes until they were cut down with a bullet or a blade.

Miriam shook her head. "I don't need to know about points on a map. I need to know what you aren't saying," she admonished. "I want to know why you boys came back the way you did." Quieter: "Some of you, at least."

The bookbinder wasn't surprised and admired her resolve—her presence here, unattended at this late hour, was evidence enough of it—so he decided to drop the pretense, the dance, pull back the curtain more than he generally would. Not all the way, of course—that would be too much, too fast, and besides, he wasn't sure exactly how the board was laid out himself—but he could see the substance bracing her scowl, so he told her the straight-razor truth as he had observed it, as one of them and not: how mud thickens blood, and vice versa, how the insides of your best friend can turn into a viscous bile. "Maybe one day you return to dust," he grumbled, his face tightening as the memories filtered through him, "But before that, you become something so much messier, so much harder to work into anthems."

He told her about how the Japanese slit GI throats and then cut their manhood off while they lay dying, how men lost arms, legs, eyes, teeth, spleens, brothers, hope; he revealed the slippery slope of being employed to kill, of just causes, greater goods, means and ends. God on your side. He told her about the caves, the tunnels, how they stretched like human fingers, in accusation and covetousness.

He described taking another's man life, a man tasked with taking your own, a man defending what you had been ordered to take, or ordered to take what you had to defend. He spoke about the blue of the Pacific and how small men were, how trivial the ground they fought over was in the framework of the immensity of the sea.

"You're still dancing around something," she alleged.

He poured more coffee. Hers, his. He was and he wasn't, an electric twinging around the cluster of round scars hidden under the tattoos spanning his back, and he found himself transported into the heat of the flames, the cold of the river. He recalled the blistered trees reaching up, and then, as if in answer to their whispered prayer, the outstretched, winged blackness, the hoary rattle that seemed to come simultaneously from the earth itself and inside his own ears. He was quiet for a long while. "At some point," he finally acknowledged, taking her a little further, "you're going to have to make your peace with the darkness. Not just its existence, but its necessity."

"More riddles," Miriam fired back weakly, two hands on her steaming cup.

"Riddles? No. I don't need to tell you every fucking thing that happened over there to help you understand what goes on right here, right under your nose." The bookbinder brushed at his beard and leaned forward, both irritated by her persistence and relieved, using the former to fortify the latter. He would take her as far as he could, right to the edge, show the pieces where they trembled. "Why do you think a place like this exists? A place like Brookshire?"

"Well," Miriam began, lighting another cigarette, "that would be to line the pockets of one J. M. Brooks."

The bookbinder cocked his head. "The developer?"

"He's made a lot of money off of other men's fresh starts."

The bookbinder watched her smoke. "He's not the first."

She shrugged. "I don't know the man, really," she said. "He's the first one I think of, mostly because of the church."

"The church?"

"The big construction. I know you've seen it."

"Yes. Right."

"I've met him, but I wouldn't say he'd know me from Eve. I'm just a trifling church secretary. Small potatoes. I handle mail. Invoices. Things like that."

The bookbinder gulped his coffee. He stood and strode back to where he kept the liquor bottles. He brought one half full of imported whiskey back to the table, poured a shot into his cup, then hers.

He sighed and took a drink. "That's not exactly where I was going."

Miriam flushed in the firelight. "Oh."

The bookbinder held up his hand. "No, it's interesting. Very interesting, actually." He looked into his cup, its oracle, pressed on. "But," he mouthed. He sighed again. "Brookshire is a special place."

"You said that already."

"What if I told you that it was becoming a uniquely *important* place?"

"Becoming?"

"Well, nobody really sets out to build a battlefield. Gettysburg was just a town. Antietam. Manila. Paris. Tokyo." He paused, considering. "Hiroshima, in its way, I reckon. Nagasaki, too." His face darkened. "We kind of broke the analogy there. Ultimately, though, a battlefield only becomes a battlefield because someone shows up. And then someone else to meet them."

"So Brookshire is a battlefield?"

"In a way."

"Because someone showed up."

"Some*thing* showed up."

"Something?" She nodded at his cup. "What exactly did you pour in there?"

The bookbinder grunted. "Maybe I should stop."

Miriam leaned forward, whispered. "Are you talking about God and the devil?"

"If it were that simple."

Miriam grimaced. "Are you the something?"

The bookbinder shook his head. "No."

Quieter, more tentative: "Are you the something else?"

He ran one finger along the edge of his cup. "I'm honestly not sure what part I'm to play." Miriam watched him hunch, as if his body were a satchel he had to haul.

"In what?"

The bookbinder took another long drink, holding the cup

low. "The culmination of things. *A* culmination of things. Their currents."

Miriam rubbed her temple and stole her own long drink. "Their currents?"

"Where does a river end? Where does it begin? Even if you try to touch one small point of it, it's never the same. We set dates. A war began on alpha. Ended on zed. Someone signed a paper. But it was building up for years, sometimes centuries. And we are still feeling each bullet today—will for some time to come."

"You boys saved the world," Miriam retorted, bringing it back to the more immediate past, a context she could grip, that held palpable for her. She could feel the warmth of the coffee and the whiskey coursing through her, starting in her middle, then out through her arms, her fingers. The two figures sat across from each other under the light of the lanterns, balancing their cups in the same way, neither blinking.

"If only," he replied gently. It was as if they were not so much arguing as walking into a harsh wood together, tracking each other only by their voices. "I think there is a great difference between saving and surviving—but in this world, if you achieve the latter, you get to claim the former."

"So nothing is real?"

"It's *all* real. But perhaps we should not be so quick to accept that one victorious crumb quenched a hunger older than we can remember." He met Miriam's gaze. There was always more—allegories that weren't allegories at all, truths that underpin the myths to underpin the truths. "Back in Japan, the old ones talk about how the world was born when the gods churned the sea with a *naginata*—basically a kind of spear. Everything we know comes from a weapon. We nourish our children with the meat of that which we kill, the fruit we cut from its branches. Murder is the root of life." The bookbinder put his cup down on a worktable with a placid clang. "Maybe we should skip the parades."

The bookbinder laid his palms down on the table; he watched the oil light attach to lines on his skin, those of time and those of ink. "The men you sit next to in church defended themselves, and attacked, and killed, and mourned, and stole—stole from the guilty, but also from the innocent, from those stuck in between. They staved off starvation on the calfs of others, found release in the wives and daughters of others, blinded themselves from their sins by convincing themselves that they were more human than the enemy, that they were gods—not *God*, of course, because that would be blasphemous, but *kami*, the sort that have the one true God's ear—and so, when they grew tired of the battle and wanted to end it once and for all, they conjured the thunder, prayers answered, two big clouds, two cities gone, snap of your fingers, the kingdom, the power and the glory, amen.

"They did all that—they were *sent* to do all that—and then they were asked to come home, to pretend it never happened, to be content mowing their lawns, fucking their ordinary wives." The bookbinder's voice lowered to a sandpaper rasp. "They put the little gods back in their cages and expected it to work out fine."

Miriam's arms were crossed against her chest. She was trembling. "And you? You weren't a part of 'all that'?"

"I was," the bookbinder answered, nodding into the firelight. He licked his dry lips. "I just never made it back."

⌄

"I'd like to show you something." The bookbinder led Miriam into the shadows behind the workshop. There was a click, and then a naked bulb over the basement stairs zapped bright. She blinked, flinched. He started up the narrow staircase and, after a short hesitation, Miriam followed.

A door opened and they were on the main level of the house. Here the bookbinder deftly moved about the floor plan despite the darkness. Another flight of stairs led to the top floor—the bedrooms. Miriam's chest fluttered as the stairs creaked under the weight of her guide. She took a deep, hitched breath and followed.

There were two rooms on that floor, to the left and the right, a narrow bathroom between them. The right room seemed lit only by the moon, and this was where the bookbinder led her. Miriam drifted along behind, a tissue caught in the pull of a fan.

A large window stood open, and she could hear all the sounds of the summer night echoing against the wood floorboards and the walls—crickets, frogs, a neighbor's chime ringing softly in the wind. A dog's plaintive bark. She watched the bookbinder's outline climb through the window and motion her toward him on the other side.

Miriam stepped to the window and looked out, down. The sloping roof was just three feet below; with the bookbinder's help, she positioned herself onto its angle. She could feel sweat on her brow and her body, and she blushed, glad for the moon's shadows, the night's shroud. The bookbinder crouched, and she lowered herself beside him, smoothing out her skirt. When she allowed herself to look up, Miriam let out a tiny cry—laid out before her was almost the entirety of Brookshire, the lights of her little corner of the world twinkling like stars below her. It was the town she moved through every day of her life; it was something brand-new. "It's beautiful."

"Worth fighting for?" the bookbinder asked. "I come out here most nights—I like to watch them go to sleep, even when I can't. There's wickedness, but there's also hope."

Miriam turned toward him. "Why Joe?"

"He found *me*."

She knew he could see her in the darkness better than she could see him. Her sigh came from her diaphragm, a surrender. "Just don't let him get hurt."

They perched on the slanted roof for minutes or hours, watching lights blink off, watching the little skirmishes end, if only for a spell.

It was near midnight when Miriam returned home, both her children asleep. She was relieved to find them so peaceful, but a touch jealous, disappointed they had not waited up, feared for her like she feared for them.

13

⌄

Near the westernmost entrance into Brookshire—a road
called Cardinal Way, off Highway 450, where the two waves of
earth fashioning the town's slope converged into a small valley—another strip of businesses, anchored by the town's drugstore and soda fountain, popular in the afternoons among the
neighborhood youth, stood watch, an outpost. In the summer
months, time stretched, and teens bopped in and out almost
as they pleased, peppered among the other locals—some for
an early respite from the heat, others for dates or late-evening
treats. The counter was always occupied but rarely crowded.

Tess hovered at the far end, drawing from a cigarette and
a strawberry milkshake. She closed her eyes but could still
feel the other customers around her, their shifting stares; she
already was growing wary of the way boys—and sometimes
most assuredly *not* the boys, their fathers even—would linger
on her body when they thought she wasn't looking, irritated
more by the mendacity than the stare itself. The stare could
be okay; sometimes the stare even delivered a small twinge,

and that was a little more okay. It was confusing, but since her mother kept insisting that she was in a confusing time (Tess was never sure whether Miriam saw her as the subject or object of that phrase), she figured she could only veer right into the inevitable.

Let chaos reign, Tess thought, pulling a shaky drag from her cigarette, exhaling, sucking the milkshake from the straw, an assembly line. The little bell over the door rang, then again; Rebecca St. Pierre and her daughter struggled through, the child robotic and uncooperative. *At least she's not screaming this time*, Tess thought, and then instantly admonished herself, gazing down past her skirt and into the heavy shadows under the counter. She noticed she could not see her own feet and wondered what else of her might be gone.

A part of her despised Rebecca in the way she despised many things, a muddled sort of loathing, the kind of grayish-brown sludge that comes from blending strange combinations and textures, porous skins; even now, glistening like a pig, struggling through a doorway, left foot, right, *one-two-three-four*, Rebecca was the most gorgeous creature Tess had ever seen. It was the struggle—hair tumbling just so, browned skin from the hot afternoons of yard chores meant to give her house a mask of working order, the way each hint of a line on her young face was a promise of substance, the whole tableau held in place with the green fire of emerald eyes—that infused her beauty, rather than detracted from it.

Once inside, Rebecca placed both hands on her daughter's shoulders. Ava, otherwise still, danced the bookbinder's meditation balls in her palm. The chimes caroled low, a frequency carried to another plane. Tess watched Ava take in the entire store, one panoramic photograph flash—and likewise caught the child's slight quake, an errant, thick clang of the chimes.

Rebecca had almost maneuvered the girl to the nearest stool, whispering gently behind her ears along the way, before Ava froze; her mother collided into the girl's back, releasing a small groan. The child glowered at Tess struggling to disappear behind nicotine and sugar at the end of the row, her blush the shade of the milkshake before her.

The soda jerk, a young man with a tycoon's energy, tried to coax the stock-still child along. "Hey there, sweetheart," he cooed, his eyes lifting to the mother: "Hiya, Mrs. St. Pierre," he offered, his voice now guttural but retaining the same over-ripe sweetness. Tess wanted to vomit her tainted shake right there on the counter. Everything was suddenly too treacly. Too wrong. She stubbed out the cigarette.

"Hello," Rebecca replied, an afterthought, her eyes, too, now focused on Tess, wondering whether Miriam Hollanger knew her daughter smoked—and in public, no less. The girl looked sickly, she surmised, but this thread was disrupted by another ring of the bell. She turned, Tess turned, the whole counter turned; the bookbinder cast his great shadow across the pharmacy's doorway.

He took a step forward, halting inches behind Rebecca, her spine straight, her face locked over one shoulder, and though neither of them moved for however long the beat, Tess swore to herself later that she saw the space around them quiver, like the air around a smoldering, sun-drowned street. An exotic detail she listened to on evening radio shows and could picture in her mind—the roads of Cairo, perhaps. Those of Bethlehem. Places much closer but still out of her reach—Death

Valley. Salt Lake. The West, whatever that was—she imagined a frontier Main Street, a large black bird flying across the white-hot sun, its blinding caw radiating in her ears.

Tess exhaled. Time caught back up with itself, and the man slid by, muttering apologies. Only when he passed between Ava and Tess did the child pull her eyes away from the teenager and become once again pliable in her mother's hands.

The bookbinder commandeered the empty stool next to Tess. The voice on the AM radio behind the counter was carrying on about the heat wave, how there was no relief in sight. "What can I get you, friend?" The soda jerk met him as he sat, a little too much of the jackrabbit, rubbing his hands with a cloth.

The bookbinder waved him off and crossed his inked forearms over the counter. "Nothing for me. I just came in to speak to *her.*" He nodded toward Tess, the girl recoiling against the wall, stunned. She tried and failed to correct her ever-deepening blush, now far past strawberry milkshake. *A true code red,* she couldn't stop herself from thinking, which made it worse. She noticed Rebecca trying to navigate Ava onto a stool without seeming to pay too much mind to the exchange. "Hello, Tess," she heard the man growl, closer. *Too close.*

Tess's mouth moved before any sound came out, like when a soundtrack didn't quite match the film. It happened sometimes in the movie house in Appleton. "How do you know my name?" she asked, enunciating each word as if relearning to speak.

"You look like your mother." Down the counter, Rebecca's eyes darted up. She fussed with Ava's hair.

Tess squirmed farther into the wall, trying to burrow into it, through it. "How do you know my *mother?*"

The bookbinder stared ahead at the shelves of dishes and appliances behind the soda counter. "We've had occasion to talk." He scratched at his beard. "I like her. I know your brother, too. Actually . . . he's the one I'm looking for today. I saw you through the window there—figured you might know where he is."

"Who?"

"Joe."

"Oh. Yeah." Tess swallowed air. "Probably playing ball."

"Where?"

"On Warbler Avenue. This side of it. But it's not really a baseball field. Just an empty lot that backs into the woods."

"Got it." He eyed the ashtray beside her. "Hitting those pretty hard?"

Tess stiffened.

The bookbinder leaned closer. "What are you drinking?"

"Strawberry milkshake."

He shook his head. "No, child. What are you *drinking*?"

Tess bit the inside of her cheek. Took a deep breath. From twenty feet away, Rebecca could see her shoulders slump.

"Bourbon."

"Interesting choice with a milkshake."

"Are you going to rat?"

The bookbinder held her gaze, made out the small lines forming around her pupils. "Be careful, kid. There's quicksand all around this place, and a person could get lost in it if they don't know what they are dealing with." He sighed. "Maybe even if they do."

The bookbinder stood. "I came here looking for your brother, and you've helped me, for which I am obliged." Then, under his breath: "Watch yourself, Tess."

⌄

The bookbinder squinted at the sunlight, the little bells of the shop's door tinkling in his wake. He hesitated on the corner, one big hand cupped over the back of his neck. Straight or right; straight was the longer way, parallel to the highway and wrapping around the farther edge of town, while right was twice as fast at least, the obvious shortcut, straight down via Tanager Way. His stomach heaved at the mere thought of the street name—such a bright, small bird associated with such horror. It was fitting in its macabre way.

The reasons he would want to steer clear of that part of town, that square white-brick house, had surprisingly little to do with the stories the neighbors of Brookshire told each other of its sordid history. They had a canon, and with minor variations here and there, its opening act was pretty well accepted: On Easter morning, the year of our Lord 1944, Paul Dyson, a war hero in Guadalcanal and a hell of a mean drunk, brutally beat and raped his wife Charlotte in their marital bed—an act so ferocious that it induced a miscarriage of what would have been the couple's first child.

The second act of the story, though, grew quickly murky, and usually relied on the testimony of a friend of a friend, someone who knew an Appleton cop or overheard someone or other in the know late at night, after tongues got loose. Charlotte Dyson wasn't in very good shape for questioning, this thread went, but by what the detectives could gather, Paul Dyson shot himself after he realized what he had done. She was short on details at the police station, but her cryptic words had been handed down through the years: "I didn't stop it," she was to have said again and again. "I let him." No one was sure whether she was referring to the suicide or the rape; no one was sure it mattered.

What didn't add up, though, and what those people in the know still shook their heads at, was how *two* bullets went through Paul Dyson that morning, both from his own gun. Charlotte supposedly spoke only in flashes, one image not necessarily tied to the next—she would often get stuck on something, repeating it until she wore herself out and fell quiet. The detectives would try to nudge her back to the timeline, but she'd pick up the tale somewhere else entirely. If they pushed too hard, she began to falter. Best they could figure, Paul's first shot didn't take; it tore through his neck but didn't kill him, not right away. He must have scared himself sober, they thought, smeared himself across the walls, the floors, as he bounded through the house, a trapped antelope bucking against the barriers of his sudden prison. At some point, and it couldn't have been long—a handful of seconds, tops—Paul Dyson most likely realized there was no turning back, stuck the gun in his mouth, and fired true.

There was always some doubt, of course—adrenaline could explain only so much. Charlotte was briefly a suspect, until a check of her hands convinced the Appleton authorities that she had not fired a gun. And, over the years, alternative theories were advanced—a gunman offing Paul for something nefarious the ex-officer was into recurred as speculation, sometimes with J. M. Brooks serving as the invisible hand behind it all, sometimes without. Even a Good Samaritan angle was considered—someone walking by, overhearing the assault, the woodsman appearing to save Red Riding Hood from the wolf only to fade back into the trees. The power of the straight line, though—the rape, the miscarriage, the suicide, *boom-boom-boom*, one right after the other, all fitting together, even imperfectly—usually won out.

And then there was the third act: the ghost story. In their own way, he figured, the people of Brookshire were most right and most wrong about this piece of the Dyson puzzle. There *was* something in that house that shouldn't be, but like the audience in Plato's cave, they couldn't see past the shadows on the wall—or, in this case, the bloodstains. What those stains represented—what held them in place—was so much worse than one dead soldier's troubled soul. The bookbinder feared he alone could appreciate the dark hum that emanated from the Dyson house—and, more importantly, could sense that it was getting stronger. Sometimes, in the quietest parts of the night, he could even feel its outmost waves from his rooftop on the other side of town.

In the end it was a combination of his own pride and a faint scratching just inside his own head, a rustling that heralded a yearning he couldn't place or wholly grasp, pricklier than just idle curiosity, that moved the bookbinder. He turned right, toward Tanager Way.

As he approached, he could feel the hum intensify, its vibrations running across every surface he passed, every physical thing, as if it were eliciting a shudder from Brookshire itself. And, almost as if in answer, the scratching inside him correspondingly ran deeper, sharper. The bookbinder, with each step forward, felt pressed between the two; the overpowering taste of metal burst across his tongue, under it, like he had swallowed a mouthful of pennies. He shoved his hands in his pockets and pushed forward.

When the bookbinder set his boot on Tanager proper, it was as if the little white house itself reacted to his hubris and struck back. The hum stretched itself beyond its bounds, took on new dimensions, intricacies. The bookbinder could detect more clearly that it was no steady entity, but many bundled black weeds competing, growing over each other's roots. It was the inverse of the girl's—*Ava's*—earthy song, repelling where she attracted. He could feel the snap of its revulsion and fear, how threatened it was. Perpetually so. The metallic taste blossomed into an abrupt, intense nausea, all push and pull, disparate urges curling around his bones, tightening like vises. He braced himself against a young poplar tree, clutched his head with his hand, alarmed by how suddenly soaked both were—thick, briny drops of sweat burst and fell from the bookbinder's face and beard into some stranger's lawn.

Something licked inside his ear, leaving words behind, typewriter hammers: *Are you a coward? Or just fucking slow?* The bookbinder grabbed at a handkerchief from his back pocket and tried to wipe his face clean. The voice floated back, tickling both against his eardrum and beyond it, an echo caught in the tree branches. *Come inside.* His mouth ran as dry as his brow was wet; it was not *her* voice that beckoned him, but *his*, mocking her. History recalibrated. The black fluttering thing in his brain crashed against the confines of his skull, and he collapsed against the tree, barely big enough to hold his mass. He slid down its trunk, scraping all the way down, his eyes burning, soaked with sweat.

"What's the matter, boy?" The voice was no longer in his head, but next to him. He felt a man-size shape hovering, a blur, a spot in the haze. "Scared of a little blood?" The bookbinder snarled and swung at the spot. "You should have heard her *asking* for it."

He screeched, a raw cry of agony and sedition.

Everything clicked silent.

The bookbinder blinked open his eyes, darting them back and forth—there was no one else around. He sat alone on a curb in the shadow of the poplar and rubbed his hand over his face. Eventually he gathered himself, standing up with some caution, still touched by vertigo. He cursed under his breath; if he was indeed the *something else*, it didn't bode well for anyone that he couldn't make it close enough to knock on the fucking door.

The bookbinder took a long look up toward the house where, all those years ago, Paul Dyson had wrestled his demons and lost. With a heavy head, he improvised a new route, staggering through a maze of cross streets to eventually land on Warbler.

⌄

By the time the bookbinder arrived at the empty lot that doubled as a ball field, his nausea mostly dissipated, the spot had been abandoned by the day's champions. Worn down by tennis shoes and the summer sun, the grass was a sad sight, patches in the dust. He spun in a slow circle, aware he wasn't completely alone, and noted the tree line eastward, past the edge of the field, placing it on his mental map of Brookshire—he knew these old oaks ran behind the houses along the southern side of Warbler Avenue. He also knew exactly what sat among them and why it might captivate a young man.

As he suspected, the bookbinder tracked size 7 Chuck Taylors into the trees. He cleared his throat and rustled some brush. Joe Hollanger soon ambled out, looking more tired than aroused.

The boy didn't feel the need to explain his emergence from the forest—just started talking, normal as anything else. "My mom changed her mind—she said it was okay if I came back to the shop."

"I know." The bookbinder pulled out his pipe and leaned against a tree.

Joe sat in the dirt, pulling out a crumpled pack of cigarettes from his shorts. The bookbinder arched an eyebrow.

"I've been doing it all along," Joe asserted, as if that clarified everything. The bookbinder shrugged and lit his pipe, handing Joe the match. They smoked for a moment. "What changed?" Joe finally said.

"We came to an understanding," the bookbinder answered.

"Did you do it to her?"

"What?"

"She came in my room smelling like the shop and whiskey." The boy blew a crooked smoke ring. "Just tell me if you did."

"No, I didn't 'do it' to her."

They looked at each other for a hard moment, until Joe's eyes trailed off, something close to satisfied.

"What do you know about such things, anyway?"

Joe turned back in the direction of the house on Warbler, the one with the girls that came in and out all afternoon.

"What do you know of that house?"

Joe blushed. They mostly kept the blinds down, but not always. And the windows were usually cracked, for the heat, so he could hear almost everything, at least—the moans, the way the women begged for it, what sounded like empty ass-kissing, even to him. He looked up. "The other day I saw Chief Hillary."

The bookbinder gazed deeper into the woods. "Is that a fact?"

They smoked, together and alone, enjoying the small respite of the scattershot shade. Joe held out his arm, studied where the light attached itself, like golden paint, rolling across his arm as he rotated it. The bookbinder watched him, struck by an echo of another life—crawling on his belly, the taste of blood in his mouth, metallic and warm. Fear and death all around, almost like a blanket. Like a blur. He remembered hiding from the moonlight, lest the glisten from his weapon's barrel gave him away.

"Why do they do it?"

The bookbinder spit and stuck his pipe back into his mouth, talking through it, as he often did. "They need the money."

"No," Joe said. "The men." Then quieter: "Do you?"

"Do I what?"

"Go there."

"No."

"Have you ever?"

"What?"

Joe stubbed out his cigarette, frustrated. "Gone *there*."

"No."

"Ever? No whorehouse or cathouse?"

The bookbinder shook his head.

"I wouldn't want to, either," Joe said.

"No?"

"Seems too sad." The boy's voice was low.

"It can be a hard life."

"I was talking about the men."

"So was I."

A long silence extended itself between them, the sort that

was a kind of sound. Joe shielded his eyes and looked up at the bookbinder. "Were you looking for me?"

"Yes."

"What for?"

The man tapped out the embers of his pipe. "Orders are starting to pile up. I could use an extra pair of hands. Consistent—on the clock. Pays ten cents a day."

"All day?"

"Mostly. You're always free to say no, or walk away."

"No, I'll come."

"You sure?"

"Yes."

"All right, then."

They shook hands. Joe spat.

14

The bookbinder didn't heed the knocking at first, for the storm that was raging. By the kerosene glow, he carefully stitched together the signatures for a collection of Jingika verses, the whole book no bigger than a wan smile. He thought of little things, their power.

The wind whipped against the walls, a giant wolf huffing, puffing, as the darkening edge of day turned into a black, blustery night. Rain kamikazed the porch's tin roof while the bombast of thunder trailed flashes that pierced the windows, the light shifting from warm to something beyond cold, beyond burning. He squinted, his concentration on a single needle passing through paper, the delicate sabotage of binding.

Instinct, a radar older than men and the stories they kept, scratched at his focus. He paused, holding still the folded pages in one hand, the needle tethered to thread in the other. The pelting rain surrounded him and his walls.

There was something else, though—some other note beyond

the ear, without syllables, a cry that coursed through him as an electrical surge. There was the storm and what authored it. *Who.* He dropped the needle only to stare at it. He put the signatures down.

He walked to the workshop's door and put his eye to the peephole. The long, screened porch was empty, leaking, its gutters overflowing. He pressed against the wood to see farther out, around to the porch's entrance off to the side. And then: *Boom-boom-boom. Boom-boom-boom.* Rhythmic, an ancient heartbeat pounding through the ramparts of this near-empty house. *Boom-boom-boom.* Something living. Something resolute.

The bookbinder made his way toward the dark center of his dwelling; he preferred not to turn on the lights, comfortable navigating the steps to the second floor and his few possessions upstairs without being able to see or be seen. Something about old habits and hard dying.

He traversed the narrow hallway, past the den and into the pitch-black living room, in total control of his body, an efficiency of movement; topside, the sound was clearer, distilled, shook everything: *BOOM-BOOM-BOOM. BOOM-BOOM-BOOM.* The bookbinder unlocked and pulled open the front door. The world screamed.

Rebecca St. Pierre, drenched, shivered on the landing, her hair plastered flat, her face a waterfall, her eyes—shining with anger and trepidation and life—the only light. Her blouse was soaked through, stuck to her skin. Her chest heaved, as if she had been running for miles, years, galaxies. Her face twitched, recalibrated itself, then twitched again; trying to remember where she was in the world, or forget forever, she wrestled with what she was doing here, on this step, staring into the eyes of this wild, stained man. He was a kindred creature she could not equate—she knew without knowing that they were both here for the same reason, even if one or the other didn't exactly know it yet. Didn't exactly not. She let out a sigh like a growl and kissed him, kissed him hard, opened them both to a hurt of which most could only dream.

Her thin arms wrapped around his tattooed shoulders, she read his scars—with his around her waist, he felt her bruises, pulled them to him, pulled her hips to his. He pressed against her, everything firm, everything charged. She bit a whisper into his neck, inhaled, breathing in his musk and the air around them, all cedar and ozone and the promise of the end of the world. He pulled her into the house and she lunged, hooked her legs around him, gaining leverage. She grabbed his face in both hands and kissed him again, tasted his mouth, his tongue, felt his beard claw at her face, pure want, pure war. A *caw* against the illusion of peace.

The bookbinder kicked the door closed, the house shuddering in its slam, the pair thrust into blackness. He could feel Rebecca's searching mouth against his, her fingers grasping at the skin of his arms, his back, trying to reach in him, through him, trying to clutch bone. They became something clumsy, banging themselves into furniture, careening against the walls, lurching across the floor.

Her kiss was wet, hungry; she smelled of rosewater. The bookbinder's body throbbed against her heat, his breathing equal parts purr, snarl. He carried her up the stairs to the top floor, each step precarious, each a chance to fall backward into hardwood, to careen back to earth, to collapse under the weight of themselves, this monster they had formed.

They staggered to the left bedroom, where the bookbinder kept his meager twin-size bed, barely more than a cot. They threw themselves onto the mattress, mouths still entwined, ragged dolls, elaborate traps.

On her back, caught between the bars of his trembling, veined arms, she scurried, almost like a crab, leaned up on her elbows, green eyes burning, neither of them knowing where the tears ended, where the rain began. She snatched at her own long skirt, scrambled for the hem, hitched and bunched the material, reached under. She tore off her panties, maneuvered them around her long, bare legs, flung them to the floor. She grabbed the man's belt buckle, loosened it with shaking hands, something in her off the rails, something in them both a mountain road, a series of switchbacks, the very edge of life, nothing but oblivion all around. She pulled open his khakis, her eyes still searing into his, branding one another—angry there was so much need, such impossible depths to scrape against—grabbed him, his hardness, with both hands and guided him between her legs, the very edge of her. He entered her slowly, in one long motion, and she cooed, dug her rigid fingers into his shoulder blades, drew blood.

Their movements became torrential, reckless; once inside, they kissed again, teeth gnashing, tasting every corner of each other. Borders fell—he lost where he ended, and she the same, each thrusting, each moaning, her sweat his, his blood hers, and when they came, old engines rattling off switchbacks, time held for as long as their bodies could bear it, until everything curled, everything collapsed.

⌣

Three blocks over, on Sparrow Lane, the Hollanger family had barricaded themselves against the storm. Joe and Tess sat at the big picture window, lulled by the pulsing sheets of rain that turned their street into a cascading river, a big muddy surge carrying chunks of debris down the hill. Though their house had been built years ago, Sparrow remained one of Brookshire's last unfinished streets, with empty lots peppered all the way to its edge, where the big new interstate was planned, a road to connect the coasts or cut America in half, depending on how one deciphered a map.

Miriam thought the lots remained unsold because of how the mud carried everywhere, deposited itself in every nook, leaving the impression of something ruined. Most people grasped only the surface of things, she thought. Folks bought up cheaper lots at the bottom of a slope because they couldn't see the inevitable flooding that would occur in basements that hadn't been built yet. They shied away from Sparrow Lane, where the water ran harmlessly by, because the street was always dirty. Miriam knew people would eventually buy up these properties when there were no others to secure, when the choice was taken from them, and then, later on, when her new neighbors would hear others complain about having to bail water every time it rained more than an inch in a day, they would think themselves lucky. And maybe they would be right in their stupid way—one was either a slave to fortune or a slave to chaos, the way white is all color and black is its absence, both, in their way, the same extreme.

A web of lightning cracked across the sky, followed by a guttural boom; the storm wasn't just near; it felt right *here*. Miriam inched toward the center of the house, her fingers tracing a wall, and gently admonished her children for hovering against the window, to back away—a request that only made them turn to her blankly, then back to the glass, so close that she could see their breath fog its clear. She had switched off all the lights, cautious of a surge. She had been afraid of thunderstorms since she was a little girl on her parents' farm back on the Eastern Shore. One afternoon a bolt had hit their barn, and she remembered the way the structure had shuddered and screamed—an old cow inside keeled over, dead before it hit the ground. A bad omen in an already bad time.

Her children didn't complain; the darkness helped them see the storm better. They shared no words, but Miriam could catch the common awe in their profiles each time their faces were lit by a strike; they looked momentarily younger than they had in a long time. So much had changed in just the last year; Tess had gone to bed one night her little girl and had teetered out the next morning a curvy young woman. It felt that quick, that shocking. Not just boys had taken notice, but men—grown goddamned men—now proffered an attention her daughter had never known before. It could not be easy, Miriam knew, her oldest child trying desperately to keep up with the woman the world had already compelled her to become.

Even Joe, already a quiet boy, had grown more complicated, more taciturn. When he ran around in shorts, Miriam felt herself repelled by the darkening hair on his legs. She knew he needed things she couldn't give. She trusted the bookbinder as far as she could, but it was a trust spiced with apprehension. There was an edge to him, even sharper than the surface—the outlandish tattoos and muscles—his own sort of river that he kept below his kindness, the sort that cut rock. She shook her head; she did not know on what road the peculiar man would lead her son, but she knew that it did not end with Joe smelling like liverwurst, or selling insurance to people who never risked anything in the first place. She would have to make her truce with that.

Miriam took a step into her living room, and then another. The closer she came to the window, the louder she could hear both the pounding of the rain and the creaking of the house. She could feel how flimsy her protections were, and goose bumps broke across her flesh. She swallowed air, hands shaking, and took a few more stilted steps forward, stood at the window with her children, let out a shriek when lightning crashed right in front of them, a sound drowned out by the thunder before the echo of light had even faded from her near-blinded eyes.

⌣

Roy Dickerson seized a drink from the tumbler on the nightstand and winced. "You really need to stock better whiskey," he declared, setting it back down. Mae rested on her side, head in upturned palm. "You're not paying for the drink," she said. "I'm the premium." He grunted as she touched his arm.

She rolled over onto her other side, the sheet slipping down the length of her. Alabaster and South Texas. *A winning combination*, he thought. She stared at the windowpane, listening to the rain and wind beat against it. "It's really coming down now. You might as well stay a bit. Pour another shitty drink." Even with her back to him, Roy could hear Mae's impish grin. She was a person who happened to the world, not the other way around.

"You're not pushing me out of here tonight?"

The madame rose from her bed, wonderful parts of her bouncing over to the window to lift the blind. She stood before the glass as naked as the day she was born; Roy could see the plump outline of her breasts in its reflection. Mae normally preached discretion because of the neighborhood, but the storm provided cover. "You think anybody's coming over in this mess? I'll be lucky to keep the girls awake. I just hope it breaks soon."

"Aren't Thursdays sort of quiet anyway? Payday's tomorrow."

Mae pressed the window with her index finger. "You know better than that," she purred. "And you know we take credit here." She turned back to the real estate agent. "A man's needs should not be dictated by the punch of the clock. What are we, an assembly line?"

Roy took a long drink, caught a burn, and coughed. *What are we?* He had been coming to Mae for months now, first because of the excitement of it all; he had sold her this house, and he knew the score, could read it in the way she cascaded across his office, a perpetual advertisement for her wares. He didn't come right away, though; it took a while to build up to it, the tall redhead holding his stare around town, the scent of lavender that she carried with her—strong without being overpowering, just enough to register, to get wedged into his weakest moments. He jacked off in the cramped office bathroom late at night after everyone else had left, imagining her on top of him, all her curves rippling across him, pulling him along, deeper into the ocean, carrying him to climax—after which he opened his eyes, saw his seed swirling around the toilet bowl, his dick in his hand, a naked bulb swinging overhead.

It was not like he had never stepped out on his wife; he had plenty, usually over in Appleton or destinations farther out, traveling "on business," showing a house out "in the sticks." His dalliances had started in Italy, where he was stationed, before they were even married, and never stopped. The trysts were nothing, maintenance, a working man's prerogative—so long as he remained discreet.

The brothel on Warbler Avenue was different, though; it manifested as pure consumerism—he got what he wanted, when he wanted, convenient to home. He only went with Mae and made standing appointments to ensure he never had to wait. He loved the arrangement and, in time, began to love her.

He knew she fucked other men, though not as often as the other girls, classifying herself as "semiretired." He was not jealous—she was a service professional, like him, a one-way street, the customer always right. What Roy loved about Mae was how he knew what she would say in any given situation, whether she was actually there or not, how she took hold in his head, a secret soundtrack only he could hear, keeping him company throughout the otherwise mundane days. He was both tickled and unnerved by the fact that the person he had the most in common with in the world was a whore.

He looked at his watch on the nightstand. "I should go," he said.

"In this rain? Noah wouldn't go out in this shit."

Roy stood up and grabbed his pants. "It'll be good. It'll wash the stink off me." He glanced at Mae, regretting what might have conjured a small wince, but she was smiling wide when she kissed him. "Good thinking, cowboy," she agreed, and winked.

⌄

Father Jim stared at the ceiling, waiting for leaks that didn't appear. He listened to the white noise of the rain against the rectory, shut his eyes, and prayed for a sleep he likewise knew wouldn't come. He had to piss again. It would be the third time since he retired to bed. He threw the covers off.

The priest shuffled down the hallway to the bathroom, not bothering to close the door. It was just him living here, had been that way for almost two years now, his only human support two layman deacons. The diocese promised an associate pastor when the new church was built, and he knew he could use the help, even if it meant he would have to close the bathroom door when he got up in the night. He stood over the toilet for ten seconds, twenty, counted from seven backward, slowly, and then finally heard the tinkle of water against water. He sighed, relieved.

Father Jim flushed the bowl and made his way to the kitchen, extracting a fifth of vodka from the icebox. He grabbed a coffee mug from a cabinet and filled it up. Prayers didn't always work, and sometimes one needed to take matters into one's own hands. He drank in heavy gulps, then poured another cup.

He walked over to his canvas chair with the shiny arms— it had been Father Thomas's before he caught the cancer and died in the room where Father Jim now slept. That had been a steep, swift descent—from spiritual father to something bloody coughed, wan, inhuman; the disease couldn't kill the man fast enough. Jim had watched the whole thing, prayed for his friend's death as an act of mercy. God would not take Thomas, though, not right away, and the surviving priest forced himself to believe his predecessor and mentor had earned a special place in heaven for the intensity of his final suffering, if not for his lifetime of compassion and service.

Father Jim lit a cigarette and pulled an ashtray near. Things had changed so much—and they seemed to be changing ever faster every day. *Progress*, he thought. The cars were faster, the kitchens in the magazine ads looked like they belonged in rocket ships—they had even built a newfangled bridge that spanned across the *entire* Chesapeake Bay. He winced at the thought; he would have to cross that literal bridge sooner rather than later. He had promises to keep on the other shore. He carried some guilt for the infrequency of his visits since Thomas passed, but the daylight seemed to be getting away from him lately, his congregation growing and, he suspected, growing more restless—the Saturday confessions, at least, were becoming more colorful.

He stole another swig from his cup, the warmth already starting to spread across his brow, make everything slow again. He could not be comfortable in his own skin without making the house a home, making it cozy, making it blur. He was a good priest, but the nights stretched in contrast to the velocity of the days, and God took longer than the drink ever did.

A burst of lightning crashed nearby, and the outline of the new church scalded his vision. He blinked. Brooks had been around again today, and it seemed like there were more and more contractors working longer and longer hours. Cousins of cousins. He thought he had caught sight of a pistol tucked in one man's waistband the other day, though he couldn't be sure. The building was changing every day, however, growing into some new shape as it struggled to its final form. A month ago Father Jim had feared the new sanctuary wouldn't be ready by Christmas; now he thought it might be done next week. There was much yet to do, but as Brooks had said and said again, there was a lot riding on this project, and he was happy to use his vast resources to help move it along. Father Jim knew there was something self-serving and lecherous about the developer's interest—that this was not the way it was supposed to be. He was losing control of the construction, depending too much on a stakeholder he didn't trust. He feared himself becoming untethered from his own parish.

He toasted his mug to the window, a half-smoked cigarette between his lips. He was being paranoid. *Everything's as right as rain.* His laugh was raw and his eyes grew heavy.

⌄

All across the lowlands of Brookshire, men cursed the sky through the dropped ceilings of their basements, the asbestos in their walls. The flooding was everywhere, whole families left with no resort but to bail out by bucket, a losing effort before it was begun. The unlucky rolled up their pants, splashed through the cold, filthy water, as if their homes were rickety ships, as if they all might sink back into the earth.

Tensions rose with the waterlines; once-cordial neighbors turned away those asking for help, angry to have to defend the urge to look out for themselves, their own. Frightened wives locked themselves in their bathrooms, or slept in tiny beds curled around their children, some of whom brandished their own welts and bruises. The storm slackened the armors that were already imperfectly held in place, and men from house to cookie-cutter house selfsame mirrored each other, ankle deep in mud water, chain-smoking like dragons, untethered from time itself, from the protections they had fashioned since coming home.

⌄

Ava watched her defeated father glare back at everything in the room but her. She understood; she could see all the individual pinpricks of his suffering, the ruinous cross fire of snakebites that extended up and down his soul. He had wanted to fight for her, had indeed fought for her the only way he knew, but his fighting got them nowhere but bone-tired. Stopping proved worse, giving him the chance to see that when he wasn't fighting, he wasn't anything. She saw all of this. She bore all of this. She watched the inky gossamer thread itself through the pinpricks and divined the pattern being stitched.

She didn't stop any of it. She let it happen. To him. To her.

Sam lit a new cigarette with his last and took a shaky drink. He could see the traces of a child, the toys scattered about, the dolls and soiled clothes, but could not locate the child; nothing added up, each primary color, each flowery print, a kind of deception that chafed at him in places no salve could calm. Every day it took more and more liquor to steady himself, to build a moat, a safe harbor. He lived in a place that both masked his rage and provoked it.

He had witnessed men—*fucking boys*—dying in the cold forests of Germany, their red punctuation splattered against the snow, had seen a skinny kid's eyes blink after the top of his head had been blown clean off, watched his mouth move, speak some oath or other that never mattered, that no living soul would ever remember. He had shot men and been shot at. He took lives, same as so many others around this town. They almost never spoke about it, the veterans long since sent back home, only late at night at a place like Wilson's or around somebody's handmade basement bar, and only in vague mutterings, euphemisms. The Germans, the Italians, were real and guilty as such, finite in time and space, but men like Sam St.

Pierre were amorphous, collective—a nation, a wave, a front. Indistinguishable from each other, they did what they had to do. Communal orders.

But Ava killed him. Each animal wail—each time she struck the furniture, the walls, *herself*—shaved his already frayed nerves. She was a hurricane he had unleashed on the world, on himself and on his wife. He knew they all despised him for it. He knew they all felt the same things he felt, because that was as far as a man like him could see.

He couldn't stomach the doctor's sympathetic prognosis that this was who she was, not a matter of getting better, but a challenge to be faced. Sam didn't need another opportunity for heroism—he had medals enough to choke on. He had enjoyed a place of honor in local parades before even enlisting, before returning from the fatherland something flickering, a bent wick in a wind most couldn't or wouldn't see. He was the handsome high school star, the pitcher who was going to cross an ocean and give the Krauts his killer fastball, right between the eyes. That was not how it came to be and never possibly could have been. His horror could never fit inside the borders of a nickel comic.

Once back home, he tried to pick up where he'd left off and married Rebecca, a local beauty to match his own, neither knowing in which direction their spirits traveled, how the light behind their eyes corresponded only imperfectly, temporarily, with fate conspiring to make one wane while the other was just beginning to ignite.

When their daughter came out blue and silent, it was Rebecca who took charge as much as the doctors. They got the baby breathing, but she still didn't cry. No smack on the ass and welcome wail to the world. It was touch and go, so much that Rebecca even had the priest called in, rushing over after offering the second Easter Sunday Mass. Somehow the child pulled through that day, but when Ava didn't develop as the world deemed she should—as *he* did—it was Rebecca who rose to the challenge of raising her. She researched old journals and texts to the point of exhaustion, examining afflictions and cures, relevant or not. She experimented with theories and remedies, sometimes on herself. She observed her daughter so closely that she sometimes forgot when or where she was—she monitored what worked, what didn't, what broke through— like positioning the antenna of one of those newfangled televisions with the precision of a surgeon. Rebecca was the one who never gave up on Ava, never lost faith that some chemistry of love and devotion would click open the lockbox and expose all the girl's treasures.

She pushed to settle in Brookshire, one town over, to be that much nearer the city and its better doctors, and Sam soon found himself even farther, fainter, on the outside, looking in. He ignored the diagnoses, pretended the child was like all the other children, punishing her when she behaved differently, hitting her when she hit herself. When that did no good—in fact, changed nothing save speeding the half-life of his wife's disgust—he double-timed it down the metaphysical mountain, every man for himself, something between a full surrender and hoarding for a last stand; he abandoned his daughter without moving an inch. It was a tenuous arrangement that depended on copious amounts of booze. Sam swallowed another long drink.

He mostly stayed out of their way, these women aflame, curling into the womb of his basement or escaping to his secret haunt—living underground either way, only appearing topside for shifts at the plant or on holy days of obligation. But sometimes, like tonight, the drink did his talking for him, carrying him up on a head of its poison steam. Sam didn't remember all of what he said to his wife—something about dinner tasting like vomit—but he did recall his finger thrust in her face, punctuation to his tirade. And her eyes shining back at him, full of hate and something even more complicated than that. *Something like a promise kept*, he thought, not wholly knowing why, only that it made him angrier. So when Rebecca stormed off, he barreled for the door to block her; in the end, though, he proved too drunk to do anything but shout more empty words, swing at her and miss.

Almost as soon as the door slammed behind her, the rain started in sheets. There was no easing into it; dark clouds had threatened, but the deluge was instantaneous, as if a pipe had burst. It wasn't raining, and then it wasn't anything *but* rain.

Lightning flickered around his house on Phoebe Street, and Sam stumbled back down into the basement, left Ava upstairs, hugging her legs and gently rocking, for an hour, then two, then three. He drank and smoked, waiting for the screams, the stomping, the crashing of plates. *This ill-fitting little girl. His.* It was during such episodes that he most stood apart from himself, just out of reach, unable to hold his tongue or his hands.

And it was in this space, of being both in and outside of himself, that Sam first started to hear the chorus, soft but resilient. He walked the streets of Brookshire, tracking the song, their luminous call, and traced them to the abandoned little house on Tanager Way, older than most. He now craved nothing more than to visit those voices, accept their smooth counsel, let them sing him toward a sort of peace, the numb relief of loosened reins. His present circumstances, though, a cocktail of the last remnants of parental devotion and the implicit danger of the tempest—both the one in the night's sky and that which he caught in his absent wife's eyes—kept him stationed behind his own walls, minding his daughter, in theory if not fact. So, instead, Sam St. Pierre fitted himself into a bottomless cup and worked himself toward oblivion.

Ava, though, one floor above, understood the storm. *How could she not?* She heard everything, the words that defined her—*disabled* and *retarded* and *idiot*. She answered all the time, constantly, but no one could hear her, because she lived on another frequency; she remembered what she showed the man like stained glass—the one in the woods with pictures on his arms, and then pictures behind *those* pictures—how she had taken his own memory, and then just *pushed* it a little: It *was* just as he had seen, like she was flying through a storm in the deepest night, the world speeding one way, her hurtling another, the friction scraping her every thought. She had offered him just a taste, and even that was almost enough to collapse him, big as he was. Or, at least, was *now*; she could see him in all directions, frontward and back.

Ava's torment was not that she was blocked from life, imprisoned, but that she was completely tender to it, to every thought in every mind in every house; there was no perspective when there were all perspectives, skipping across all the futures and all the pasts, all on top of each other. She was the light of the stacked and nested worlds of time and space, a kind of pinprick herself. It could have been too much to bear—very nearly was—but she had been born precisely for this theater: *Something arrives. And then something else to answer.*

Ava thought of her mother, all the many versions of her mother, and the stained-glass man who now held her in his arms. He was wiser than most, of course, if that was what you could call it—but even he had limitations, could see only so far out. Even he still supposed he had to be a kind of hammer, when he was really more of a prism, an instrument for the light and shadow to dance through, to change and be changed. He would get there, though. She would help him when it was time.

Ava stared down through the floorboards at her father dozing in his chair, his glass, precarious like him, loose in his grip. She dragged a chair screeching across the kitchen's linoleum, and then across the wood floor of the front parlor, leaving two jagged scratches in her wake. She set the chair next to the big picture window, climbed up, raised her arms, swung them down.

Stopped the rain she started.

15

~

The little bell over the door clanged.

Stan Chandler's wrinkled face lifted before his eyes did, still locked on the newsprint spread across the counter. He pulled a drag from his cigarette and placed it down in the full ashtray beside him. He cleared his throat, squinting into the sunlight through the glass of the door.

"Haven't seen you in a spell."

The bookbinder examined a new bench vise displayed at the front of the store. He bounced it in his hands, judging its weight.

"Been a few weeks."

Stan turned a page. "Hear you've been keeping busy." The bookbinder stopped and turned to Stan, who was back to reading his *Post*. The old man plucked his cigarette, took another drag.

"I'm not sure what you mean."

Stan puffed and shrugged. He licked his yellowish index

finger and thumb to turn another page. "Business going well, I take it?"

"*Ai.*"

The man at the register stubbed out his butt and folded up his paper. "Been pretty busy here, too." He looked around the empty store. "Present lack of company excluded, of course."

"Of course."

"Folks been having a lot of trouble on account of that big storm last week. Lot of flooding. Lot of damage. Been good for me, though I hate to say a thing like that. Others' misfortune and such." Stan sank back on his stool. "Something like that—the force of it—I've never seen anything like it. Didn't seem wholly . . . *right.*"

"Right?"

"Normal, I guess." Stan held out his hands as if to shape something, then let them fall back to rest. "It seemed a little *unnatural,* don't you think?"

The bookbinder set the vise back in its place. "Sometimes things look one way only because people don't know any better yet."

Stan snickered dryly, a snapped branch. "Well, you have me there." He held his hand high to the ground. "That's still pretty lofty thinking, though." He lowered his hand down to chest level. "I'm talking about things down here. Close to the ground." He paused. "Things you can touch. Things that can hurt a person. The kind they can more or less see coming."

The bookbinder stepped to the counter. "You would be surprised how connected the two usually are."

"Oh, not that surprised, really." Stan studied his own cracked hands. His voice grew huskier. "I've had enough rugs pulled out from under me, to be sure." He straightened, popped his knuckles. "A lot of folks talking, and a lot of folks got hurt by that storm," he confided. "You should be mindful of that, at least. Tread softly. I might be some dense hardware man who doesn't know shit from Shinola, but I know who you are. I've known since the minute you stepped in the shop that first time. Different, sure." He twirled an extended finger at the bookbinder. "Those big muscles and the drawings on you. The beard and hair. Older, too—been some years, but hard years it looks like. No offense."

Each locked into the other's hard stare; the bookbinder almost nodded.

"The eyes, though—they were the tell. Not exactly the same, but not so different as the rest." After a long beat, and realizing he was still standing, Stan pressed on. "I might not know *why* you're back here—and I probably don't *want* to know—but I suspect you don't need too many folks digging too deep."

"I'm not hiding." The bookbinder's tenor matched his slate expression.

"Hiding in plain sight is a kind of hiding. A clever kind, but it's still hiding." Stan shook out a new cigarette and lit it. Inhaled and exhaled. "Have you seen the priest yet?"

"Why would I?"

Stan nodded and took another long drag. "Because he was there. After—he was there. He helped, too. A lot, actually. *After.*" He blew a plume of smoke, regarding it as it vanished before him. "But that's his story to tell, not mine. I only told him what I thought he needed to know—God knows, literally, all the sins that man already has to carry with him. A whole town's worth, I imagine."

He took another drag. "If I were you, I'd go see the priest."

⌄

The bookbinder had already recognized how Stan Chandler was right about the town at large; the storm had loosened an acidity in Brookshire—a highball of roused, dark humors. The hum had upped its wattage again, almost a bracing; he felt it everywhere now, casting itself at a low frequency, but there just the same. There seemed a sheen now, a hazy dusting that colored the tensions in everyday interactions, heightened and tweaked them. People waved less, glared more. They poured that extra finger of the preferred spirit they didn't need. They swore under their breath, in their hearts, curled their lips into sneers as they passed each other on the street and parked on their stoops. It wasn't relentless and it wasn't always overt, often crouching just at the edge of notice. The Appleton police had started running an extra patrol or two, but simply chalked the surge in illicit activity up to a hot, listless summer.

The bookbinder lowered his head and adjusted his rucksack, following his own shadow along the sidewalk. He could feel insolent eyes on him. Stan Chandler's words echoed in his head: *Tread softly.*

Farther down the road, he could hear the laborers working on the church—it sounded like an army, all hollering the Lord's name, in vain and otherwise, no second thoughts given. They had two cranes running on opposite ends of the sanctuary; this was J. M. Brooks's show now.

The door to the rectory, a little entranceway cut into the side of a hill, was unlocked. The bookbinder smelled must and the old incense meant to cover it. Across the room, Miriam Hollanger sat at her desk.

"Hello," the bookbinder said.

"Hello," Miriam replied, peering down at a stack of bills and forms on her desk.

"Is the padre in today?"

"No," Miriam said, taking a deep breath. "I'm sorry, but he is not."

"The car's here." He pointed outside. Father Jim had use of a donated Ford Mainline, with which he made his rounds.

"He doesn't always take the car." Miriam lit a nervous cigarette. The truth was, Father Jim hadn't yet come downstairs. Everything was dark when Miriam had arrived at eight thirty, and she had stomped up the stairs to his living quarters without any sort of response. She'd known the priest was alive only from the serrated sound of his snoring through the door.

It was happening more often. The Friday before, Father Jim never came out of his room. When Miriam checked on him, a thick voice called out that he was feeling a little under the weather and to please cancel his appointments, with apologies. An empty fifth of vodka sat on his small kitchen counter. She walked around the living room, avoiding all the dust as best as she could until she stood over his reading chair. Cigarette burns pockmarked its arms, and when she touched the cushion, it was damp. She leaned down to sniff it, instinctively, then sprang back. Vodka and piss.

The man never snapped, never lost his temper or had an ill word for anyone, even if Miriam thought he should. To the outside world, he was just kindly Father Jim, and there was no disingenuousness to any of it; he *was* kind. Something, though, had seeped into the basement of his heart. It wore at him, made him cover his hands in his cassock so no one could see the shaking.

Some people thought the drink was the demon, but not Miriam. The drink was the medicine, the demons swimming there anyway; one horror did not preclude the other, and wet or dry, the man would still choke on himself. The bottle was just a sword, but it came with its own price, and no matter which way you cut things, Father Jim was losing.

Once, years back, Miriam had asked him about his nights at Wilson's. The pastor had smiled, she remembered, and patted her hand. That was the flock, he told her; those souls most in need of the Gospels spent their nights in a darkness punctuated by bursts of neon and tobacco smoke—so that was where he was most needed. He would rather be home reading a good book, or better yet, *the* Good Book, but passing the proverbial bottle with desolate men was how he could be of the most service. And though he was telling the complete truth when he recited these words, he also wasn't, all at the very same time.

Miriam set her cigarette in an ashtray and rustled papers, daring the bookbinder to say something.

"I see," he said.

"I can tell him you called."

"Miriam?"

She looked up at him. *How dare you*, she thought. *How dare you walk in here and act like I don't hear about every salacious thing that happens in this town.* She said none of this, gave him the warmest smile she could muster. "I'll let him know you stopped by."

The bookbinder watched her, then lifted his rucksack from the floor. He nodded and turned, leaving the rectory. Miriam clutched for her cigarette and smoked in silence, chastising herself as much as anything. She was not a schoolgirl anymore, she reminded herself, and had little time for riddles shaped like men. The tremor of the cigarette in her fingers, though, betrayed the heat that coursed beneath her rationalizations.

⌣

When the bookbinder returned to his workshop, he found Joe at the farthest table, hunched over his work. A young blond woman sat alone in the corner.

She waved cautiously, turning to the boy with his back to her.

"He's a little shy," the bookbinder granted.

The girl's chin fell, her face darkened. "We've met before, I think."

"I see."

She made a motion between the bookbinder and herself. "But I don't think we've ever met."

"No, I would say not."

"But you gave me something a few months ago. A gift, I think. A book of recipes."

"Ah. Yes."

The woman's lip trembled. "It was perfect." She wiped the bridge of her nose and snorted, embarrassed. "I never thanked you, and now—" She took a deep breath. "I have a request." Her accent thickened as she struggled for the right word.

"Another book?"

She nodded. "Something I can send back home." She began to curl in the chair, catlike; the bookbinder impassive, she caught herself and reverted to upright. "I'd like to let my mother know I am well." A pause. ""Without saying too much," the woman whispered. She narrowed her gaze. "I can pay, of course."

The bookbinder stroked his beard. He looked to Joe, the

boy either ignoring them or desperately pretending to. "I don't think I want your money."

Joe flinched. The woman, too. "You—you don't?"

"No."

She looked at her hands. "I understand." She flattened her skirt, stood. "Well, thank you for your time." Her voice cooled, grew sparse.

The bookbinder shook his head. "No, I think you misunderstand. We'll make the book."

The prostitute narrowed her eyes. "But you don't want money?"

"No."

"What do you want?"

The bookbinder glanced at the back of Joe's head. He spoke in low tones. "I'm more interested in other things you might have to offer," he said. He pulled his pipe from his pocket. "Let's go out on the porch."

The woman's shoulders slumped, and she nodded. The bookbinder shut the door behind them; Joe, left inside, tried to concentrate on his sewing, but his mind was a chain reaction of ricocheting notions that quickly worked themselves up to an incoherent scramble.

⌄

When the bookbinder reentered the shop a few minutes later, he was alone, his pipe dangling from his mouth. He walked to where Joe was feigning concentration and waited for the boy to say something.

Joe kept his eyes low. "You don't have to creep." He cleared his throat. "So you're going to make her book for her?"

"No. You are."

Joe twisted back. "*I* am?"

"It's the least you can do for all she's done for you."

Joe reddened, a blush so strong it seemed to radiate against the walls, rivaling the lantern under which he worked. He pressed on, sweaty palms and all, trying to navigate the needle and thread through the edges of the octavo.

"Are you going to do it with her?"

"Who?"

Joe tilted his head to the door. "*Her*. The . . . lady. 'Take advantage of her talents.'" Joe mimicked the bookbinder's voice. His face was bunched up, as were his skinny hands, punching the needle through the paper.

The bookbinder almost admonished him but thought better of it. "No, Joe. I'm not going to *do it* with her."

"You sure?"

"Yes."

The boy gritted his teeth.

"What?"

"Nothing," Joe muttered.

"You've got something on your mind."

Joe thrust the half-tied signatures down on the table. "You did it with Mrs. St. Pierre. Everybody knows it."

The bookbinder regarded Joe. He leaned back against a paneled wall. "Where did you hear that?"

"Folks saw her leave your house after that big storm. Someone told my mother that she looked—"

"She looked what?"

Joe made a face. "She looked like she got a good workout."

"I see."

Joe banged his hand against the table. The bookbinder could feel the rage and fear, the powerlessness.

"Why don't you ask me what you want to ask me, Joe?"

Joe balled his hands into fists, then stretched out his fingers. His voice grew pensive, wounded. "My mother came here late once, too."

The bookbinder nodded to nobody in particular. "I thought we already went over this. Your mother and I just had a drink and talked. At *that* table. About you, in fact."

Joe swallowed, breathed. "What about Mrs. St. Pierre?"

"That is my concern." The bookbinder stood up; the conversation was over. "You're going to have to trust me, Joe." He headed to the back rooms, then paused, not looking at the boy. "It's not always easy—I can appreciate that."

Joe stewed at the table for several minutes before he picked up the half-finished book and got back to it.

⌣

Later, when Miriam returned home from the rectory, the bookbinder was once again sitting on her front steps, this time smoking and staring up at the thin clouds passing over.

"Where's Joe?"

The bookbinder raised his eyebrows. "Working."

She leaned against her railing. "Are you a big shot now or something? You should trade tips with Brooks."

"I was thinking that myself." The bookbinder took a pull. "I wanted to talk to you."

"I'm flattered. About what?"

"I think you have heard some things."

Miriam waved her hands, shook her head. "Your business is your own. Nothing to do with me."

"I want to explain."

"You have nothing to explain. You are a grown man. I don't care."

"If you don't care, why are you mad?"

Miriam banged the railing. "I'm not mad!" She shook her head again, then, defeated, dropped her purse. "I'm a little mad. But not why you think."

"No?"

"No. I'm mad because of your nerve. You come here, to *my* little sleepy town—yes, I get it, we're a little sleepy town. You come here with your"—she wagged a finger at him—"*all this*, on top of your talking like some sphinx, spending money no one knows where it comes from—"

"That's nobody's business."

"That's right. That's *right*. You don't owe a soul here an explanation for who you are or where you came from. But the other side of that is that you can't look down on those same people for being curious. You can't swoop in looking like you look and talking like you talk, sticking strange books everywhere like Easter eggs, turning people's lives upside down—" Miriam took a breath to calm herself, recognizing that each word served as a tell illuminating her own bluffs. She pressed on anyway. "You can't be a mystery and then be surprised when everybody tries to solve you."

The bookbinder worked his pipe in silence.

"And another thing."

"There's more?"

"There's always more." Miriam sat down on a step, kicking off her shoes—one, then the other. "Be careful." She shrugged.

"You boys run around here all night and day like headless chickens, sticking your rods wherever you please, into those girls down on Warbler Avenue—and, yes, I know all about that place, thank you very much. I'm not stupid."

The man flashed a small grin behind his pipe. "That was never in doubt," he mumbled, without taking it from his mouth. Miriam glared at the bookbinder, then down the length of her street. She seemed at a threshold and decided to cross. "I need a drink. You want one?"

"Please."

She got up and stepped over him, resting her hand on his shoulder as she passed. She unlocked the door and went inside, her shoes and purse left scattered on the steps.

A woman pushed a stroller up the hill toward him, to where Kingfisher Street met Sparrow. She stared until she was close enough to see the bookbinder was staring back, then quickly looked away. He watched her maneuver the stroller left and up the cross street, breaking away from him, pretending not to notice him at all. He gazed back up at the few translucent clouds marring an otherwise never-ending blue. He could hear a car or two rumbling along Meadowlark, the men from the early shifts returning home.

The storm door banged behind his reverie, and Miriam handed him a glass, then retook her place a few steps down. They both drank long swigs, giving the whiskey time to settle and warm their throats, their bellies.

"You were saying I needed to be careful. As you share a drink with a scandalous man in your front yard."

Miriam shrugged. "That die has been cast. It would be worse if I snuck around. As I was saying, you men can—"

"I got that part."

Miriam put her glass down and folded her hands. "It's something else when you make a cuckold of a husband. That's a married woman you're running around with. I may not think Sam St. Pierre is worth the dirt it would take to bury him, but that doesn't mean he still doesn't have friends in this town, or at least a few drinking buddies left." She sniffed and took another nip. "They're probably as unhinged as he is."

"He doesn't concern me."

Miriam turned around to face him head-on. "That cockiness—you think you know better. Just because you sit on your roof doesn't mean you can look down on everyone."

"It's not down. It's *through*."

She wagged her finger at him again. "See—*that*. That dismissiveness. I know you've got your eyes in the stars, but it's the thing swiping at your ankles that is going to trip you up." Her face dimmed; she turned back out toward the street and its fine layer of dirt, a complement to the clouds. "And that little girl. That poor little girl." She took a drink. "I just hope you really know what you're doing."

Miriam stared into the amber oracle of her glass. They both held silent for a long while. The widow finally spoke again, her voice pushing through her teeth: "Why not me?"

The bookbinder tapped his pipe through the railing, into the bushes. He slid down a step, shoulder to shoulder with her. "Because *you're* still married, in all the ways that matter."

Miriam was still. "He's dead," she whispered. "He's dead."

"You found something more powerful than that," he replied, and she shook her head, then nodded. The bookbinder stared at his own tumbler. "I know I can't beat that. I wouldn't dare try."

Miriam smirked bitterly. "You could have tried a little."

She sighed and wiped an eye. "Who am I kidding—I don't have time for you. I've got problems of my own."

"Tell me."

"You don't need to humor me."

"Try me."

Miriam turned to him, examined him examining her. She blushed. "Fine. My daughter."

"Tess."

She started. "Yes. *Tess.* I've been hearing things there, too." She expected some reaction from the bookbinder, but he remained still. She squinted at him. "You don't look surprised."

The bookbinder looked on ahead.

"I don't catch her often, and even when I do . . ." Miriam's voice faltered. She bit her lip. "That's the cruelest trick, you know? You're given this gift, this responsibility. You watch them grow, you worry constantly, worry *them* like little rosaries—you think you're helping them grow . . . and right when it really matters, right when they can really take flight and do some real damage to themselves or the world—then you find out that you were powerless all along." Her laugh squeezed out tears. "You find out you're useless. It was all a shell game."

She put her fist to her mouth, trying to hold it all back. "She scares me. She scares me so damn much."

Miriam leaned over and wept against the bookbinder's chest. She realized between hitched breaths that she had not cried, really cried, in years—and this made her cry even harder. "It gets so bad," she said over and over. "I don't have any idea what I'm doing." The bookbinder held her until she took one long, fluttering breath in, and let it go.

"What are the neighbors going to say about this, you in my arms?"

"Screw them." Her head dropped, long strands of her auburn hair hanging down, loosened from their bun, and she found herself tracing the tattoos on his right forearm, the hand holding the whiskey. "What does that mean?" she asked, pointing to three Mandarin pictographs just below the inside crease of his elbow.

He twisted his arm to get a better look. "Eternal."

"Eternal?"

"Well, that's one way to explain it. Not everything is an exact match. Asia's a long way away, after all."

"Try me."

"It's a bit like I told you before, about rivers—how a river runs. It's always moving, always churning, always working. It's *doing*. It has a purpose, to carry itself from here to there. It has an *eternal* purpose." He took a drink. "The mission never ends."

Miriam sat up, wiped her eyes. "I get that," she said, reaching for her purse to grab a cigarette.

⌣

After the bookbinder had been gone long enough to get wherever he was going, but not too long, so as to risk him being on his way back, Joe got up from his work, made his circuit around the workshop, running his fingers over spines, pretending he was after nothing—even to himself—but knowing he was after something, the old leather book tempting his curiosity, pulling him closer.

He made his way to the shelf, his blood pumping in his ears, and took another quick glance at the door. The bookbinder had taken to leaving Joe alone in the shop for long stretches, and Joe, as a boy his age is wont to do, soon took to snooping, investigating what secrets a man like the book-binder might keep lying around. Truth was, Joe mostly rifled through the books looking for nudie prints, but one afternoon he came across this severe-looking tome and heaved it down.

He did again now and laid it on a worktable. He ran his finger over the three raised markings. One more check of the door and he opened the cover, the first handful of pages, then stared at the thing buried there in the cutout, the strange way it was all black, all shine. He thought of his father, and the bookbinder, too—of what it meant to be a hero, of what you had to take and what you had to leave behind, the sad symmetry and the balance.

Joe peered into the book for seconds, minutes, hours, days—until he slammed it shut and returned it to its place, always in arm's reach.

16

Even tucked into the middle of a common shopping strip, Father Jim deemed Wilson's bar a wood-trimmed, old-world comfort in an increasingly paved world, the architectural equivalent of a rearward glance over the shoulder. It was a cave for storytellers, a campfire.

Near the end of July, the weather settled on humid and hot, men drinking ice-cold beer with one hand, dirty handkerchiefs dabbing at their brows with the other. They hunched over Wilson's pride, the hand-carved bar that ran the length of the establishment, and his spindly iron tables. They sunned their wrinkled skin under neon booze signs lining the walls rather than the star slung low outside them.

Father Jim watched Wilson sip on his water with lemon, a damp towel across the back of the barkeep's neck. He did not partake of his own stock, choosing instead to make his profit on the thirst of others. Three fans whirred high from the ceiling, like buttons holding the ceiling in place, and the men studied their drinks, the glasses into which they poured themselves.

Conversations circled around the strange lights in the sky, the ensuing newspaper stories. Father Jim listened silently from the far end of the bar.

"Did you even read the damn articles?" a hoarse voice finally blurted out, exasperated.

"You can't believe those vultures. They're selling papers."

A theatrical smack against the bar. "The guys in the—what do you call it?"

"Airport?"

"Yeah, the airport, but the thing, what do they call the thing?"

"An airplane?" someone shouted to a smattering of laughter.

"No, smart-ass! The thing, with the radar—"

"The tower."

"Bingo. The *tower.* The guys that work in the tower saw them, plain as day."

"It was just the weather!" There was a murmuring from the crowd in Wilson's. Another voice, overenunciating the words, ill fitting like cheap false teeth: "A *temperature inversion.*"

"You don't even know what that means, George!" someone hollered, and the men laughed again.

"Screw all of you!" the man yelled back, forcing Wilson to take a step from behind the bar, raise his hands. "Hey, hey," he said calmly, bringing at least the temperament, if not the temperature, of the room back down a few degrees.

"My brother-in-law works at National," a thin man with thinner hair announced from his seat at one of the tables. "He says he saw 'em, at least a couple. He said the radar guys caught seven blips or whatever. He only saw two, but they sure wasn't the weather, he says. They were orange and glowed and moved in different directions. And they were *fast*, brother." A swig of beer. "He says he's buddies with one of those tower guys, you know. He says this buddy took some numbers, you know, measuring where it was and then where it went and the time and all that. He says if the numbers were right—and I mean it's this guy's job all day—then those things were moving seven thousand miles an hour."

"Jesus."

"Jesus got nothing to do with it. I tell you . . . this world." The men in the bar grew quiet, pushed to ponder their place in a universe where something could travel seven thousand miles an hour, the speed of a bullet, the speed of release.

The little bell over the entrance announced the bookbinder. The men turned, some thoughtlessly grabbing for their beers, others settling back in their chairs, their stools.

The bookbinder stepped forward, the faces around him beginning to take shape. He noted Roy Dickerson standing by the jukebox and nodded his way. The real estate agent dipped his head in return, somewhere between an acknowledgment and another drink.

The bookbinder's boots echoed across the scratched wood floor, as if he carried a weight greater than his frame. The world flashed around him, and then his boots were thunking against mud, the darkness of the bar the darkness of the past, the forest, the river, but it wasn't the past or the forest or the river—it was *now*, and these men were *his* men, his unit. They were scurrying through the obscura, artillery screaming all around, overhead, through skin and bone. He blinked and saw a corpse with half a head where a boy had been, a tanked man. The body drinking next to him, the bald, skinny one with a brother-in-law at the airport, looked through him with black-ball eyes. Dean Martin crooned into the middle of a dogfight. The bookbinder blinked again and he was in an oven of a saloon, men sweating and staring at him. He took a deep breath to locate himself. He stepped to the bar, and as his eyes focused, he recognized Sam St. Pierre drinking alone.

The bookbinder leaned in to Wilson. "Double Canadian Club, please," he said, and the bartender nodded. Sam sat oblivious, hotboxing an endless series of cigarettes, listening to the game on Wilson's radio. The Senators were hovering around last place, but not completely out of striking distance, only five games back. There was hope yet for them to play above their means.

Sam bunched his soiled rag in his free fist and slowly began to perceive the density of the figure to his left, the shadow it cast even in this den held together with shadows. Recognition dawned sluggish at first, then all at once, and the half-blitzed man inhaled half his cigarette in one long pull. He coughed, but out of the cough tumbled sharp words clamoring over themselves, razor blades choked from the smoke cloud: "You have some fucking nerve."

A chair squeaked. The bookbinder shifted his body only to accept his drink from the bartender, fish a few coins from his pocket, and place them on the bar.

"I said—"

The bookbinder leaned down, a long strand of hair falling from behind his ear. "I heard what you said," he muttered so low only Sam could hear. And then, closer, even lower, typeset punched into the cuckold's ear: "You cannot possibly fathom the depths of my fucking nerve."

Sam reddened, then jabbed his cigarette butt into the

ashtray with a sweaty, arrhythmic hand. The bookbinder straightened; he pushed himself from the bar and took a hard drink, two thrusts of his Adam's apple, and wiped his mustache clean.

"I didn't come here for you," the bookbinder growled, as if he could have meant this particular social visit or a much broader purpose altogether. Either way, he left St. Pierre drunk and gnarled over the bar, staring into the mirror behind the lined-up liquor bottles.

The bookbinder made his way through men who begrudgingly let him pass. Stan Chandler had warned him to be careful. Miriam, too. The town's dirt was collecting on his step, under his nails. *Again.*

He navigated until he was beside Father Jim, the priest's own shoulders hunched over the bar. "Is this seat taken?" the bookbinder asked, and Father Jim replied with wide, tinted eyes. He fanned out his hand: *Be my guest.*

"You can be a hard man to nail down, Padre."

Father Jim's wince landed as a wan smile. "Then I'm not doing my job." He took a drink.

"A little birdy told me I should see you."

The priest lifted his head, the embers at the end of his cigarette brightening. He examined the man beside him, the incongruities. "Yes," he exhaled cautiously. "I guess that makes sense." He coughed into a fist. "Folks around here have a lot of questions about you."

"I meant the other way around."

The priest chuckled gloom. He touched his collar with his hand.

Around the bar, some of the men had moved on, back to talking about UFOs, or baseball, or their shitty jobs. Some, though, kept their attention on the two men in the corner, the priest and the freak. "Is there somewhere else we can go?" the bookbinder asked.

The priest laughed again and stole a long drink. "What, you don't like the attention after you make such an entrance?" The bookbinder shook his head. "I don't think I am who you think I am."

"I don't think I know *who* you are. Or what to make of you at all, exactly."

"Is that a problem?"

"If it were, I'd be in the wrong line of work." Father Jim stubbed out his cigarette. "The things I *know* imprison me. Any hope I might yet muster rests solely in the unknown." The priest's voice was already getting wobbly.

"Father, that's what I need to ask you about."

"Pardon?"

"A thing you might know. Something that happened here a long time ago."

Father Jim lifted his head at this, but before he could say anything more, a young man burst into the bar. "It's on fire!" he hollered. "House fire! You can see it from the top of the hill!"

Chairs screamed against the floor. Wilson flipped off the transistor. "Slow down, son," he instructed in a voice as calm as if he were counting out change. "What's on fire?"

The kid looked around the bar; he had the floor. Realizing what he had to say, he now wished perhaps he was not the one who had volunteered to rustle up the men at Wilson's. He tried to be vague. "House fire. Down on Warbler Avenue."

A man pushed through the crowd. "I live on Warbler! Which house?" He was up in the kid's face. "*Which* house?" he yelled, growing frantic.

"It's not yours."

The man was beside himself, cheap whiskey on his breath. "How the hell do you know which house is mine?"

The kid swallowed. "It's Ms. Mae's house, sir," he whispered.

"What?"

Louder: "Ms. Mae's house is on fire."

The men shuffled their feet. Someone cleared a throat. Roy Dickerson's face lost all its color, but he didn't move; he just stood there with his hand on the jukebox, as if by letting it go, he might fall out of gravity, shoot off at seven thousand miles an hour.

Father Jim was standing now, one shock already overriding the other. "It's faster if we cut past the restrooms." The bookbinder hesitated, then chased the priest out through the back door, across Meadowlark and into the cross-hatched streets of Brookshire just as the sun was beginning to set.

Back in Wilson's, everyone waited for everyone else to move until there was a bellowed "Fuck it" and footsteps headed for the door. One man followed, and then another, and soon a whole flock of tipsy, oil-stained husbands and sons and brothers were running down the side of the highway, sirens from the volunteer fire department half a mile up on their heels. The truck overtook them at the turn-in, and then they were following it, a makeshift foot brigade to the rescue.

⌣

Father Jim's shortcut proved true, and the two men landed on Warbler Avenue, chests heaving, before the volunteer truck. What raged before them was the most poetic sort of horror, a home aflame, the tongues of gold and amber reaching up, hungry for air, for more of everything: 1402 Warbler was burning, and burning fast.

The bookbinder fell under its spell. He closed his eyes and it was Okinawa all over again. Villages blazing in every direction—houses, barns, temples—and the screams of children and cows riding the waves of night. He rode the current below, wet and convulsing in the river at the center of all the fire, floating backward, his blood in the water and the water in his blood, watching the structures of men shiver and collapse. It was a baptism for him, washed away from the world or the other way around.

He opened his eyes: a suburban whorehouse alight. *America*. Dusk was just beginning to lose hold, and bodies and shadows, bastards all, flickered past. He heard the fire truck sirens approaching.

There were young women, girls even, in the lawn, half dressed, choking, spitting into the grass, trying to expel the smoke from their chests. The redhead, the one called Mae, stumbled off in a trance, her gaze held to the fire, hypnotized.

The sirens' wail grew louder, the smoke billowed, and the materializing crowd fell back, overpowered. Father Jim found his voice, louder than in the bar, and he was yelling for help, trying to pull those overcome by the smoke to safety. The bookbinder's eyes began to tear, but he pushed forward, tracking a sound just beyond the mechanical wail, just on its edge—a human scream. It could have been thousands of miles away, a decade ago, just as likely as in the world around, but he pressed on, fanned smoke from his face. After a pass of his arm, he caught a white exclamation point flash in front of him, human shaped.

"Wait!" he tried to call, his voice busted glass. The shape

ran back into the house, and he took off after it through the open front door.

Inside—all brightness and heat. The walls fluttered and danced, monarch wings creaking haunted lullabies as the flames traveled through them like ghosts, disappearing, bursting back out. "*Stop!*" The figure—the blond prostitute—turned, glanced at him, and then stepped deeper into the chaos, toward a row of back rooms.

The bookbinder felt a blackness over his shoulder and swung around, fist clenched; Father Jim started, held up his hands. "Get out of here!" the bookbinder roared, but the priest shook his head.

The bookbinder pulled off his T-shirt, tore it in two. He handed Father Jim a remnant and took one himself, putting it over his nose and mouth. They pushed on, the hairs on their arms, their eyebrows and lashes, singed by the air around them.

They burst into a back bedroom, almost dark, and Father Jim screamed. He had grasped the doorjamb for balance; the bookbinder could smell the priest's cooked flesh.

He crawled on all fours, knowing she couldn't have gotten far, bumping into something soft. He ran his hand over the obstacle: a leg, then a waist, then ribs. He crawled over the woman's face; she was barely conscious but held a manila envelope tightly in her hand. "Stupid girl," the bookbinder snarled. "Stupid, stupid girl." Just as he stood, picked her up, a barely audible mew escaped the corner of the burning room. He turned to Father Jim staring into the same corner. "Shit," the bookbinder muttered. He leaned the woman against the bed. "Stay with me." She nodded weakly. He crawled over.

Another woman was crumpled in the corner, twice as big as the blonde. The bookbinder struggled to drag her back across the bed. "Padre, I need help," he coughed out, and the priest rushed over, took her legs. "Listen to me!" the bookbinder barked into the blonde's ear, taking the envelope from her hand and stuffing it down his waistband. The young woman's eyes fluttered drunkenly. "You have to put your arms around me," he ordered. "And hold on." She nodded, grabbed at his neck. He took the other by her shoulders; Father Jim grabbed the collapsed woman's ankles.

The beams of the house were screaming now, begging to be allowed to collapse. Father Jim whispered a small prayer, the bookbinder's voice clattering in his head. *Hold on*, he thought. *Please, Christ, just hold on a little longer.* He could have been praying for any of them, all of them.

My God, the priest thought. The woman was so heavy and his arms were so tired and his hand hurt more than he could imagine something hurting, he just wanted it gone, wanted to be rid of it, chopped off, and the bookbinder, this sinew of a man, was teetering, out of breath himself, one body draped over his back, another in his arms and they were leaning, all of them leaning, and the floor itself was bending under the strain, they would crash through it at any moment, or the one above would fall on them, it wasn't a matter of if but when, Father Jim's breath choking on his heartbeat, too far up his throat, and just a few more steps, they were going to make it, they were never going to make it, the house was squealing, a siren, the siren was squealing and—

Outside. Father Jim expected to see a light at the end, a pure white, but only the beginnings of night and the deep blood bruise of the fire truck lights under all the flashing emerged. He wanted to draw a long, fresh breath of air, like bursting through the surface of the water, but it was nothing like that—it shifted only from completely stifling to *almost* completely stifling, a moderate improvement; he lost his balance and felt his body tumble down the porch, caught only by the firemen racing in just as his menagerie stumbled out. Heavy gloves held him up, marched and deposited him on a lawn across the street. The priest dry heaved a chalky black cloud. A fireman called out and Father Jim tried to wave him off, but he took one look at the priest's mangled hand and hollered for help. More trucks had arrived, along with police cars, a hearse as a makeshift ambulance. The army of half-drunk men from Wilson's was also there, doing whatever they could, snapped to an attention that had been latent for years: helping victims out of harm's way, pulling heavy hose from the truck, carrying gear. Chief Hillary was there, barking orders, looking out of sorts, like he wanted to be anywhere else in the world but here, caught in the glare of his own red and blue lights.

The brothel faded in and out of sight behind the tongues of flame, as if it were deciding in which dimension it existed. Father Jim thought he saw it smile something fierce; he screamed as someone put a press on his red-raw hand.

He leaned up on his elbows, looked around for something to focus on beyond the pain. He watched the half-naked bookbinder kneel beside the blond woman, shaking her gently, shaking his head. Father Jim's stomach sank as he deciphered the scene, the bookbinder now hovering over the woman, and then back again on his haunches. He watched the bookbinder's glare alight along the horizon, the eyes bright, even from this distance, finding nowhere to land.

No, the bookbinder thought. *Not again. Not another.* He gazed down at the woman, thin as a rail but also as sturdy, and saw only another soldier, another confederate lost along the way, the sacrifice once more backlit by resolute fire. Her already-pale skin was already veering blue under the grime; all he could think of was how he had ordered her to hold on, and she had, somehow. How it didn't matter in the end.

A fireman approached from behind, and the bookbinder spun on him, growling, spittle loose off his lip, his bared teeth, his fist cocked, already back in the battle.

"Whoa, big fella!" the fireman exclaimed, his hands up in peace, his mouth a crooked *o* under his heavy mustache. "I'm on your side."

The bookbinder shook his head and stumbled back. Beyond the fireman was enemy territory now, the villagers wary of the Americans and their violence to end violence, something like white magic to defeat the wicked, a naked hypocrisy playing out among the elements. *God on your side.* The flames roared, a cacophony, all whipping on top of each other, those of then and those of now, the bookbinder barely hearing himself croak "You're too late" over the chaos, before he shook his head, patted at the envelope in his pants. "We're always too late."

Father Jim bore witness to the strange man stumbling away as the fireman dropped beside the young woman, removing his helmet. She had not moved in forever, and the priest's eyes trailed from her still body to the bookbinder's burdened slouch, thought him timeless by the light of the fire, a keepsake so old and priceless it must be tucked away and taken for granted, lest you drive yourself mad trying to account for him.

Father Jim turned away from that scene, catching sight of the other rescued woman in the other direction, the heavier one, sitting up and responding to a crowd of ladies. He took some solace in the fact that it was not all for naught, his and the bookbinder's efforts, but not too much, for a tear, or perhaps a few of them beaded together, cut a course down the ash covering his cheek, his stubbled jaw.

The fire burned wild, and the whole town watched the brigade battle it to a sort of uneasy truce. Rebecca St. Pierre arrived, Ava too big in her arms, her husband eyeing them from the edge of the crowd, then snapping suddenly awake, walking to her, his teeth bared in the effigy of a smile; she kept her own hurricane buttoned up, every urge inside her driving her toward the bookbinder diminishing into the distance, the ash that marked his skin even from this far, the taste of the smoldering wound that was his remembered kiss.

Miriam Hollanger, too, had arrived, arranging blankets and food for the newly homeless, harlots or not, and also noticed the bookbinder's exodus, the blond girl lying still in the grass; Miriam wanted to go after him but glimpsed Rebecca and her bristly husband, the electricity of it all—a standoff pulsing in the shadow of a catastrophe that was just starting to dawn on her, them—and she held back, instead throwing herself into the tasks at hand, making herself useful.

The men from Wilson's smoked cigarettes and rubbed the grime from their brows. They said nothing, reverting to another life, a time when it was better to make yourself small. Some mingled with their families. A bottle appeared and was passed around. Each took their share.

Rachel Dickerson stood in the middle of the street, too close to the fire in one of her typical hatch-pattern dresses, staring down Mae, her red hair and bright eyes matching the flicker of her waning home. Roy Dickerson stepped off the curb, gave a quick glance to his lover, put his arm around his wife's shoulder, and led her away. Everything in Mae's face

shattered and rearranged itself in an instant, too fast for anyone to register what had happened.

There was a creaking roar, something unholy, and a platoon
of firemen yelling to get back, run, and then one last shriek, a
cry between pain and pleasure—absolute surrender—and the
whole frame of the house collapsed on itself, the second floor
through the first, and the first into the basement, and 1402
Warbler was no more.

17

"What does this one mean?" Rebecca ran her finger along the inside of the bookbinder's arm, past the blackbirds, the nymph clutching a ledge, the steamer made of words: *So we drove on toward death through the cooling twilight* and *Despair has its own calms.* Past *And miles to go before I sleep.* Her nail traced a Mandarin character, the first of three, just below the bend of his elbow.

The bookbinder twisted his arm, trying to focus on the markings, *through* them, through the blood, the bone, the bed, the floor, the level beneath, the workshop, *down, down, down,* into the rock and clay, the desolate rivers that run deeper than dreams. "It means I lost something once," he said, facing her. "Gained something else. For better or worse."

"Something or someone?" she asked, a beat too quickly.

"It's complicated." He sank back into the pillow, staring at the small settling cracks in the plaster ceiling.

"So am I," Rebecca replied, the covers falling from her

body. She walked to the open window, the moonlight a luster on her skin, her breasts, the tuft of hair between her legs.

She took a deep breath. "Do you think me a whore?"

"No." He sat up. "I think you a mirror."

Rebecca laughed sadly. "No. You're not the one who's married, remember?"

"Did he hurt you?"

She turned to the bookbinder, her frown almost a pout. Her eyes, though, held stern. "I don't need you to protect me."

He grunted, knowing this to be true in ways that she had perhaps not yet fathomed, and of which he was just beginning to discern the edges. In the immediate and the mundane, though, he could not make out any new bruises on her body—the older ones pastel, diluted watercolors in the lunar light.

"He didn't hit me, if that's what you're worried about. He didn't touch me."

"What *did* he do?"

Rebecca traced letters on the glass. "I used to do this as a schoolgirl. I would spell out my secrets in letters written directly on top of each other. It would make this sort of picture—not so different from some of yours." She nodded toward the man and his markings. "My own private code. My favorite color. B-L-U-E, one on top of the other. What I wanted to be when I grew up. S-E-N-A-T-O-R. The names of boys I liked."

"Senator?"

"I would have written *astronaut*, if such a thing existed at the time."

"What's stopping you?"

Rebecca pursed her lips, stared at the moon above. "You are either teasing me, or a very foolish man."

"Why?"

She glided to the bookbinder's meager nightstand, took a cigarette from her case, and lit it. Exhaled silver-blue smoke. "Not in this world," she contended.

"The world is a big place, bigger than we can see. I think sometimes we forget that."

"And a woman like me can rule these exotic lands?"

"Something like that, yes."

"I'd love to believe you." Rebecca thought of that receding little girl carving codes into paper, all hand-me-down frock and possibility, and the woman who now stood naked in the moonlight, smoking a cigarette before this man who was not her husband, her spiteful deadbeat husband, this man who was not the father to her broken little girl. And yet he had said *mirror*, and she could not be sure he was wrong.

She had worn so many roles over the years, some of her own device, some a conspiracy of her circumstances. They all chafed in their own way and their own time. *Daughter. Lover. Wife. Mother. Protector.*

And now, in some quarters, at least, *adulteress. Jezebel.* She turned to the bookbinder.

"He called me a 'filthy whore like all those other whores.' What else? Oh, yes—*soiled.* A soiled bitch." She blew smoke. "Perhaps I have more than one mirror. Perhaps he can see me now."

"What exactly does a man who can't see past the lip of his own glass know?"

"Oh, I imagine whatever the whispers are, he knows. Or thinks he knows." She paused. "In the end, that's all that matters."

"How do you mean?"

She turned to the bookbinder, genuinely surprised. "He doesn't love me." She took a long drag. "He can only mimic it. He can only play the part. It's more than even that, though.

His reality is not the same as yours or mine. He made a choice to fracture from it, to protect himself."

"You sound as if you feel sorry for him."

Rebecca shook her head. "I have empathy for him. I don't want to say *sympathy*, because that would mean I find him pathetic."

"Don't you?"

She thought for a moment, shrugged. "I don't think I could do that to someone. To him. Like it's done to me."

The bookbinder was still, his face an inquiry.

"You know . . ." Rebecca bobbed her head dramatically. "'Oh, *poor* Rebecca St. Pierre, struggling with her idiot child.' Or 'There goes Rebecca, bless her heart. What a lot the Good Lord has put on her.' What a lot of shit." Another drag.

"If anybody has to feel anything about me, I would want them to feel empathy. I'm fine with people wanting to understand, but I don't need them feeling *sorry* for me." She turned on the bookbinder, her eyes brighter than even the spark from her cigarette. "I don't need *you* feeling sorry for me. I'm not your damsel, either." Rebecca stubbed out the butt.

The bookbinder remained still.

"My point is, I feel empathy for Sam. I hate the things he does—don't get me wrong, I *hate* them—but I *understand* them sometimes. I can see where his broken parts are, not because he is correct, but because I share some of those same wounds. Not every claim he's made against the universe is false."

"He's lost, Rebecca."

"I wonder who is familiar to whom?" The question—soft, fragile—hung before her; the night's breeze blew in, scattered the words. Rebecca closed her eyes, inhaled, then climbed out on the roof. The bookbinder, himself naked, followed.

They sat in the shadows, the shadows of shadows, holding

each against the other. After some time, Rebecca sighed. "Imagine the passion."

"What?"

"Rachel Dickerson, burning that place to the ground."

"I think it might be something more than passion."

Rebecca turned. "What do you mean?"

"It's just a sense. A pressure building."

"The pressure is always there. It just churns. The building is a myth."

"I've heard things. Kids knocking over mailboxes. Busting windows. Run-ins at the market. Things are getting worse."

"You've been talking to Miriam, haven't you?" She eyed him for his reaction.

The bookbinder shrugged. "I trust her."

Rebecca considered him, then kissed his shoulder, and it was not enough. She kissed his mouth hard and stood, an orchid among thistles. The bookbinder stared at the sky, his body crouched, a watchman, an infinite sentry. For a moment Rebecca thought she could see him, could see in both directions, where he came from and where he was headed, and she shuddered, suddenly chilled in the night air. She folded her bare arms around herself. "Did you know her?"

"Who?"

"The girl. From the fire. The one who . . ."

"Died?" The bookbinder spat the word. It left an acid taste on his tongue, but he did not shy from it; he let it sit there, settle in, burn itself good.

"Yes," Rebecca replied, soft as she could, knowing it didn't really help. It didn't really soften anything.

"A little. I knew her a little." He shook his head. "Not much at all."

"It's okay."

He shook his head harder, and she wasn't sure it was meant for her. "She helped me a little." He thought about the deal they had made on his porch. He had been wondering whether she had gone back into the burning brothel for the envelope or her friend; if the former, he wasn't sure he could bear it. It had never been worth it—there would always be another way. *Stupid girl.* "We had a business transaction."

He knew he would have to make it worth it.

Rebecca cocked her head, both troubled and not by the notion of her paramour in a business transaction with a prostitute. A prostitute who had died in his arms. Her mind raced, and she struggled to tamp it down, though she stood perfectly still, naked on the roof. "Will you tell me about it?"

The bookbinder shook his head a third time, this time so faintly she wasn't even sure he had.

"I have to go," she finally admitted, and leaned down, kissing him again. "I've left Ava alone with him too long." The bookbinder grabbed her arm, and she thought he might pull her down on top of him or toss her over the edge—she was perhaps fine with either, but he let his hand slide down her bicep, her elbow, his rough skin scratching against hers, then letting go, and she ducked back inside the window.

Rebecca dressed in silence, slipping the linen dress over her thin frame. She took the stairs all the way to the basement, the workshop, and stepped out through the unlit back porch into the dark yard, where she could become invisible for a brief respite, reappearing somewhere else, like the fireflies her daughter chased to exhaustion but could never catch.

18

Miriam clasped the phone in her neck and held up a finger for the bookbinder to wait. She finished her conversation, offered her professional goodbye, and placed the receiver back in its cradle.

"Is he here?"

Miriam peered up at the ceiling, her eyes dancing with a mixture of worry and irritation. "I can hear him moving around, if that's what you mean. But I don't think he's in any condition to take visitors."

She pulled her cigarette case from the desk, plucked one, and lit it. She leaned back, exhaling. "I've tried to explain to him that you two saved that girl. To focus on that. Not"—she paused long enough to take in another drag and let it out—"the other." She tapped ash into its tray. "You did everything you could."

She twisted the cigarette in her fingers, narrowing her gaze. "Sometimes I think he wants to do more good than this world allows. I think that's what haunts him most."

She examined the bookbinder's face, papercut wrinkles around his own eyes. She had noticed them before, but the fluorescent light in the office held them on display. "And how are you holding up?"

"Fine."

Miriam sighed—she knew he was lying, either to her or himself, but she also knew that there wasn't much she could do about it. It was as if she could literally see the skin become stone, the etchings across it iron bracing. Something above the rectory office thumped. "I don't know what set him off in the night. But everything's locked up there, and he's never done that. He'll hide bottles in empty suitcases, tape them behind his headboard—no better than one of my children trying to get away with mischief. But he's never just barricaded himself like this."

She considered the bills stacked on her desk. "Maybe it's the hand. Maybe the pills they gave him ran out."

The bookbinder stood. "I need to talk to him."

Miriam shrugged. "I told you—it's locked."

"I have ways around that."

Miriam nodded. "There's so much to do. He can't just disappear." She lowered her voice. "Brooks has been by twice this week already. In *person*. Always with a couple of thugs."

⌄

Picking a church rectory lock did not prove a challenge. The bookbinder opened the door at the top of the stairs and was hit with a wall of squalor, a blend of flop sweat and cheap aftershave, cigarette smoke, old spilled whiskey, old piss. The windows were shut tight and blinds drawn, though it had to be ninety degrees outside, August pressing itself down on the pavement.

"Get out." Father Jim's voice arrived as a hoarse creak, a match strike, his skinny arm extending out from the recliner. The bookbinder pressed the door shut behind him. Empty bottles guarded the counter of the little kitchen to his right. He switched on the overhead light, and the arm recoiled, wounded. The bookbinder switched the light back off.

He walked into the living room, stepped over a pillow, a bottle cap. There were cigarette burns peppering the shag carpet, constellations at his feet. Father Jim slumped in the old recliner, dressed in a stained robe and threadbare socks. He lit a cigarette with his good hand, mumbled something incomprehensible over the filter. He looked smaller, his eyes rimmed, rabid. He smoked in quick, thoughtless puffs, ash peppering his lap. A tumbler of something golden and warm sat beside him. "Who are you?" he asked, trying to focus on the figure. "*What* are you?"

"I'm the one who cleans up," the bookbinder growled, grabbing the tumbler.

The priest flinched again but seemed only to collapse further into the chair, taking longer, more exhausted drags from his cigarette. It was as if he had been waiting for someone to take the cup. "And here I thought that was my job." He licked his lips. "Am I supposed to know you? From some other life?"

The bookbinder's face darkened. "I hear tell you've seen my work. But no—we didn't meet before that search party. And then the fire." He gazed on a framed picture of Jesus, his two fingers upheld, as if offering a blessing. "Figured you'd be more used to that kind of thing, though."

"Clever."

"I'll make a pot of coffee," the bookbinder said, carrying the glass to the kitchen. He poured the whiskey down the sink and put a kettle on.

"What do you want from me?" the priest bellowed after him. "What the hell do you think I know?"

"We'll get to that after you've had some coffee."

Father Jim stared into an empty corner of the room. "I'm no help to anyone."

The bookbinder filled the doorway. "First, tell me about Brooks."

A hoarse laugh tumbled from the priest. "If you're asking, you already know."

"I really don't."

Father Jim grunted. "He's a very rich man. A miserable, rich man."

"Miserable?"

The priest's heavy head rolled back against the chair. "He covets. He craves things that are not for sale."

"Most of us do."

Father Jim took a deep breath, let it out slowly. He nodded, his mouth almost a smirk, but not quite. "It was a nice church. A nice little church. That's all anybody ever wanted. His crews broke ground, and he came to me—last year, he came to me—wanted to revise the plans, make it twice as big . . . this thing, this giant thing, and I said no at first, I did . . ." He scratched at his chest. "He kept on. He kept *on*." Father Jim lit another cigarette with the end of the last. "Then the crews slowed down."

"Oh, they kept showing up, but they . . . missed deadlines. Jobs weren't getting completed or had to be redone. The parish was burning through money, and then Brooks came back . . . I could read between the lines—I knew I had to play ball. So we went with his specs, expanded the foundation—a giant basement banquet hall that he owns . . . tax-free, of course, separation of church and state, you see? All of a sudden, the crews picked back up, more guys, more equipment . . . and then we were hitting deadlines, *boom-boom-boom*, but the budget . . ." He laughed again. "The budget was completely shot. I had a basement—*his* basement, mind you, with a bar and a ballroom . . . I had half a church and we were out of money." He dropped his head into his bandaged hand, winced, and let out a little cry. He took another long cigarette drag. "Brooks comes back, offers me a loan."

"A loan."

Father Jim nodded. "Yes—and not just out of the generosity of his heart, either. I don't know much about such things— but the way some of the invoices overpaid for some things, and then back again, it sure looked like laundering. Like good money for bad. Or vice versa. Either way, it was the only way to keep the church afloat, so . . . so I took it. I took it all."

The nod transformed into a slow, sad shake. "I'm in his pocket now. Like Hillary. Like this whole damn town, whether they like it or not. Whether they *know* it or not."

The kettle whistled, and the bookbinder took it off the burner. When the coffee was brewed, he returned to the priest's side, a small dining chair in one hand, a mug in the other. He handed the latter to Father Jim, sitting more upright now, peering at the closed blinds as if to try to see through them. "You never answered me," he said. "Why are you here?"

"I was told you might have some answers for me."

"Oh, yes. A little birdy. Which birdy?"

"Stan Chandler."

The priest's eyes narrowed. "I see. Well, I can't say I have

much to do with Mr. Chandler. He's not even a parishioner."
Father Jim blew on his coffee.

"It would have been almost ten years ago now. You were
here?"

Father Jim looked up. "There weren't as many folks around
then." Back down at his cup. The bookbinder caught a small,
resigned sigh. "Well, if Stan is talking, I imagine I don't have
much quarter. I'm guessing this has something to do with the
Dysons?"

The bookbinder placed his chair directly in front of the
priest. He thought of Rebecca in the moonlight, her secret
codes, his own, the gravity between them. He thought of Rachel Dickerson and the way her eyes caught the inferno's light,
holding it like a note in a song. The Nordic woman, wanting
her mother to know the *why* but not necessarily the *what* or
the *how*—more like him than he could have possibly imagined—and the calm of her dead eyes, rendering all the questions, all the answers, moot. He thought of Hillary and now
this Brooks, and the knots big and small that were tightening
all around them. He thought of the little white square of a
house that hummed and pulsed. He couldn't see everything
that was to come, but he sat just high enough to see much
more than most. "Things are moving fast now. And I think
they're related."

"Things? What things? The fire?"

"The fire. There's more, though." The bookbinder looked
into Father Jim's bleary gaze. "So much more. Would you
balk if I told you there are forces at work here in Brookshire
that would make your Gospels curl like the paper they're
written on?"

The priest coughed, pinched his face. "Try me."

"Do you believe in good and evil?"

"It's in the job description."

The bookbinder's jaw held its grim line, his eyes flint. "Good and evil. Light and dark. Black and white. Yin and yang. Imperfect christenings, but about as far as we can see. It's all the same, and it's all converging here. *Now.*"

Father Jim's tone shifted, took on the air of a counselor, traveling well-worn paths. "Tell me," he coaxed, soft, reassuring.

"It's quite a story." The bookbinder scratched at his beard. His eyes narrowed, and he seemed to the priest to be wrestling with some colossus that wasn't quite there, yet somehow right on top of them both. The hairs on Father Jim's neck, his forearms, stood straight. The bookbinder bowed his head. "Remind me—how does it start?"

The priest eyed him warily, an animal in the path of a much bigger predator, offering deference. Everything was still so foggy, so blurred, and this odd man somehow cut through the fog, not so much a light as a dagger—the glint off a dagger. Father Jim cleared his throat, a slight warming blush. "You start with 'Bless me, Father, for I have sinned.'"

The bookbinder glared at the priest, hard enough to make him blink. "Bless me, Father, for I have sinned."

"And then you tell me your sins."

"I have killed others."

"Oh." Father Jim folded his hands and, with some effort, closed his eyes, listened as the bookbinder told his tale and confessed his sins.

When the bookbinder was through, the priest blinked at his dirty socks and lit another cigarette with a shaky hand. He smoked it without a word, all the way down to the filter.

The pair sat in silence, save for the ticking of an old clock, before Father Jim finally broke it. "There is something you need to see. But, first, I'm going to need more coffee."

⌣

The bookbinder waited while Father Jim showered and shaved. He opened the blinds and stood at the window with his smoldering pipe, watching the panorama the priest could observe from his humble nest: To the left, Saint Anne's School prevailed, back in session in a matter of weeks, the whole cycle begun anew, the coming of fall, the dying of the light that precedes the rise, the rebirth. Straight ahead, he watched the trucks in the parking lot, the army of dark contractors eating their lunches and smoking. And to the right, like a sword thrust to the hilt, the would-be Saint Anne's Church, itself built on top of a small hill that rested on other, steeper hills, a king of kings. It towered over the school, over the shops farther down the highway, over everything. They were running twelve-hour shifts to have it all done by the Christmas Vigil. Mr. J. M. Brooks was covering the costs, but there was always a price.

The priest walked into the room, wearing a pressed clerical shirt. His eyes still held glass, but he cleaned up well. "We'll take my car." And then quieter, embarrassed: "May I ask that you drive?"

They settled into the parish's Mainline and headed east, away from the city, out toward the bay. They drove for over an hour and crossed the brand-new bridge, Father Jim a little dizzy, a little frightened by the height, the speed, believing mortal men were not meant to traverse water quite like this. On the other side was the Eastern Shore, its acres and acres of tobacco fields. It was a rhythmic drive, the cough of the engine against dark green leaves swaying in the breeze and the orange August sun filling the spaces the countryside allowed. The painted lines of the highway ended at the horizon.

Midafternoon had taken hold before the bookbinder turned onto an unmarked dirt road at the priest's direction, and then another, which after about a mile led to a long, ambling driveway. Carved out into a spell of weeping willows and soaring oaks was a white box of a building partially covered in ivy, and behind it several more rectangular buildings, also white, but darker, more entrenched in the forest and its overgrowth. There was no sign. The bookbinder turned the engine off. His pipe dangled from his mouth.

"We're here," Father Jim announced.

When they stepped out of the car, the bookbinder was most struck by the silence of the place. There were the sporadic notes of birdsong and a rumble of tree frogs and insects just along the surface, but beyond that only the sound of abyss, of a Styx—not the death men fear but the peaceful drift they crave. The building seemed like a waved handkerchief, a goodbye to the harried, unruly world.

"The sisters of Our Lady of Sorrows run this place," Father Jim advised, though this did not mean anything in particular to the bookbinder. They walked up the two cracked stone front steps and entered the building. A small nun sat at a desk, offering a smile that was not warm, but not unkind.

"Father McKeon." She acknowledged the priest, nodding to the scruffy man beside him. "And who do we have here?"

"This is a friend of mine," the priest deflected.

She nodded more cordially to the bookbinder. "A pleasure. Father, a word, please?"

Father Jim leaned over the desk, the nun whispering, all the while keeping watch on the bookbinder. "I realize that he's in terrible shape, but I must insist, we are simply not equipped to take in any men at this time. I know we've never explicitly had this conversation, but I thought it was under—"

Father Jim started to chuckle, startling the woman, both by his demeanor and his breath, the edges still marred by drink.

"No, no, no," he said gently, patting the woman on her folded hands. "We are just visiting." And then closer, so only she could hear: "We're here to see my parishioner."

The nun continued to eye the bookbinder, the words and scenes scratched across his forearms, those climbing up his neck like the ivy crisscrossing the lobby's small windows. "Is this wise, Father?"

The priest shook his head. "It is necessary. Whether it is wise or not, only God knows."

The nun sighed. "She stays in her room, mostly. We keep her in here, in the main building—the top floor. Same as before."

"Thank you." The priest offered her a polite nod, which she returned, grimacing. "Did you take the bridge?" she blurted as they moved from the desk.

Father Jim nodded again.

"What was it like?"

He paused. "It was . . . easy. Easier than the ferry, of course."

The nun shook her head. "It worries me," she replied softly, mostly to herself.

Father Jim led the bookbinder up a narrow flight of stairs.

"What is this place?" the newcomer asked, a tightness building in him, a radar ping.

The priest spoke softly over his shoulder. "Well, officially it serves as a hospital for women. Unofficially . . . that covers a lot of ground." The stairs creaked beneath them. "There are many touched women here, but there are also others, girls that have gotten in trouble, victims of . . . harshness." He paused to turn at a landing. "It's a place where someone can disappear." The bookbinder himself glanced about the staircase as if looking for escape routes.

They reached the top floor, walked a few paces, and Father Jim placed a soft knock on a door numbered simply "11." He opened it slowly, and they were greeted with the sound of Chopin playing on a phonograph, a nocturne in the middle of the day.

"Hello, Charlotte," Father Jim said, and everything inside the bookbinder fell like a thousand dropped books crashing to the floor—not the flutter of loose pages but the thump of bound, heavy bricks, a lifetime of stories, all stitched together, knotted without mercy. "I have someone here to see you."

The bookbinder swallowed, glared hard at the priest, who stiffened and moved aside; the bookbinder stepped inside the doorway of the tiny room. A beautiful young woman, her dark hair cropped short, sat at the window, in the soft light filtered through the oaks. She turned slowly to the bookbinder and offered a forlorn smile. "My, you look different."

"You too," the bookbinder answered weakly, all the room's air pulled from him. He turned to Father Jim, his eyes welling up.

"Do you remember Mama playing these records?" she asked.

"I do," the bookbinder replied, a small deceit. The song was familiar, if not the context. His lip trembled as his distrait brain tried to catch any one of the moth thoughts now careening about and nail it down into coherence. He flickered between the skinny youth he was and the complicated thing into which he had since been fashioned. In the end, he simply repeated, "I do."

Charlotte smiled again, a little brighter, and raised an eyebrow. "How do all of you fit in that one little doorway?"

Father Jim turned to the bookbinder, then back to Charlotte. "What do you mean, dear?"

"All of you crowded there, one on top of the other."

"There's only two of us here."

Charlotte shook her head gently, more bemused by the priest than anything. "No, there's you, and my brother, and the black one, the thing with feathers. Big sprawling thing. Doesn't make any sense how it fits in there, does it?"

Father Jim blinked, fearing he had made a terrible mistake. Much less shock than this could trigger an episode. He chastised himself in his own head.

Charlotte's voice was vulnerable, though not weak, and meandered to them from across the room, a transmission. "You brought something back, didn't you, Michael?"

The bookbinder, her brother, nodded. When last he saw her, he couldn't tell where her husband's blood ended and hers began. And he never had a chance to say a goodbye—at least not one she could register. She stumbled out to the shed and he ran. All the way to an enlistment office. All the way to the end of the world.

And back again.

"I'm not scared."

"You needn't be." He sighed. His voice was exposed wire, and he ran his hand across the side of his bristled jaw. His mouth was a wasteland, dryer than dry. The thing with wings shifted inside him.

"Paul brought something back with him, too, didn't he?"

Charlotte didn't wait for a reply. "Something terrible." She turned her attention to Father Jim, himself frozen. She straightened, read the room in her own good pupil's way. "May I speak of Paul, Father?"

"You can talk about anything you'd like, my dear."

"Sometimes they don't like me to talk about Paul here," she confided. "They say it upsets me."

"It's okay, child. You're safe now."

Charlotte shook her head slowly. "It wasn't Paul, though." She turned to the window, to the sunlight breaking in. "It wasn't *just* Paul." She paused, closing and reopening her eyes to meet her brother's stare. "It's still there, isn't it?" She read his eyes. "That cute little house in that cute little town . . . what was it called again?"

The bookbinder cleared his throat. "Brookshire."

"Brookshire . . ." Charlotte turned from them, back to the window, the sun through the trees. "Yes. Brookshire. We were only there a short while."

She snapped to attention, returning to the men in the doorway. "Every day about this time, the sun hits this window and I put on my Chopin. One matches the other quite nicely, even if you wouldn't think it." She giggled.

"That's lovely," Father Jim said.

"It's balance. There are two kinds of darkness, you know? There's the absence of light—that's one kind. But there's also the shadow the brightest light casts. That's something else." Charlotte watched the bookbinder, the space where he stood, his hands stuffed in his pockets and then outstretched, to his sides, at his neck, back again, a human smear, a blur. "I'm so glad you came."

"I thought I lost you."

The woman cocked her head just so, tittering lightly. "Oh, silly, you can't lose me. I'm your sister, and you can't ever lose a sister."

The bookbinder shook; long, exhausted tears wetted his beard. Father Jim placed a tentative hand on the man's shoulder, not sure what he would touch.

"Whyever are you crying?" Charlotte turned her round eyes to Father Jim. "Have you spoken to Paul lately?"

The bookbinder gaped at her, his own eyes pleading, a dispatch his sister could only register intermittently. Father Jim stepped forward and interceded. "He's still on active duty, my dear."

Charlotte smiled. "He's a war hero, you know?" She had grown a shade paler, if such an alteration were even possible, and her blues traveled from the bookbinder to the priest, then back, off somewhere else entirely. "The record has ended," she hinted, and softly turned away.

⌄

Walking out, Father Jim tried to explain. "She doesn't remember that day like you or I do. She doesn't understand that her husband is dead, but she at least seems to know he can't hurt her anymore." He turned so they were facing each other. "Apparently Stan Chandler called me right after the Appleton PD. But it was Easter morning, and I had two Masses to perform. And then, after, I ended up in Appleton myself, the birthing ward—an emergency. Ava St. Pierre, in fact . . ." The priest, too, had heard the rumors of where the girl's mother had been spending her evenings. "Anyway, it was a fraught delivery, and she didn't seem like she was going to make it." He shook his head. "No, she *didn't* make it—no *seem* about it. And then she *did*. I had raced to offer last rites that proved unwarranted. Thank God."

Father Jim watched the sun, well into its dive. "By the time I made it back to town, the police had already released Charlotte. They probably shouldn't have—not because she was guilty, but . . ." He looked back at the half-hidden buildings. "She was not all there. But they grew tired of looking at her, I figure—or having to look *away*—and shuttled her back home."

"Stan was adamant that she couldn't stay. Couldn't take what was to come. I had my reservations, but he was just as adamant that she was a complete innocent. Which I didn't doubt, not exactly—but it was almost like he was talking around a hole in his own story." His voice lowered. "For a while there, I even wondered if *he* had done it." He studied the bookbinder. "I can't presume—" He sighed. "This isn't perfect. But it's better than where she was."

The bookbinder looked past the priest, past the structures full of disappearing people, past the trees and miles and miles of things overgrown, things yet untouched. "Was this my penance?"

"No, son," the priest countered. "This was your absolution." He shook a cigarette from its pack. "I fear the penance is yet to come."

19

⌣

When Father Jim pulled the Ford from the curb of Kestrel Street later that night, the blood coursing through the book-binder was molten, the thing inside him agitated, all his senses inflamed. Joe's bicycle, usually propped against the edge of the porch, was gone, the books all put away, nothing stirring. The days were growing shorter but still lingered, the evenings a slow melt into night. The bookbinder heard the block's children playing through their last games in their yards, tiny cries of triumph, laughs that could punch through clouds.

Beyond that, though, beneath the sounds other men could hear, the bookbinder bore the tension of his house, a taut string near to snapping. He was no soothsayer; he could not foretell the future, exactly, but he could intuit the music of it all—so when he opened the back door to find Chief Hillary sitting in his chair, licking his thumb and flipping through one of his constructions, the bookbinder was not surprised.

A wrinkled cigarette dangled from the corner of the chief's mouth. "The Hollanger boy let me in," he explained. He took a long drag and stubbed the cigarette out on the bookbinder's table, tossing the butt on the floor. "I told him to run along home, and he did. Like a good boy."

The bookbinder straightened the tools on a worktable, pinpointing his focus on each one, straining to keep the agitation at bay.

"What's that you got there?" Hillary asked, pointing to the white, oblong-shaped item in the bookbinder's hand.

"A bonefolder."

"Sounds dangerous."

"It folds paper."

The chief chuckled. "And a knife cuts turkey at Thanksgiving dinner. Lots of things can be dangerous."

The bookbinder said nothing.

"Are you dangerous, bookmaker?"

The bookbinder set the bonefolder down with a small clink.

Hillary shrugged. "Because I'm hearing things, young man." He shook a fleshy finger. "I'm hearing things about you not playing nice. I thought we had an understanding."

"I thought so, too."

The chief stood up, popped his lower back. "The understanding was that I was going to look the other way regarding this here little illegal business venture you have going on, so long as you kept your nose clean."

"And I haven't?"

The chief picked up another half-finished book, shook his head. "No, son, you have not. Like I said, I'm hearing things. Intimidation of the citizenry. Tough talk in saloons and whatnot." He tossed the signatures down with a smack. "I don't like bars myself. Nothing good ever comes out of a bar."

"Or a brothel."

The chief glared. "Well, we don't have to worry about that anymore, do we?" He shifted, slid a thumb under a suspender. "And there's the matter of the St. Pierre woman, too? This town is lousy for keeping secrets, but the worst-kept one is you carrying on with another man's wife right under *his* nose. And there's an idiot child involved, no less?" Hillary whistled, looked out toward the porch. "Hell, it's not just your nose that's dirty these days, is it?" He dropped his thumb down on his holstered revolver, flashed a grin like a blister.

"And, so long as we're talking about brothels, son, there's the little matter of a little whore dying right under *your* nose. If we're splitting hairs."

The bookbinder's expression remained stone, masking the eruptions behind it. He gritted his teeth so hard he could hear them. "I have something for you." Mechanically, concentrating on each step, on not tearing the gelatinous old man's face off right then and there—*one, two, three, four; one, two, three, four*—he marched toward the back of the shop, through the doorway and into the shadows.

Chief Hillary flipped the holster strap loose of his gun. "Don't go getting clever, boy," he snarled, his voice lowering a register, all composed attention.

The bookbinder reappeared in the workshop. He tossed a book on the table next to Hillary, and the chief jumped at the thud; after a cold scowl, he relaxed his hand from his sidearm. This one was bigger than the last, a foot long, almost as wide, bound in a simple, coarse fabric, but with perfect lines, the edges crisp and the cuts sharp. The chief shook the book. Nothing fell out.

He tried to hand it back. "I think there's been a mistake. This isn't what I normally read."

"Open it."

The chief licked his teeth and complied. The pages were not paper but bound, glossy photographs quilted together—photographs of a nude Chief Hillary cavorting with an assortment of prostitutes, some barely more than children. One could tell they were not taken on the same day, and all were close enough that the camera had to have been *in* the room—or, at least, an adjoining closet.

The chief's face raced past red to purple, the color of burst blood beneath the surface.

"You are not my concern," the bookbinder said, speaking slowly, making sure each word hammered home. "Unless you choose to *make* yourself my concern." The old chief's hands shook against the cover.

"The negatives are safely far away from here. From me. You know"—the bookbinder seethed—"if you were ever to get clever." The last words rolled into an almost unintelligible snarl, a thunder.

Hillary's mouth moved, but the man said nothing.

"My recollection of our arrangement is that you won't be bothering me. Or anyone I choose to associate with—from here on out."

The bookbinder trudged toward the front of the shop and swung open the storm door. The chief put on his hat and passed without a word, just the cold husk of his viscous breathing.

20

Fall brought no relief from the weight in the air. The summer's heat did not retreat on cue, and windows remained open along the streets of Brookshire, betraying the boiling skirmishes inside, the dining table tyrannies. Wives covered up their welts in long sleeves before the season demanded it, and their feral children, almost-men and almost-women, revved their souped-up hot rods deep into the night. Tess Hollanger started wearing makeup as if it were warpaint, and Joe donned his Saint Anne's uniform for the last time—the navy slacks, the frayed backpack.

On Kestrel Street, Joe learned an arsenal of new skills, folding paper sheets into perfect octavos or carving intricate negatives into thin metal plates—what he saw when he closed his eyes, in reverse. The book he had started for the blond lady, the one his mother said the bookbinder had tried to save, rested on a small shelf beside his worktable, collecting dust. He promised himself—and her, too, in the small, quiet way he could—that he would finish it one day. But, for now, he could not bear to look at it for too long, let alone pick it up and put his grubby hands on it. It had become something new in the time between then and now, a relic, a kind of scar.

In the meantime Joe had taken to carefully cutting out the pages along the spine of two existing books, and then interspersing them, one after the other, so the reader was reading one, and then the next, and then the first, and then the next, until, at some point, they were reading a third. He christened these "Frankenstein books."

His mentor was present but distracted; the bookbinder often scowled in a corner, working through his pipe instead of books, or pacing upstairs, his footfalls heavy through the ceiling. The bookbinder looked older every day, and Joe suspected he spent entire nights on the roof, only descending back down at dawn.

Rebecca St. Pierre established her eye for the business and began to help with the workshop's finances, managing the books of the books. She convinced the bookbinder to try the porch as a showroom while the weather still held, and she grew less careful about her own comings and goings, less concerned with the tongue clicks of the haughtiest of her neighbors. She even brought Ava with her, the girl never without her Baoding balls. Her daughter seemed calmer here, less prone to fits. They hardly interacted in any way Rebecca could see, but she had to admit some intrinsic connection between her strange daughter and perhaps stranger lover, some palpable ease that took hold when each was safely in the other's presence.

Even so, Rebecca knew something had changed with the bookbinder, something he refused to unbolt. It wasn't just the girl who had suffocated in the fire, or the stress of Hillary's machinations; the man bent wan, big as he was, and had developed tics perhaps only she noticed—when he scratched his beard, it was as if he were feeling for his face more than anything, making sure it was where it was supposed to be—making sure it was still *what* it was supposed to be. He shuffled around the workshop like he was trapped in a dinner jacket several sizes too small. He still maintained his lumbering grace, but she could see the strain in his brow, the sketch lines under the masterpiece.

It was when he gazed directly at her, though, often from across the room, that struck her the most acutely: He held the expression of a man who had already lost everything, though all he had was only a few feet away, well within his reach. Neither way to read him struck pleasant.

Rebecca noticed Joe step away from one of his Frankensteins to pick up a spare bonefolder from the table. He made his way to Ava, and Rebecca shifted on her stool at the front of the shop, managing to bite back a warning cry; Ava would not let anyone approach her straight on without a meltdown, and poor Joe was about to learn the hard way. The lesson, though, was Rebecca's—she watched her daughter silently observe the boy slide beside her and started when Ava gently placed her little spheres on the table to pluck the bonefolder from his hand. Rebecca took a cigarette from her case and smoked against the long afternoon light darting in, somewhere between bemused and delighted by the scene. She allowed herself a small hope that this was progress, perhaps even growth—but even if it were merely a singular anomaly, a one-time respite, she would take that, too. Rebecca wanted only happiness for Ava, and she had the sense, though the girl could obviously not tell her directly, that every little crumb of it her progeny had ever enjoyed had been hard-fought. She did not think her daughter was simple like the rest of town did; she held that Ava was perhaps the most complicated creature in all existence. She would never be able to prove it, but that wasn't strictly necessary. If it were only a delusion, it was her fantasy to embrace, one she knew she had no doubt earned.

Her eyes tracked along the plane running out ahead of her, past Joe offering Ava sheets of paper that the girl took and began wordlessly folding, and caught the bookbinder buried in a shadow, staring at her child with such intense agony that she almost dropped her cigarette. Mournfulness flickered through his eyes, and he had never looked both so young and so old at once. There was a tortuousness in the arrangement of his face, the way the brow tightened around the devastated stare, like he was working out some fresh horror only to discover another behind it, a chain reaction. For a moment she thought he resembled Sam, and she squeezed her eyes shut just to quash the repulsion that shuddered through her.

Joe had already returned to his stool, leaving Ava to her craftwork. Rebecca turned to him.

"I have your pay, Joe."

Joe looked up and frowned. "But I just got paid."

"Some more of your books sold this week."

"But I've been at school—I've hardly done anything."

The bookbinder looked down his pipe. "Then don't take it."

Rebecca ignored the bark. She had commandeered a role, made herself useful. "It's yours. I'm handling the bills today, and the one who handles the bills has all the power."

Joe regarded her quizzically but nodded and thanked her. She dropped coins into his palm.

She stood and took a few steps toward the center of the

workshop, her emerald gaze now tight on the bookbinder leaking smoke in the corner. She recognized firsthand the difference between running to and running from—it wasn't fear that radiated from his bones. There was bravery in his rage, and rage in his bravery, and truthfulness steeped in both, the hardest kind that kept him from telling her everything was going to be all right on those nights when she climbed into his bed. She knew from the beginning what she was in for, the precariousness of a blood-tinged kiss; whatever this was offered no happily ever after. Theirs was a season, and the season was changing.

She turned back to Joe. "Why don't you go buy yourself a malt before it gets too cold to enjoy them?"

⌣

Joe was not stupid; he knew Mrs. St. Pierre's suggestion had little to do with his enjoyment or the shifting weather—she and the bookbinder were going to have it out. He had seen enough blowups between Tess and his mother to recognize both a pressure change and the wisdom of evacuation, lest he get swept up in it all. In this case he was only too happy to oblige and get out of the way.

He also knew it was about time. Something was off with the bookbinder, and it wasn't just an attitude. He looked to be in pain, though Joe couldn't tell whether something was wrong with the man's body or soul. Maybe both—everybody he knew was going a little bit crazy. Why should the weirdest of them all be any different?

When he pushed open the drugstore's glass door, he was not surprised to see Tess sitting alone at the counter—a lack of surprise that surprised him. His big sister had once been a constant in his life, and now wasn't, and his brain still toggled back and forth between these two realities. He hesitated at the door, unsure on which version of this alien he had stumbled.

Tess twitched and caught him hovering at the end of the counter, not quite committing to a seat. She corkscrewed her face and he shrugged in its wake, shuffling over to climb onto the stool beside her.

"What's wrong with you? Do I bite?"

"Nah." And then gingerly: "Are you okay?"

"Are *you* okay?"

Joe nodded. He eyed the tall glass in front of Tess; she tracked his gaze, frowned. "It's just a shake."

"Okay."

Tess balled her hand into a fist, squeezed, and then, very slowly, released it, opened it, so she was staring at her knuckles, palm down, her hand's minute tremble. She sighed. "What do you think you know, Joe?" She considered her brother and realized he looked older now, too. It was funny how that worked—she had not in fact left him behind. She may have turned a corner on the track, couldn't see him at times, but he was back there, keeping pace all the same.

Sometimes her mother took up so much of the space in their house—purposely tried to fill it to account for the six-foot, man-shaped elephant missing from the room—that Tess didn't even remember Joe was a witness, that he saw everything the Hollanger women did to themselves and each other.

Joe ordered a chocolate malt. "Coming right up," the soda jerk snapped, breezing by. Joe rubbed his fingers together, then stared at them.

"Just say it."

Joe looked up. "What?"

"What's on your mind? You've got that Joe face on."

"What's that supposed to mean?"

"Well, it usually means either you're trying to figure out the grand puzzle of existence . . . or you have to take a shit."

"Shut up."

Joe's tone was harder than she expected. Tess pulled out a crumpled pack of cigarettes and offered one. He shook his head, glancing around. The counter man placed the malt on his ghostly reflection while his sister lit up and exhaled. "You don't need to worry about me, little brother," she said, trying to reaffirm her advantage. "I'm a big girl and I know what I'm doing."

"Do you?" The edge hadn't softened, and Tess tried to tamp down her defensiveness. She didn't need a two-front war in her own house. There were benefits to paying attention in history class.

Instead, she collected herself and took a long look at the burning end of her cigarette. "Now, what is *that* supposed to mean?" She didn't wait for an answer. "What have you heard?" Her heart started to thump; she was surprised at how frightened she was by all the answers at play.

"Nothing."

"Bullshit."

Joe didn't want to be here, under these lights, having this conversation. But he was here, and short of running away and leaving a Joe-shaped hole in the wall like the *Looney Tunes* reels, there was nothing else to do but answer truthfully. "That you're a lush." Tess flinched but held her pose, cigarette up. "That you've been running around with greaser boys and trashy girls." Joe swallowed air. "That you've gone *bad.*"

He leaned on the last word, and Tess thought it would have seemed wholly childish if not for the austerity of his expression, the furrow of his brow. She felt shame racing to the edges of her skin, but also rage mixed with a twisted sort of pride. She reached for the one weapon she always kept ready at hand: her righteous indignation. "That's what *they* say, huh?" she shot back, forgetting the tact she had fostered just moments ago. "Well, let me tell you a little about *them*, baby brother. Let me tell you what *they*—"

She was interrupted by the clanging of the little bell and Sam St. Pierre stumbling into the drugstore. *Lush*, she thought, *might just be a matter of degrees.*

The man coughed, clearing his throat, and from across the aisles, Joe could still smell the cloud of stink, the sharp gin reek. Sam blinked at the Hollangers, then sneered, as if they were the things dragged in. Joe felt the man's eyes brush over him and land on his sister; casually, with careful effort, Sam pulled a cigarette from his pocket. "Well, lookee, lookee," he slurred. "Beautiful day, isn't it, kiddos?"

Tess took a pull from her shake and her smoke, then set both aside. She folded her hands in front of her, placing the end of her nose just on top to temper their shake. It wasn't fear that surged through her—she knew it even if no one else did. She thought of the switchblade she had started carrying around in her waistband, right at the small of her back. She had pinched it off a passed-out buster in some girl's basement.

They can look, but they can't see, Tess thought. She stilled herself and let Sam St. Pierre take his gander.

Joe beside her didn't much care for Mr. St. Pierre, one of the adults who had long since forfeited his respect—but he *did* fear him, detecting something of a rabid dog about the man, so he muttered his assent. Joe didn't want any trouble—he just wanted to sit here with his malt; for the first time in a long time, he just wanted to sit here with his sister, hold this strange, true note between them a little while longer.

"I wasn't talking to you, twerp."

"And he wasn't talking to you." Tess stirred her malt, setting the elongated spoon on a napkin.

"How's that?"

"I asked my brother if he liked his shake. He was answering me, not you."

Sam squinted and took a stool. "Feisty little girl." He exhaled, all smog, and smirked. "Or so I've been hearing." He turned to the soda jerk. "Lemonade."

The young man behind the counter nodded and grabbed a glass. Sam blew smoke in large, theatrical bursts, his head swaying to a tune that wasn't playing for anyone else. "The youngest Hollanger—the asshole's apprentice," he growled with syrupy menace, the smirk widening, stretching his face. "Been hearing things about you Hollangers. Big sis—Tess, right?" He pointed at the girl with her palms now pressed against the counter, a pose that could mean placidity, or could be coiling. "Tess Hollanger," he repeated, almost licking her name. "Been hearing you've been hanging out where you don't belong." Tess held against the urge to turn to the man, watched her knuckles instead, how white they seemed under the fluorescent lights reflecting off the counter. She caught something in the drunk's voice, a tinge of complication just beneath the obvious provocation, the teasing. There was a message between the words, but she couldn't tell whether it was a threat or a plea, or if both were one and the same.

Joe, too, stared down, but at his malt, feeling the reddening rush up so fast he thought it would pass over him and smack the wall. He heard every word Sam St. Pierre said, but as if distant, underwater. Closer, much closer, he could hear only his own inner voice, Ghost Joe admonishing real Joe, finding him eternally lacking. He thought of angels of death and first-borns, and how after all these years, the story might have gotten jumbled.

Tess's stool screeched. Joe's first urge was to climb all the way into his jacket, into another dimension where he was unrecognizable, a quantum do-over.

"How about it, young lady? You like being where you don't belong?" Sam beamed high wattage, eyes all flash and tint. "What do you say, Joe Bazooka? I bet the boys in school have been talking. Maybe even *bragging*."

Tess stood. She felt the cool of the knife's handle, hidden now by her jacket, against her back.

"It doesn't *want* you, you dumb little whore!" Sam yelped. Tess, who had started toward the overcast man, paused, struck by his words. The drunk stumbled from the force of his own bark, then recovered with a smile. His teeth snapped shut, holding the line of his sick grin. He stretched his arms out like a preacher offering a blessing, a "V" for victory.

A clatter behind the counter—the soda jerk dumped the lemonade he had just topped off. "Get out of here," he ordered in a tremulous voice.

Sam tamped down his vaudeville theatrics, grew suddenly still. His voice was balanced, as if on a tightrope. "I'm a paying customer," he replied, almost a waltz. "Now grab *me* another fuck*ing* glass of lemon*a*de."

Joe watched what he could not stop, a chain reaction, each motion punctuated by the beat of his heart, his own double-time waltz, the blood pounding in his ears. He watched the soda jerk turn his back on Sam St. Pierre, watched the drunk's sober fingers flick his lit cigarette at the young man's neck. He watched Tess glide toward Sam, her hand sliding under her jacket, out of sight. He thought of the gnarled old book with the strange markings and the secret inside, of his father on some beach Joe couldn't wholly fathom, jumping in front of a bullet, how much of that stolen soldier was in Tess, how much was in him, how things changed in tiny, important moments, the impossibly thin line between being a hero and something else entirely. He knew everything was about to go wrong, much worse than being mocked or blushing, that this was one of those tiny moments, that he had to do something, anything, and all he could hear over and over was St. Pierre's pompous voice: "Grab me another fucking glass." So Joe did— he grabbed his half-empty malt and chucked it at the man ten feet away, nailing him right over the left eye. The glass shattered when it hit the ground, Sam holding his face and staring at the mess erupted across the floor.

Tess halted and dropped her hands to her sides, empty, smoothing the fabric of her jacket.

"What the *fuck*?" Sam screamed, jumping from his stool. His hands, curled in veiny fists, dashed about him like planets with no orbit. "What the *fuck*!" Customers gravitated near the commotion at the counter, and Sam could feel his space shrinking. He twisted around slowly, a shambolic wobble, each step plodding in a tight arc. "I know how to reach you, junior," he spit, his eyes burning not on Joe, but on Tess, and, as if Sam St. Pierre had just remembered an important appointment, he burst through the drugstore's door and out into the waning day.

The soda jerk grabbed a cigarette from his pack next to the radio. He lit it, still shaking, and sighed. Joe regarded the shattered malt on the floor. "I'm sorry about the mess, mister," he mumbled. "I'll pay—"

"Don't sweat it, kid."

"But—"

"I said don't sweat it." A pause: "You want another one? On the house?" Joe looked up, and the man behind the counter seemed sadly amused, the adrenaline beginning to dissipate.

"No, thanks."

The man turned to Tess, her body still, but her eyes disheveled, wild; his amusement faded, leaving only the grim. "I suspect we could have had a much bigger mess in here. I think you saved us all a world of trouble, kid."

Joe spun toward his sister and watched her toggle between a woman and a child, right there on the checkerboard tile of the drugstore floor. Her bottom lip began to tremble, her tousled eyes catching the harsh fluorescents above, igniting like small halos. Joe bit the inside of his cheek hard to keep from sobbing when she grabbed his sweaty hand in hers for the first time in as long as he could remember, took the lead, and marched him—*them*—out through the door.

21

"There's less of you here than the day before," Rebecca finally said. "And I know that couldn't make any sense to anyone except you—but you won't talk to me. You're going to do whatever this is alone. And you're going to make me watch."

The bookbinder peered up from his corner. She stood on the other side of the room, her feet set, braced for the world and whatever bend it now had for her. The easiest thing for him to do would be to ease her mind and promise that he was fine, that he was right here, same as he had been and would be. Instead, he just looked on from his stool, his breathing forced, his deep-set eyes almost radiating, pushing her, making her spin fragile words she at first never intended to say.

"This is how it starts to unwind—with secrets."

"There are no secrets."

"No?"

"There are no *new* secrets."

"What does that even mean?"

The bookbinder rested his broad back against the wall. His

jaw tightened; he sighed, and Rebecca struggled to transcribe the codes in how his chest collapsed with the exhale.

"They are the same secrets as always." He stared at the table before him, trying to pull the right words from the scratches. "They are just pushing to the surface. They won't be held back much longer."

"Have I done something?" She took a step. "Have I *not* done something?"

His voice trudged across eons to rustle between them. "I think I have been unfair to you." He shook his head and closed his eyes.

"Let me help."

"You don't understand." His voice almost cracked. "There's no *room*." In the span of seconds he suffered hours of bit-back confessions. He imagined the release of telling her every-thing—that what she thought she knew was but the shape of things, and how the shape of things itself was full of falsehoods, whole dimensions missing from its physics. He opened his eyes and saw Okinawa spread out before him, just one of an infin-itude of graveyards, the bullets like shooting stars, the river a baptism, the sky blue black against the light of the burning village. The sky, though, was not the sky, or not *just* the sky, but feathers, thousands of feathers, and there *it* was, converging on itself, hovering just above him as his mortal blood ran into the river and the river ran into him. The beast grabbed him by the chest with its three brawny legs just before he sank all the way under, clutching him dripping in its gawk.

He first guessed it was through chance—*dumb fucking luck,* he thought bitterly—that it found him among all the other in-terlopers—that it overtook *him*, encased *him* in its desolate pitch—but he had grown to realize that the universe never leaves such things to chance. It had marked him the moment Paul Dyson died, simply waiting until he ran right to it. It was all part of the same clockworks as everything else, the gears grinding despite—and in anticipation of—the little prayers of men.

The bookbinder didn't know how this act would end—only that it would end, and soon. He trembled, then tried to gather his bearings by staking himself to the present. Rebecca hadn't moved—she had only grown paler where she stood. He, too, felt weak; the bookbinder opened his mouth only to snap it shut, holding his revelations like a plague behind his teeth.

Rebecca stood both with him and apart, the chasm denser than the oxygen in the room. It threatened to choke her right then and there. For a moment she thought she might drown standing up; for a moment she thought it might be a fitting end.

That moment passed, anger taking its place. "You *are* a fool," Rebecca declared, not wholly convinced but aware that, though there be only one kind of strength, there are infinite variants of weakness. "And the same as the rest." Her condemnation arrived hoarse from stifled tears grating against those fallen long ago.

"Goddamn it!" she screamed. It landed as a groan, an ellipsis, Rebecca catching sight of Ava in the corner, her daughter gurgling and mumbling nonsense, folding paper, watching all their infinite futures play out on top of themselves.

⌣

The bookbinder locked the shop; there had been no proper goodbye, if that was what this was. Ava was the last out of the door, pulled by her mother, and when she twisted in his direction just past the threshold, he was stunned by her flat countenance contrasted against the electric acuity of the eyes—she wasn't scared by what she saw inside him; she wasn't even surprised. If anything, he felt a pull toward her and back again. The peculiar energy of a building storm. Maybe even something like regret.

Toward and back again.

Alone, he poured himself a glassful of whiskey and lumbered upstairs to the den, a mostly empty room where he kept only a small chair and a hi-fi on a side table.

He twisted the power knob and inhaled the machine's crackle, positioning a wax record on the turntable: Chopin's Nocturnes, Op. 9, No. 2, in E-Flat Major. His hands lined with calluses, he set the crooked arm over the spinning black lake. He was entranced by the visual; after a few pregnant moments, the notes spilled out into the room.

The bookbinder stood at the window and ran a rough finger along the sheers, the sinking sun thick and orange against his skin. He closed his eyes and swallowed a long, deep drink. He returned to that distant night once more—his second stain, which splayed across everything he touched, in every direction—the perverse quiet of the river, louder than most metropolises because you could hear your own heartbeat, a bass line just beneath the crickets, the thump of the water in your ears. Occasionally a wind would rustle past, a timeless urge shaking corpses for loose change. And then there would be another rattle of gunfire from one side or the other, the distinction not mattering much anymore.

The bullets that delivered him into that river, itself a cleave across the skin of a broad Okinawan forest, entered from

behind, hot fingers piercing his flesh, pushing him from their
smolder into the ice water below. He never saw his assailant;
he never confirmed if it was friend or foe, an objective or an
accident. That, too, didn't matter much in the end. A means
to an end, it turned out. The inevitable, indefinite one. The
one still unfurling.

The record skipped—in the sun-drenched room, in the
blotted-out river—and the beast stretched itself against what
was left of him, the ragged, blood- and water-soaked remnants
of his uniform, his rucksack, bunched in its triplet claws.

When it screamed, inches from his face, the wicked *caw*
blew out his eardrums, his pupils. He could smell only the
ancient rancidness of its breath, entire epochs stained into its
blistering wind.

And then he felt something wriggle against his lips, spread
his teeth apart, farther—*impossibly* farther—until he felt his
jaw pop on one side, then the other, and still this wriggling
pressed on, pressed *in*, oily feathers squeezing themselves
into the crevices between his stalled organs. He tasted all the
beast's collected fury and dread, tinsel from the warpath, metallic like treasure, like the barrel of a sidearm, until that sensation, too, burned mercifully away.

He died by the sound of beating wings, and woke again
to a likesame song, a dark rustling against bone and muscle, a
pulsing. He was found on the brink of life in a wedge of rocks
and dead branches and mud, an inadvertent nest just outside
a small village that had somehow managed to endure the shell-
ing. Or at least survive it. A child discovered the pale, broken
giant, unaware that the tall creature wedged in the riverbed
was nearly twice the size as when he entered. Her parents
pulled him into their meager hut, a death sentence for them all

if he was discovered. The family, and then the town, tended to a body that had no business healing, but healed nonetheless, the bookbinder-to-be recuperating on a threadbare bed of straw.

Yatagarasu. The word was a familiar stranger in a foreign tongue, and from its harsh taste he came to understand more exotic words, ancient ones from the time of the Exalted Man and the Exalted Woman, and then all the words of all the languages of men and more.

When he peered out of the little hut's square window, he could see so far that the horizon curved.

His nightmares seemed to last centuries and were as real as waking. He would rouse himself from dirt and straw with dried blood caked across his knuckles, having punched the hard-packed floor through the night, the borderless quilt of lamp-black hours stitched over him.

In time the man had mended enough to walk again and leave the little village; the war, though, had already ended, civilization moving on without him. Listless, he found himself lingering in the dark corners of the island, guided by impulses he could hardly understand, unquenchable hungers. He landed in Tokyo proper, a haggard feast, and learned the carnal benefits of being a ghost, of no longer existing among the countable things. He fell in with the joyless, passed his time trading on the horrors of others, their shame, the bad dreams they buried in the rebirth of their national ones. There were plenty of secrets in the East after the war, and even more across Europe, where he eventually migrated. He found quick wealth bleeding *Sturmbannführers* of their selfsame stolen plunder.

He also discovered a respectable trade, one that occupied

his hands without bloodying them. Needle and thread and paper. A small squall of creation in the larger tempest of oblivion. That inevitable, indefinite endgame.

Always, there was a beacon, a siren song shared with the beast, calling them both from their knotted core. Seasons passed, whole years, and neither goaded the other too hard toward it, instinct validating the presentiment that some storms must gather before being unleashed. The bookbinder's return to America, his march with the sun, was an ambling funeral parade that played out over the better part of a decade. His return to Brookshire was likewise not coincidence but a culmination, not the first or the last, just one of the universe's endless challenges to itself. Light and dark. Yin and yang.

Charlotte Dyson in her little room had been half right: Her husband, Paul, had brought something back with him. Her brother, though, was brought back by something else.

22

The harder Tess tried to drown everything away, the harder it washed over her; her whole life was a ricochet. She tugged from the bottle as if at war with it, a compromised master trying to prove incontestable might, ward off a coup. She touched her neck, her hand burrowing into her jacket, and she stroked the angry thrust of her own throat as she guzzled the cheap whiskey. *Watch yourself*, she thought, the bookbinder's simple warning, months old now, replaying in her head. *Watch yourself.*

"There's nothing to see," she announced to the empty elementary school parking lot, slurring, struck by how far away her own voice sounded even though she was touching its cords. The sky was darkening, bruising as fast as the pain was fading. She tripped on a memory of her father sitting in his leather chair between deployments, half asleep, a lit cigarette between his lips, a great distance in his eyes. Tess turned away from the image, turned inward to find herself looking at a long black pool in her middle, a wound that had tried to clot but proved too big. She examined the inky abyss left by a war she had not experienced, yet was her defining experience. She stole another drink to flavor her lips.

Apples and trees, Tess thought, almost a non sequitur, trying to take comfort in the cliché, in the surface of things. It didn't hold—it never did; she wondered what was so wrong or right with her that she couldn't seem to skip across her days like a rock, just like everyone else in this town apparently could.

She felt sorry for herself, and the shame of that momentary lapse towed her down even farther, darker depths, where the strangest fish lived, the blind ones that never bumped into anything. That was where her dad was, she imagined, chewed on and leading some ghostly pack of lost corpses; even though she knew his remains were safe in the ground of Arlington, her stomach turned.

Tess held it back and down, and she bit on the inside of her lip until the world settled itself once more.

She lit a match on the third strike, squinting as she put it to her cigarette, and cursed as she watched headlights pull into the lot. She considered dropping the smoke and the bottle and running back into the tree line, but the reality of her current state nipped such an adventure almost before it began; she lifted her butt a few inches off the curb, then felt gravity yank it back down again. She swallowed another long drag in anticipation of her comeuppance.

The headlights expanded, washing over her frame; there was a sudden brake, a brief idling, and then a continuation of the turn as the sedan swung around and slid gently into a parking spot. There was another pause, as if a decision were being made, and then Tess registered the driver door opening, slamming shut.

A figure sauntered toward her, Tess's pulse rising with each approaching step, her insides a betrayal of her stone-still veneer. The figure lit a cigarette of its own, and she deciphered the face of Roy Dickerson in the quick flicker; she sighed with so much relief that it escaped through her teeth as a frail whistle.

"Tess? Tess Hollanger? Is that you?"

"Hi, Mr. Dickerson." Tess half-heartedly tried to bury her thick tongue. The syllables overlapped each other anyway.

The man cast a look around the empty pavement. "What in tarnation are you doing out here?"

"What are *you* doing out here?"

"I'm . . ." Roy Dickerson stammered and faltered, sure his answer would sound as ridiculous to her as hers would surely to him. He decided to stick with the truth. "Well, I come out here some evenings to look at the stars. I mean, they cleared out a hell of a lot of the trees here for this place." He did a little spin. "Might as well take advantage." He eyed the outline of her bottle, now close enough to see Tess and her accoutrements more clearly. "Your turn."

"I'm looking at the stars, too."

"In the bottom of that bottle?"

"No place better." She thrust the bottle up toward him. "Wanna see?"

He took it, gazed at it, at the weight of its meaning, second-guessing himself. "Does your mother know what you're doing out here?"

"What do you think?" she answered, not quite playfully.

Roy shrugged and took a long drink, then a seat on the curb next to the girl. "It's not safe, a girl out here alone," he said.

"I can take care of myself," Tess doubled down. "And who

says I'm always alone?" She offered her chin in adolescent defiance.

Roy snorted and took another drink.

Tess blushed, then inhaled a last drag and snuffed out her cigarette as elegantly as she could muster. "So, really, why are you here?"

Roy bounced the bottle in his hand, then set it down. "I was telling the truth." He took and let out a breath. "I come out here sometimes after my rounds, smoke a few cigarettes, gawk at the stars, find a quiet space." He scratched at his neck. "Ah, what am I saying? You don't need to hear this shit." He tossed a piece of gravel, listening to it clink against its brethren.

"Why don't you just go home?" Tess caught Roy's flinch before she had even registered what she had said. She knew from eavesdropping that Roy's wife had been sent to a hospital somewhere across the bay, and his two small children were staying with their aunt, Roy's sister-in-law. "Sorry," she mumbled.

He waved her off. "It's fine," he said. "It's just that some empty places are less empty than others, you know?" And then, quieter: "Some are supposed to be empty."

Tess nodded, more to herself than to him. She felt the urge to change the subject. "Lotta high jinks on this side of town." She wasn't even entirely sure what she meant, or why she'd said it.

Roy cocked his head and Tess shrank. He looked hard at her. "What high jinks might you know about, young lady?"

"Nothing," she lied, instantly made to feel like a child again, put in her place. The liquor kept her tongue from holding, and she tried to fill in the uncomfortable silence. "I just hear things."

"Hear things, huh?" Roy Dickerson was looking out into the night. "Like spook stories?"

Tess nodded weakly but wasn't even sure he saw her. They both understood intuitively that they were referring to the same haunt. In truth, the Dyson house was almost always on Tess's mind these days, its steady hum and almost-song; she had the sense that she had even started dreaming about it, if she could have remembered her dreams.

He softened a little. "I do not understand that fucking place." He winced. "Sorry."

Tess waved him off, W. C. Fields in bobby socks.

"The bank won't tear it down, replace those goddamned walls . . . nothing. Then Brooks gets his suspenders too tight, berates me for not being able to sell . . . misery, basically. *Tragedy.* It's goddamned cursed!" Roy sighed. He had been keeping the place up as best as he could, cutting the grass, trimming the hedges, the little things he could do to try to help it sell after the bank took over. No matter what he did, though, the stains would not vanish. He had scrubbed and stripped the drywall, painted over the stains with fresh coat over fresh coat—done everything but demolish the albatross wholesale—with the only result being that what had once been a deep burgundy was now a smeared, translucent lavender. He had replaced the carpet two times over, but rust-brown circles still bled through from underneath. "None of those bean counters believe me, but none of them will set foot in the place." Roy snorted bitterly. "Even after all these years, it's still easier and cheaper to blame me, I guess."

"And now, on top of it all, some asshole has been using the place as their personal lounge, bottles and cigarette butts strewn all over. Even piss!" He turned on her. "Know anything about that, Miss Hollanger?"

Tess stared at him with dull vacuity, her mind racing behind her eyes, as fast as it could muster while thick on cheap booze, conjuring and dismissing alibis, excuses. She had sneaked into the Dyson house a few times herself—perhaps more than a few. She went a little farther each time, first sticking to the basement, then the top of the stairs to the kitchen, and then later, the main attraction, the matching mile markers of Paul Dyson's last moments. A life turned *here*. Ended *here*. And there were those voices inside the pulsing of the walls. They seeped from inside the drywall, masculine, one on top of the other, entangled; she found herself stirred by their doleful croon, the way each note drew from a molten anger just underneath the creaks and whirs of the physical world. She couldn't make out the words, but she absorbed what they meant, the grimy, delectable truths they confessed, urges that fired along the scars tattooed across her insides.

Before Tess could lie to Roy again, a thought struck and he leaned over the girl, grabbing the pack of cigarettes resting beside her. She squeaked, surprised. He read *Pall Mall* across the label and tossed them back on the ground. "Wrong brand," he muttered. "I wish I could catch the son of a bitch." He lit one of his own. "I wish I could get one fucking thing right." Roy's voice faltered on the last word.

Tess started to ask him what he meant exactly, but she caught his head drop, nestling itself perfectly in the curve of his hunch and decided to leave well enough alone. She put her hand on Roy Dickerson's back and patted the man like a stray, struck by the fact that, the older she got, the more she realized that there wasn't really anyone worthier running things—the people supposedly in charge were just as screwed up as the kids, if not more, and nobody was minding the store.

⌄

Later, when Tess lurched through the front door, it took all her strength not to swing into the room, hanging by the knob, vaudeville style. Her mother was in the kitchen, and Tess heard the woman's shriek before she saw her. "Where the devil have you been?" Miriam demanded as she snapped off the radio. Joe was in the front room reading a comic; turning to his sister, he instantly comprehended her state—completely smashed and in no condition to survive this face-off. With a quick flick of his head, he showed his sister the path to salvation, and while she rushed down the hall to her room, using every ounce of concentration she could manage to keep from falling over her toes and onto her face, her brother ran interference in the kitchen, distracting his mother with some breathless story he supposedly heard from one of the neighborhood kids about a so-and-so doing some-such-thing he shouldn't have been do-ing, being somewhere he shouldn't have been—a rambling, twisty tale without much of a point, and less of an ending.

After letting a minute pass, maybe two, before grasping the conspiracy of Joe's story, Miriam pushed past her son and marched down the hall to Tess's room, only to find it locked from the inside. She jiggled the knob and raised her fist to pound on it, then slowly dropped her hand. She stared at the chipped paint and deduced that there was no vital truth she wanted to discover on the other side. They were all back home under her roof, having survived another day. That would have to be good enough.

23

Morning burst quickly, and the bookbinder spent his first conscious moments staring at the white of the wall in front of him. His mouth emerged dry and thick, and when he licked his equally parched lips, he caught the sick-sweet flavor of old spirits on his mustache.

The beast was growing impatient, its incitement building into something rawer that tore at the bookbinder's insides the more he tried to steady it. Discovering Charlotte alive had only made it worse, more immediate; he could feel not just the flutter now, but the unsheathed talons, the triplet razor-sharp claws digging first for purchase and then, inescapably, release.

A black hole roamed the little house on Tanager Way, and the monster inside the bookbinder yearned fiercely for its taste. Its host, and the resonance of his humanity still intact, was more reticent; the bookbinder understood destiny, inevitability, as much as—*more* than—any other, but, despite his cold calculus, he had still faltered, unable to stop himself from planting something like roots. Fashioning a makeshift tribe.

He had dressed himself in hubris through the mistake of caring for others. He had let his defenses down, ruining everything; he had come to love his neighbor.

He thought of Rebecca, the scent of her body, all roses and rain, and realized that it was he, not the thing inside him, who was the true monster, who had been led by selfishness and appetite. He had had no business involving the woman—though he had to concede, even in this harsh season of self-loathing, that their intersection had occurred not solely at the places of their want, but also through the vehicle of the peculiar eight-year-old to whom they were both beholden.

The bookbinder's mind drifted to a life that could never be, and he closed his eyes to strike it away. The vision rippled, colors and shapes torn away until it was Rebecca alone, encompassed by the black. It crept on her, spindly fingers sharpening into swords of onyx that slowly pierced her skin. He shut his eyes tighter, and the hellscape became that much more real, a waft of copper mixing with the floral scent, the soft and wet.

He inhaled, exhaled—*focused*—and the vision eventually passed like a cloud; he loosened its hold by surrendering to it. He was here. He was in this room, hungover and full of wrath. He had assembled the components of a kind of peace—and all it had proved was that nothing was over and nothing was new. If a corner had been turned, it only led to the same fucking cell. The same all-encompassing war.

He stretched, and the world wobbled; he centered himself in the chair, running a hand over his face, registering the stench of pipe tobacco on his fingers. He desperately needed a shower.

The bookbinder's own stink triggered a thought, a crack

across his surrender: *I am here. I am here.* As long as that were true, as long as this frame could still collect mud and musk, he still had some say, not wholly a slave to fortune; he could help these people yet. He thought of Stan Chandler, his hands cutting across his chest in pantomime—the ones down below, trapped under the caprices of gods. He caught his hazy reflection in the window's glass, and the town waking up beyond, through his outline; he admired the contrast, the symmetry. He might be waning, but the town could yet rise.

The bookbinder contemplated Chief Hillary, a loose thread he could pull. He already had leverage on the old cop, but it admittedly promised finite returns: Hillary was nothing more than a fat mosquito in a cattle car, a pest drunk off easy meat who thought himself magnificent. There was another, higher up the food chain, though, who held the mosquito in his pocket, whose greed impacted all of Brookshire. Another who shifted the fates of people the bookbinder cared about, for better, for worse, like tin soldiers.

The bookbinder dropped to the floor and began his morning push-ups. He would shower and drink a whole pot of black coffee before heading to the rectory. It was Rebecca's voice that played in his head, an aria: "The one who handles the bills has all the power."

⌄

As he returned from his rounds, Father Jim opened the rectory door to discover the bookbinder hovering over Miriam, the man's broad shadow tinting his secretary's arms and the papers on her desk the same shade of gray.

"What's wrong?" In profile, Miriam was a hawk, and when

she faced him, she looked right through him and his collar. She saw him not as a conduit to God, but a man of her species, a broken one at that, and he both loved and resented her for her verdict, more the former than the latter. Even the resentment, he suspected, was a sort of love.

Father Jim was not a man who lied, and his dishonesty, if it could be called that, came strictly from omission. He had long since forgone such defenses against Miriam Hollanger. The bookbinder was a different animal altogether, but he garnered that same unnerving trust; they shared a secret now, the pair of them, the confessor and confessed, yet somehow it drove the priest to know the other less, much as one small answer opens doors to bigger, more hopeless questions.

Father Jim sat down in a folding chair generally reserved for waiting parishioners. He ran his hand through hair just threatening to thin. "Old Mr. Kish," he said, "poor man."

"Who?"

"Mrs. O'Connor's father. Lives with her and her husband. This is the . . . third?" He paused, scratched his neck. "*Third* time she's called me to give last rites? I suspect I'll be back there a time or two more."

He fiddled with his hat in his lap. "I suspect she's mistaking the loss of his life for dying," he said slowly. "It's not always a straight line." His face darkened as he thought of Ava St. Pierre, the other extraordinary occurrence that Easter of 1944. A birth and a death, all in the same hospital bed. On the same day. *And yet she walks among us still.*

The priest looked up at the two across from him, noting the intimacy with which they stood beside each other. He felt a small pang of jealousy. He knew about the bookbinder and the girl's mother, and he had also heard—not heard, but been accosted with, *warned* about—the rumors around this man and his own secretary.

He didn't believe them, of course—not because he was naive or because he didn't understand lust, but because he was beginning to fathom something about these two creatures and the depths they carted with them. There was a connection between the bookbinder and the widow, no doubt, but a connection born of loss—of the spirit rather than the flesh. Father Jim knew that ground was easily muddied, but he also knew that Miriam was not the only one, that he had seen the same pulse between the bookbinder and Charlotte, a shared song beyond the vibrations of skin and bone, the collective nocturne behind the human heart.

"Father?" Miriam cocked her head with concern.

The priest caught himself, apologized. "I must have been lost in thought." A pause. "It must be a horror to lose everything in that way. The poor old man believes himself a child of ten in Hungary."

The bookbinder thrust his hands in his pockets. "Sounds like paradise," he contended, his face empty. "To travel in that direction, to end in the beginning, to fold yourself back into a place before the universe got its hands on you."

Father Jim smiled and nodded, shook the hat in his hand again. "And to what do we owe the pleasure today?"

Miriam shuffled papers on the desk. "He's signing up for a booth at the bazaar," the secretary lied. The bookbinder shot her a look that she didn't acknowledge. "He'll be selling his books in the parking lot come nine o'clock sharp on Saturday morning."

The bookbinder stared at the back of her head for a moment, scratching his beard. "Yes."

"Excellent!" the priest exclaimed, genuinely happy even though he knew it to be a ruse. "It should be a lovely morning."

The bookbinder turned to him. "There's one other thing, Father," he said, now Miriam's turn to flash a look left unacknowledged.

"What's that?"

"I need to borrow your car."

"Certainly. I'm free for a few hours. Where do you need to go?"

The bookbinder's mouth bent into a small, sad grin. "I don't think you should go on this particular field trip, Padre."

The bookbinder strode through the pristine doors of the building—an ugly construction, he thought, one of those modern designs, a cube made up of squares, mirrored windows meant to catch the sun and throw it back in your face. It was a building that put a lot of effort into pretending it wasn't there.

Inside, a pretty brunette in a pressed yellow dress greeted him, and he watched her try and fail to tamp her scowl at his feral appearance. She was a child, fresh out of high school, at best, but he could sense she came from a certain amount of money—not the highest strata, but enough to have inherited a particular perch in the world—and he could already see in her expression those fortification lines forming, the moats dug. She wasn't a Brooks; no, this girl was a step below, but ambitious, and easy enough on the eyes to carve herself a place. Precarious, though—the bookbinder made a mental note and approached. "I'm here to see Mr. Brooks."

She flashed a professional smile. "Of course, sir." A little extra dollop of syrup: "You have an appointment?"

"I do not."

The girl feigned disappointment. "I'm sorry, but Mr. Brooks is an incredibly busy—"

He raised his hand and her breath hitched. She bit her lip, but her eyes danced. "I appreciate that," he whispered. "Tell him I'm a friend of Chief Nathaniel Hillary. Tell him I'm the bookbinder from Kestrel Street."

The girl stared back blankly, but he only nodded, his eyes never letting her off his hook. She picked up the blinking phone on her desk, pressed a button, and plucked at the cord. She turned, muffling her voice. "I'm terribly sorry to disturb you, sir." She listened. "Yes. There's a man here—he doesn't have an appointment, but he's very insistent." The girl flashed her eyes at the bookbinder. "He says he's a friend of Chief Hillary?" Another pause. "Yes. Well, he said he was a . . . a bookbinder, I believe?" She nodded, her eyes glassy. "One moment. I'll ask."

She put the receiver on her shoulder. "What is your name, sir?"

"He wouldn't recognize it."

The receptionist's face fell. She was quickly sinking out of her league—she could neither get her employer the answers he sought nor for the life of her understand why a man like Mr. Brooks was still entertaining this stranger, who was beginning to frighten her. The bookbinder remained perfectly still.

She turned away again. "He won't say, sir." She lowered her voice to a whisper. "Long hair. Beard. It looks like he's wearing an army jacket." She waited.

"Are you sure?" She twitched, put her fingers to her mouth,

wishing she could pull it back. "Yes, sir, of course. I'm very sorry. Right away." She dropped the phone into its cradle. "He will see you now. Tenth floor." The girl at the desk blushed but said nothing more.

The bookbinder thanked her and made his way to the elevators. *Precarious.* Precarious can sometimes prove useful.

⌄

"A drink?"

The bookbinder was almost as tall sitting as J. M. Brooks was standing. Barrel-chested, with slicked hair and a black suit of hard lines, the businessman had the look of a steam engine. He spoke like one, too, each syllable a punch at the air around him.

The bookbinder nodded from his seat.

Brooks walked to the sidebar and poured a brandy for each of them. The office was traditional in a way the building that housed it was not, with a bearskin rug and fine walnut paneling. Taxidermy and wrought iron sconces decorated the walls. Heavy drapes softened the perfect square windows.

"You know, I've heard a lot about you, son," Brooks said, handing the bookbinder a glass. "Not all of it good."

"I imagine I could say the same."

Brooks cocked his head, grimaced—then grinned to take its edge off. "Is that a fact? Well, I appreciate that—I'm a big believer in handling things head-on." His smile was playful, but his eyes were steady.

"Cheers." The bookbinder raised his glass and took it to his lips.

Brooks sat behind the big hand-carved desk, directly across

from the bookbinder; somehow they were still eye to eye. Brooks folded his hands. "So, in the spirit of handling things head-on—I'm assuming you're here because you want something."

"I'd like you to make sure Hillary stays out of my way, to start."

Brooks's laugh was an empty graveyard wind. "Out of your way?"

"I've mostly handled him myself. But it occurs to me certain junkyard dogs won't let a leg go even when in their best interest."

The businessman's face broke into a grin. His voice was triumphant, patronizing. "Son, Chief Nathaniel Hillary is a lawman." He raised his hands in innocence. "I couldn't interfere with his duty if I wanted to." Pressing his hands together: "Though I do admit that I'm growing curious what your 'way' might be, and why he needs to stay out of it."

The bookbinder leaned forward, silent, resting his elbows and veined forearms on the polished surface of the other's desk. His breath steady and low, almost a cool purr, a metronome. Brooks played his thumbs against each other, his eyes landing on the top right drawer every few beats to avoid the Sphinx's stare. He broke the tension by standing up and taking a stagy drink. "I hear you make books?"

The bookbinder held his silence.

"Do you read them?"

"Ai."

Brooks placed his glass back on the desk, licked a dollop of liquor from his finger. "Well, that's all well and good. Books are fine. But real life . . ." He started again with a nod. "What interests me, what is most important, perhaps, are not the books that are written, but all the many that never are."

He tapped the desk. "You strut in here"—he spread his arms as wide as they would allow—"into this beautiful space with all these beautiful things, and you think it is something that just *happened*. You can only see the book, *J. M. Brooks, Millionaire*. You have no idea all the things I've done to get all this—all the work, all the sacrifice, all the stories that brought me here."

"The same can be said the other way around," the bookbinder interjected.

"I earned my spot on this side of the desk, young man. Your ignorance of the circumstances does not change that fact."

"You could say I'm uniquely familiar with your circumstances."

"How's that?"

"You are not the first man in my path to serve unbridled appetites."

The businessman's face was slate, a mask like the side of a mountain. "Oh, so you're the hobo Jesus who's going to give me a lesson on how the world works? The second fucking coming!" He flared his arms in mock drama. "And I've been lollygagging all this time to have my soul saved! By a bookmaker in the suburbs!"

Now worked up, Brooks reddened, straight to crimson, hints of blue around the edges of his eyes and flared nostrils. "Do you have any idea what I do here?"

The bookbinder leaned in again. "Firsthand."

"So you're a businessman?"

"This isn't business. This is profiteering. With a side of bribery, corruption, code violations, and other spiders I haven't uncovered quite yet."

"You son of a bitch." Hot spit flew from Brooks's lips.

"Do you have any idea how many millions of men have come back from hell itself itching for nothing but normalcy? Three squares, a roof, a couple of kids, a pretty wife to screw now and again?"

"I was there. 'Hell itself.'"

Brooks stiffened, putting his square face back in order. He grabbed a cigar from its case. "I thank you for your service."

"Anytime," the bookbinder hissed.

"So you understand?"

"Understand?"

"The urge. To settle down. To find peace again. Security."

The bookbinder sat back in his chair and surveyed the room: books never opened, decorative tinsel, animal heads that had been procured, not hunted. "Yes."

"That's the itch. I provide the balm." Brooks's voice grew more confident in the comfort of his sales pitch. "I build the framework that allows our boys to become kings of their own castles—in clean, safe, beautiful environments. We create impressions—*perspectives*—you see? We make safe streets for our boys who made it back."

"Safe?" the bookbinder sneered. "You're exploiting the victims of war."

"Victims?" Brooks tugged at his lapels. "No, they're heroes."

"They're *all* victims. The man with his guts hanging out of his middle is a victim, but so is the man who shot him. *Speared* him. Neither asked to be there. Dig farther back into the circus, most everybody is taking orders from somebody else. A salute and no questions asked, all the way to the top—these are the ways such things are won. And, even there—even *there*—the guys signing the checks and deploying the planes and pushing the buttons, the so-called first movers—almost each of them is the victim of circumstance, of a series of bad choices where only bad choices were available because of some other foolish guess somebody else made somewhere even further down the timeline. Victims, to a man."

"I'm not a victim."

"I know," the bookbinder rumbled. "War always seems to work out fine for its masters. Until it doesn't."

"Fuck you." Brooks tapped his cigar, straightening his short spine.

"I've seen decent men and women getting screwed out of their savings for shit work, faulty materials, bad sewage and drainage, police harassment, frau—"

Brooks cut him off. "You've got it all figured out, don't you?" He took a puff of his cigar and tapped the desk with his free hand. "Why are you here? What are you going to do about these things you think you've figured out?"

"I wanted to look you in the eye, man to man. Tell you to your face that I can offer them a different cure for the itch. *My* way that you're now curious about. A kind of *scratch*, instead of a balm." The bookbinder narrowed his stare. "I wanted you to see *me*."

"Is that some sort of threat?"

"More like fair warning."

The developer's face pulled tight behind his pallid smoke. "That's why you came here? To *warn* me?"

The bookbinder ran his finger leisurely along the edge of Brooks's desk. He took his time crafting his own pitch. A retort, a counter. He closed his eyes as he spoke. "War is a kind of hell; you're right about that. It's everything that you can imagine—all the violence, the blind hate, the stolen youth, all of that born of this fear, not of death, because that's going to come, but *losing*, not for yourself, but for everybody left behind, the people depending on you, whether they know it or not. You're a line in the sand, or the mud, or the snow, and if evil gets past that line, if evil can tip the balance and that's the legacy left for the world to suffer . . ." The bookbinder opened his eyes, stood up. "You put a single drop of ink in a glass of water and the whole thing turns black. That's the power of evil, and that's how this game gets you—the only way to protect the good from the evil is to become blacker than the evil itself."

He rested his weight on the other man's desk, marking territory. "You're right about another thing, too. You can't imagine the books that haven't been written about me, about what I had to do to get to this place in time and space, across this desk from you." The bookbinder was standing in a tenth-floor office; he was thousands of miles away.

Brooks's voice was cautious, but sharp. "Maybe someone should. Or maybe you're not worth digging at. Maybe someone should just end the fucking story."

The bookbinder scratched at his temple. He could feel the beast's excitement rise and strained to temper it. He spoke slowly, the speed of a lazy river. "It's just you and me and that pistol you keep in that drawer over there." He nodded and leaned in. "The only question is, can you pull that gun out and get off a shot before I jump across this desk and bite out your throat with my bare fucking teeth?"

The bookbinder saw a primitive fear blossom in the developer's gaze, and the mere sight of it released a pang, a shift he could barely hold back; he bit his own tongue silently behind tight lips and held the line. He studied the face across from his, past the extant panic, read the wrinkles around the eyes, the codes buried in them, understood the reach of stockpiled money, their webbing; justice called not for a quick, bloody resolution, but symmetry, an unraveling worthy of the empire. The last thing the bookbinder needed to do was make this miscreant into a martyr. No, J. M. Brooks would be awake for his own amputation, and once the screaming had ended, the bone saw would be pulled from his own twitching hand.

The two men remained there, frozen—the bookbinder hunched, the businessman erect in his chair, a Tao for the ones trapped down below—until the former eased, turned, and stepped out of the opulent office without looking back.

24

⌣

In that autumn of 1952, the lingering warmth abruptly hardened into a chill, as if Brookshire had reached a tipping point. The breeze became a wind, and the wind struck hard on the October morning of Saint Anne's annual fall church bazaar. The *I Like Ike* signs and, to a lesser degree, the Stevenson ones, peppered intersections and front yards, paper snapping against the stakes affixing them to the dirt.

The bookbinder huddled beside a folding table decorated in haphazard stacks of books, all shapes and sizes. He sipped from a paper cup of coffee between pulls from his pipe. Joe kept busy arranging new piles around him.

They were testing out the new automatic church bell, nine strikes to announce the hour; whole families pulled up in cars built like tanks, children climbing over themselves like sewer rats to get to the games and prizes, the clickity spinning wheels. The parents, hungover and bleary-eyed, trailed behind, toeing gently on the asphalt as if they had confused themselves with creatures who could accidentally puncture the world. More arrived on foot, bands of well-shod vagabonds trudging up the hills of Brookshire to reach the church grounds at the top, armies that looked both ways before they crossed the street.

Crowds gravitated to the bookbinder's table. It seemed that everyone in town who had not already trekked to the basement store on Kestrel Street strolled by—some just to browse at the exotic collection, or gawk at its keeper, but several laid down a cut of the previous day's paycheck for the artist's wares. Husbands and wives alike took the bookbinder aside to whisper discreet custom orders. Others just thanked him for services rendered.

Tess passed in the morning chill, buzzing alone in a swarm of teens, looking worse for wear. Joe watched her from behind the table, his face an undersize portrait of parental concern.

Their mother zipped across the Saint Anne's School parking lot with a clipboard clasped against her chest, checking in vendors and making sure the concession stand had enough buns. Miriam was a field general, barking orders she was halfway to completing herself before anyone else could sufficiently hop to. She paused at the bookbinder's table long enough to ask after Tess and tell Joe to tuck in his shirt. The boy shrugged at the question and nodded at the command.

Miriam took a quick step forward, then stopped on her heel. The bookbinder watched the color drain from her fingers as she clutched the clipboard. She looked hard at Joe, but it was not an anger that radiated from her expression—her eyes betrayed softer cousins: helplessness, apprehension. A forlorn shade of reconciliation blossomed in her voice. "You're not helping her, son," she reproached—quiet, blunt, as if she were rebuking a mirror. The bookbinder watched Joe try to bury his wince, staring hard at the toes of his Chuck Taylors.

Father Jim ambled about the tables, thanking all in attendance for their support of the church looming in the background. The structure was complete, the contractors now
hustling over each other to get the interior ready for Christmas
Mass. The income and donations from the bazaar would help,
but Saint Anne's was still in snowballing debt to its great-
est patron, J. M. Brooks; in fact, Brookshire's namesake had
called Father Jim just the past week, quizzing the priest about
his relationship with a certain vagrant bookbinder who had
paid Brooks a disconcerting visit. *Did he know anything about
that?* Father Jim nodded toward the bookbinder and tapped
his table with an index finger, but he didn't linger.

By late morning, when the St. Pierre family arrived, the
crowd had thinned. Sam and Rebecca walked apart, together,
similar to so many of the other married couples at the bazaar,
Ava between them and in front, the head of an asymmetrical triangle. The bookbinder observed the brood as it roved
across the lot. It was an ancient precept that the number three
was magical: The trick, the loophole, the bookbinder had
discovered, was in the definition, the varying concentric and
overlapping threes of which one could compose a life. Every
man was perhaps less a king than his own illusionist.

Ava halted at the bookbinder's table, turning to peer right
through the man many times her size. Rebecca almost tripped
in her heels, a skinny bedlam of frozen and fluttering limbs;
her husband stopped just as abruptly, awkwardly, his neck
twisting almost like a corkscrew, molasses slow, as he took
in the scene before him. Joe, heart picking up steam, glanced
to the bookbinder for a tell, or any kind of guidance; his employer gave him—them all—nothing, simply stood statue still.

Ava broke the stillness, pulling a rectangle from under her

jacket; she displayed a book of her own device. The book-binder knelt before her and gently took it from her palm. Completely without cut edges, the girl's creation was constructed of careful folds that, when opened, revealed the shape of an eight-span bird in flight, fashioned entirely out of uncountable tiny creases. He turned the object around in his hands, studied it from every angle, unsure how it was even crafted. He recognized it as something beyond even his expertise. His lack of surprise was buried in the gasps around him.

The bird with bent edges burst into star-flash as Sam St. Pierre slammed his fist into the bookbinder's forehead. The attacker howled and grabbed at his broken knuckles, his face writhed in pain. The origami book fell to the ground, and Ava also began to scream, not like a child but an alarm, steady and piercing. Rebecca woke from her stupor, pushing past her husband without so much as a look at him—tobacco sallow, sad-eyed, and holding his own hand like a sack of marbles.

"You horsefucker," Sam spat through his teeth, under his daughter's shrill racket. His whole body shook as he tried to scrape all the spite he could muster into words. The words left him wanting, though, and after a few moments of gnashing and sputtering, all impotence and no release, he simply croaked, "You can have my filthy whore wife, but you don't get my daughter, too." He teetered on his feet.

The bookbinder rose to his. He rubbed his temple and regarded the cuckold as if a childish trinket, something that had once been important but now held little worth. The bazaar traffic had stalled under Ava's screams; everyone still in attendance watched them, watched Rebecca cooly turn and kick Sam hard in the crotch, crumpling him, raining punches on his back and head until the bookbinder pulled her away. No one came to Sam's aid, each spectator looking away, halfway wondering whether another would step in, help him up, but after a few long moments on the ground, Sam staggered to his feet and straightened himself as best he could. He stumbled back in the direction of his house, the bazaar a silent chorus bearing witness.

Rebecca shook herself from the bookbinder's grip. She glowered at the shape of her husband just cresting the hill in the distance. Ava had hushed, and when her mother reached out her hand, the girl grasped it.

The bookbinder took a step toward them. "Don't."

Rebecca spun her head so it was in profile, perpendicular to the man, not quite looking at him. "It's my home, too."

"Please."

She turned back to the crest of the hill but didn't move, hesitant, thresholds both seen and unseen before her. "I told you—I don't need you to protect me."

"He's dangerous. It's madness."

The lines of a sad smile broke across Rebecca's jaw. "Why stop now?" She spun on her heels to face the bookbinder. "I'm not scared," she lied, squeezing Ava's little hand.

"He'll hurt you."

She shook her head. "With a busted hand like that?" She touched the bump blossoming on the bookbinder's head. "You take care of you, and I'll take care of me. I thought that was the way it had to be?" She tried to smile again, but it was a flickering thing, a poor connection. She guided Ava from the table, and then from the school parking lot, back into Sam St. Pierre's orbit. The beast pitched itself against the bookbinder's skull.

Miriam appeared, grabbing his arm. He ground his teeth. "I need to—"

"Do what she said," she interjected. "You need to do what she said."

"I can't leave her to him." Even the bookbinder wasn't wholly sure which *her* he meant.

Miriam exhaled, reminded of her own powerlessness, the foxholes around her own control. "You can and you will. This is her fight—it always was. She has every right to fight it her way." She gently bit the inside of her cheek, an old habit. "If we're lucky, you're leaving *him* to *her*."

The bookbinder glared at her; she shook her head. "I'm not saying it's smart or right or anything like that. I'm not even saying it's not crazy. But if you"—she paused, hitching on the word—"if you actually care about her—if she's more to you than a reflection of your own fairy tales—then you will risk her like this." Miriam's voice dropped low. "You will risk her like I risked mine."

The bookbinder's glare softened, fell upon the folded bird on the asphalt, half collapsed back into a book. He bent down to pick it up, turning it over in his hands.

"What is really going on?" She studied him studying the tome. "What is that girl to you?" When no answer arrived, she sighed and squeezed his arm. "Joe, help your boss pack up," she ordered. And then to the man beside her: "You go home. And you *stay* there until you hear different."

25

As she descended the hill the along the sidewalk of Robin Road, Rebecca realized she could not hear her own footfalls, or those of Ava, for the thudding of her heart and the pounding in her head. She had offered a false front of confidence to the bookbinder, but here, when no one was looking, all the possibilities of what waited for her just inside her own front door spiraled and churned to the point of almost felling her. Her hand still tightly grasped in Ava's, she imagined she appeared soused in the noon sun, bumbling down the sidewalk, a jalopy jangling in fits and starts.

She understood that Sam had been whittled down by inertia and drink, leaving a brittle scarecrow version of the man she married. He was mostly bark these days, and even the bark had become a slurry, feeble hack. He *had* just taken a shot at a man twice his size, though, so there was still some powder in the keg. She rationalized that his punch at the bookbinder had probably been his best shot—she was sure she had heard multiple bones snap on impact—but she could not wholly convince herself that she was not in danger. That Ava was not in danger.

Or maybe he wouldn't even be there. That was as likely as anything, and he had flown the coop over much less. She couldn't count his fugitive nights anymore—those had only ramped up in frequency in recent months. She had entertained the notion that he, too, had taken a lover—had even hoped for it, if she were being honest with herself—but she also knew that was unlikely, unless there was a woman in town who could be satisfied sitting and watching him drink. He hadn't been able to perform his marital obligations for years, though she'd heard tell of his foul boasting during some of his intoxicated tirades. It was a mask, like everything else. *How many masks*, she thought, a kind of question but also an exclamation, as if from one of the Victorian romances she so loved as a girl. *How many masks we wear!* She tightened her grip on Ava, craving her daughter's complicated, frosty warmth.

There was another side to the heart-thud and head-pound, though: A part of her *wanted* this face-off, pined for the Band-Aid to be ripped off, come what may. Hers had become a world of eggshells with interludes of freedom—of a better dream—but even that seemed to have been wrenched from her. Now all that was left in the embers of her days was an equilibrium of cool tension, empty of relief.

She knew all her rage didn't rest at Sam's feet; she could not hide from the fact that many of those eggshells were the product of this beautiful, strange creature beside her, the thing in the world she loved above all else. She tried not to think of other roads, of the things she had lost along the way, and she certainly never spoke of them out loud; she was sadly bemused, though, whenever she heard someone say they would die for their child. *That would be a respite,* she would think behind her polite nod, her arcadian smile. *Try living for one.*

The guilt, when these resentments emerged, was so intense that it sometimes buckled her. It was often Ava who came to her in those moments, laying a serene hand on her mother's head, or just looking at her in that unblinking pure way, as if her gaze were the first gaze and all the other gazes from all the other creatures were just pale imitations of the crux. The fact that it was the object of her resentments who brought such silent comfort made the shame both more intense and more bearable, all at the very same time.

There was a tug on her wrist, and Rebecca realized she had stopped in front of her own lawn. They were home.

⌣

Sam leaned over the kitchen sink, wrapping his mangled hand in ice, and Rebecca noticed the way his body lurched and twitched, even when he barely moved, every component incongruent to every other, a series of fault lines. The shifts were inevitable, the oncoming quake a fact of her—*their*—existence. She planted her shoes into the shag carpet of the front room, shoulder-width apart—a bracing, a challenge. Ava stood motionless; behind her eyes, though, all the convergences of all the variables played before her, marshaling a charge throughout this little space, a tiger's cage with a few meaningless portraits left hanging on the walls.

Sam cocked his head when he heard them but did not turn, his face twisting up and out toward the little picture window overlooking the neighbor's backyard, the crisscrossing laundry lines. He imagined Brookshire as nothing more than a kind of stable, and he pictured himself out past these boundaries, these chain-link carve-outs, galloping free, his breath harsh steam in the chilly night, the onyx chorus a symphony, the soundtrack to his escape.

But he was here, trapped in these walls with these two bitches, one of ice and one of fire. "You've embarrassed me for the last time," he hissed as menacingly as he could.

"I imagine you're right," Rebecca answered, low and calm, and Sam flinched. Where he had expected defiance, he heard in his wife's voice a new quality that elicited a chill that ran up from his tailbone: steadfastness. This was righteous indignation—not the cartoonish version native to blurry nights at Wilson's, but a sword dipped in a noble poison.

Sam turned and looked his wife up and down—the glistening eyes, the balled fists, pearl necklace, heels. A different kind of uniform, another front. A smoldering. One of them, he knew, didn't belong.

He tried to conjure words, something memorable, something worthy of the moment, but the rage and pride and fear tripped over each other, across his fungal tongue—all that escaped was a blurted, raspy bleat. He felt his cheeks flush as he charged.

Rebecca heard the yelp but did not move. Sam's ambush was swift but brought only glancing blows—he awkwardly tried to lead with his left hand. He worked to grapple with her, overpower her, but the busted hand flared with each effort to grip, and she was able to slide free each time. Ava backed away from the melee, crouching into a corner, hugging her knees and waiting for what came next.

Sam lunged and Rebecca stepped aside, grabbed at his head and used his own momentum to slam him into an end table. He seethed, eyes wide, the whites cracked with vessels, a sick grin out of place beneath them. She felt a moment of pity, but Sam rose and was on her again, this time swinging with his right fist, with abandon, and though she was able to fend the punches off—she saw the firecrackers of pain that shot through him with each swing—he would not relent.

BOOM-BOOM-BOOM. The knock distracted them both, so that one of Sam's punches sneaked through Rebecca's crossed arms. It was enough to knock her back and create a space between them. *BOOM-BOOM-BOOM.* They faced each other on the shag, chests heaving, eyes burning. There was a holler on the other side and then another loud knock.

Rebecca straightened and ran a hand over her forehead, then against her skirt. She flattened her hair and answered the door: Miriam Hollanger stood in the frame, her own slate eyes dancing. Ava's book of folds rested delicately in the woman's unsteady hands.

Miriam looked past the lady of the house to Sam—a human traffic jam, all bad angles. She spoke too loudly—to both, neither. "I believe your daughter left this at the bazaar."

The two mothers exchanged a knowing look. Rebecca blanched, looked down at her shoes. "Thank you," she said.

"Of course," Miriam replied, leaning into the awkward pause. "Mind getting the door for me, dear? I don't want to damage this beautiful thing." And with that Miriam had invited herself in. She marched across to the little dining room that branched off at the house's far end, gingerly placing Ava's book down on the table. She stepped back into the front room, its heavy, soundless air, and looked to Sam, then Rebecca. "Everything all right here?"

Rebecca nodded a lie.

"Right as rain," Sam answered, drawing out the last word.

"Good." Miriam nodded back. "I thought I heard quite a commotion coming up here, but it could have been any-thing—these walls being so thin, you know?" Her own heart was pounding, sweat running under her pressed clothes, but she held her eyes on Sam scratching at the back of his neck, grasping that he, too, wanted desperately to be anywhere but here—particularly with her studying him like a mangy dog. She leaned into that, too. "I tell you, it has been *quite* a day already." She turned to Rebecca. "Might I trouble you for a glass of water?"

"Of course." Rebecca fought off the urge to curtsy, catch-ing the rhythm of this mannered performance. She touched Miriam's shoulder as she passed into the kitchen, a small, thoughtless motion that was anything but, an acknowledg-ment among allies.

Miriam and Sam both turned to Ava in the corner to avoid looking at each other. "You really shouldn't have come all this way for that little thing." Sam held his bad hand in his good hand, both crossed in front of him.

"Oh, it was no trouble," Miriam almost sang back, treacle sweet.

"Hell, you could have left it with *him* if he liked it so god-damned much."

Miriam tilted her eyes back toward Sam, all daggers. "How's that hand, Sam?"

His chin quivered, jaw clenched, hot blood surging to the surface of his face. He took a step toward Miriam just as Re-becca arrived with a glass. He stared at it with a flicker of rec-ognition. "You know what?" His voice was gravel. "I'm feeling a little parched myself." He lowered his hands. "I'm going out for a spell." He tramped across the living room and hollered "Don't wait up!" before slamming the door behind him.

Miriam fished a jittery cigarette out of her purse and lit it. "I can stay as long as you need."

Rebecca closed her eyes, shaking her head. "He won't be back."

Miriam blew smoke. "Are you sure?"

"If I know Sam—and I realize that is debatable at this point"—Rebecca sighed—"he's gone." She looked about the room, at Ava crouched, as if seeing it all for the very first time. "There's nothing left for him here. There hasn't been for some time. But after today—after today, he can run with abandon. The last gate has fallen."

26

It is said that, in its gloaming, the sky and everything beneath it exist in their most fragile, true state, both more and less than they are—men almost hidden, the gods almost revealed. Contrasts soften, the luminous and the gloom passing at their closest convergence. It is an hour where sentient creatures, like the stars they mimic, are most susceptible to their own divergences, their petty victories, their transient defeats.

The world was streaked with indigo as Sam St. Pierre trudged along the streets of Brookshire. He had been booted from Wilson's again, though he couldn't remember why. Perhaps hot words had been spoken. Perhaps he had lost his balance. It hardly mattered.

Sam could picture the bartender's mouth, rimmed along the top with his neatly trimmed mustache, the lips twisting themselves to form two words, similar in sound and inflection, but so common to Sam's nights that he didn't need to hear them to make out what was being said: "Go. Home." He understood the surface of Wilson's order perfectly; its underpinning, however, had lost all meaning for him. He had swayed there under the whir of the fans and the neon for several strained moments, focused only on the bartender's teeth. Then he'd turned and left.

On Tanager Way, there was a path Sam had learned through familiarity, by which he could trace the outer rim of the farthest hill that made up the Dyson's front yard, tight along the heavy hedge line—he had learned a man could make his way toward the backyard without being seen. It was both a trick of the shadows and a matter of angles, no neighbor in position to have a straight sight line to this particular point. He was surrounded by walls and edges, traveling along a gap in the rest of the world's perceptions.

Drunk as he was, the house seemed to stagger to him as much as he to it, a kind of white-brick wave closer with each hitched step, each flick of his eyelids. He knew he was stumbling, but he also knew it didn't matter if everything else was, too.

He could make out the side window of the den, though, the thick black behind the frame, and he knew so long as he kept that window in the center of his vision, headed slowly toward it as the hedges brushed against his back, he could pass as a kind of makeshift ghost; the grass just beneath its overcoat of yellow and amber leaves was a tell, thin along his route if anybody ever bothered to look, but no one ever did—not even Roy Dickerson with his half-assed guardianship by default.

Something flickered where no flicker should have been, and Sam froze. He blinked his bleary eyes clear, trying to collapse his threadbare focus on the black square at one o'clock, almost straight ahead. He found himself instantly back to his nights of sentry in Germany, every godforsaken inch of him tuned into the glint of a Kraut rifle muzzle, the snap of a twig. Adrenaline coursed through him, providing its fleeting sobriety.

He saw it again. Not a muzzle but a device just as familiar: the glass neck of a bottle. A neck grasped in a small, pale hand. A pinprick of orange light, the dot of a cigarette, rounded out the constellation. Someone was in the Dyson house. Someone who didn't belong.

❧

Tess took a fierce swig from the little bottle, just inside the window. One long gulp and then a second until she almost choked and spit it up. She pulled from her cigarette to wash it down. She wasn't drunk but aspired to be; her face was red and pinched as if she had been crying, though her eyes were empty of tears.

After the bazaar, she had ridden out with a pack of teenagers she could hardly call friends—acquaintances, maybe, or even better, she thought, *familiars*—and she'd landed in Appleton with a pack of these familiars, sharing swigs from a jar of moonshine around an afternoon bonfire out on some outskirt property. The wrong boy had gotten fresh, the right one hadn't, focusing his drawn-out lips and hands on some brunette cheerleader instead, and when Tess quietly meandered into the woods at the edge of the acreage and never came back, she was sure someone would notice eventually, but she was just as sure that she didn't care.

She walked the five miles of back roads it took to return to Brookshire, but once on her own terrain, she had no interest in actually going home. Her mother was many things, but she was no fool, and so long as the woman wasn't distracted by some other confederate's minor tragedy, she would be right there hovering between the living room and the kitchen, eyeing the escape routes and attending her own. She would want to know where Tess had been, and with whom; it was an unnecessary, melodramatic chapter that Tess, a harsh editor, had no intention of writing just to cross out later.

Instead, the girl swiped a half-pint from the liquor store when the man behind the counter wasn't looking and bought a pack of cigarettes when he was. *Equilibrium.* She took to the streets as the sun veered toward the horizon.

The chill came quickly with the twilight, the air around Tess prickling her skin, even with her jacket pulled taut around her. She found her curbside throne in the empty elementary school parking lot but couldn't bury her shiver there. She tried to will herself warm, as if each shake were a confession of vulnerability. She huddled over herself, miserable, and considered shelter. A glint of a vision cut into her thoughts, and the decision was made before she even had a chance to weigh her options; Tess stubbed out her cigarette and headed for Tanager Way. She had long since memorized the route and settled into a quick, easy step; it was like catching a trail in the snow, like when she and Joe used to go sledding down Sparrow Lane after a blizzard. Once, a few years back, she had slid under a parked Oldsmobile and slit her leg—it took six stiches to close and she still bore a scar on her shin. She remembered hobbling up the hill in agony after the impact, and waving to Joe to stay put; her brother misread the sign, though, and she watched his saucer ape her path, rotating ever so slightly, so that the back of his head lined up with the jagged underside of the sedan as the saucer bore down. She had to tackle him—knock him clean off—to save him. She remembered the screech of the metal saucer meeting the metal exhaust. She ran an index finger along the curve of the bottle nestled in her jacket pocket.

Tess twisted the basement knob of the Dyson house— it gave. She was no longer surprised and, once inside, let a mouthful of bourbon and the hum of the house conspire to warm her bones. She wandered through the dwelling, feeling less like a trespasser than on her previous sojourns. She gravitated to the den, under the second sunset of Paul Dyson's blood spatter, and stood by the window, savoring sips from her bottle, letting time begin to stretch itself. She didn't fear being seen; there was something to the house's walls that made her feel protected. It was a place of long-gone lives, horrors played out before hers had taken their final shape—there was a commonality of broken things not properly set. It was a pocket in time, and she could be invisible here. Sometimes that was what she craved the most.

And just as she settled—just as she felt the little click inside her head, the one that loosened all the padlocks—something shuffled and banged just beneath her. She stopped, the bottle tipped, just kissing her lips, her cigarette hanging between her fingers. She tried to focus through the warm blur, straining to hear soft tiptoe steps. She chided herself for her imagination—for still being a scared kid susceptible to neighborhood ghost stories.

The kitchen door—the one that led to the narrow basement stairs—creaked, and she cursed herself again, this time for the opposite impulse: her naive lack of vigilance in the wake of danger. She could bolt for the front door, but that would expose her to whoever, whatever, was creeping her way.

She had seen enough of the detritus of men—spent cigarette butts, food wrappers, crushed beer cans—to know she was not the house's only earthly trespasser, but that didn't ease her mind; she wasn't sure another lone wolf of Brookshire was a better option for her in this moment than the monsters of her fancy.

Tess pressed her shoulders against a wall between windows, hiding herself in the young night's long shadows. She drew a concentrated breath to try to slow her pulse, convinced her telltale instrument was pumping so loud, it would give her away.

It didn't matter. The voice that carried from the edge of the room was forced, a badly tuned guitar. "No use hiding," it declared. And then the voice was on her, corporeal, covering her cheeks and the tops of her ears, the breath both rank and antiseptic, as if cheap mouthwash had gone ripe. Tess tried to hold her gag. "What is it with you Hollangers?" Sam St. Pierre seethed. "Bad pennies always showing up where you don't belong."

Her flesh rippled against his touch. He laughed something both fake and full of locusts, as if he existed somewhere between shame and a ravenous pride. It was instinct, rather than any coherent plan, that coursed through Tess in that moment; she dropped her half-pint, and when the hand gripping her slackened at the bottle's crash, she pulled the switchblade from her waistband, flicked it open, and slashed at where Sam's laugh had erupted; she felt the blade catch against its target, surprised and not by his scream.

Tess felt her body lifted—and then she was soaring backward, slamming against the far wall and losing her hold on the knife. Sam was back on top of her, straddling her, the pinks and wan yellows of his widened eyeballs caught in the moonlight just breaking through the window. He put his hands—one bare, one bandaged—on her neck and began to choke her. She turned to face him; if she was going to die, she was going to make him watch—she was Sergeant Joseph Hollanger's daughter, *goddamn it*. Blood from Sam's cut cheek dripped on her blouse and the lapel of her jacket.

The skin around Sam's face swelled and sank behind an undecipherable expression, and he loosened his hands once more, this time yowling into her face. "I told you it didn't want you!" he screamed. He threw her against the wall again. He was staring at her, wild-eyed, his good hand clutching the wrist of his bad one. He staggered. "Get out of here, you little bitch!" His lips pulled back into a sprawling, ridiculous grin, and she thought she saw a single word press through his teeth from deep in his throat: *please*.

Tess scrambled to her feet and broke into a sprint, a cacophony of voices on her heels. Not just Sam's, but others behind him, overrunning him—strangers, *familiars*, cursing her, mocking her, catcalling her, mongrel-size spiders scrambling along the walls. The words themselves were nothing new in their way, but it was all new, concentrated umbrage at all creation for not being what it was supposed to be, and for her, a citizen thereof, not being what they wanted her to be. Sam chased her, possessed, overrunning his own limbs, careening into drywall like a crazed marionette. Tess took the basement stairs two at a time; she almost tripped but caught herself with the railing, and Sam collapsed on all fours at the first-floor threshold, hollering incantations at her that almost but not quite turned into coherent obscenities.

Tess swung back the basement door and broke out into the

spangled night; its stark contrast of star-shine and the obscura between, the cold burn of its air scratchy against her lungs, drove her on, urging her away from the blur and toward her mother's house, her home.

⌄

When the door swung open, Rebecca knew everything had changed. An alien, crooked smirk was plastered across Sam's face, and above it, almost in effigy, a crescent of drying blood. His skin stretched in some spots, sagged in others, almost rippled. His eyes were glassy—not drunk glassy but *gone* glassy—and he gripped a switchblade tight in his busted hand; she could see he felt no pain. Whatever was inside him felt no pain. The milky orbs blinked at her, and then down at the knife; Sam snapped the blade closed, slid it in his pocket. There would be no victory for her here, no fending off whatever had taken hold of her husband.

Rebecca found herself counting the punches like sheep. When she came back to consciousness, Sam and Ava were gone.

⌣

27

The bookbinder paced, as he had for large swaths of the afternoon and evening, the light yawning and bending itself across the workshop. The telephone finally rang; he realized in the space between tinny trills that he had been craving its call as much as dreading it. His head throbbed.

"Get over here. *Now.*" Miriam Hollanger's voice was mostly steady, wavering only at the edges. The bookbinder, though, picked up on its angst immediately. He lunged for his jacket before even hanging up.

The beast jumped, too. The bookbinder grabbed a chairback, suddenly dizzy with exertion. He was a barge rocking on a dark river. He was its skeleton crew. He was the river. All these truths were converging on him, themselves, in the moment. He scanned the room, its tools, half-constructed books lying about the tables—he allowed himself to briefly admire this thing he had built, messy as it was. He tried to memorize as much of it as he could bear to keep.

⌄

The bookbinder clutched his jacket at the neck, trudging toward Sparrow Lane. The wind felt almost pleasant against his aching head. Leaves blew about, the trees deconstructing around him, tearing themselves apart. He had once read that the leaves were, in fact, always yellow—or orange, or red—the green just a kind of film that masked their true colors until it eventually burned away. He didn't know whether that was exactly accurate, but it seemed about right.

The night had fallen, and all the lights were on in the Hollanger house. Miriam swung open the door mid-knock. Her eyes widened when she took him in. "Good lord."

"I'll be fine."

"You look like you're going to keel over." She stepped aside. Tess was in the front room, crumpled on the slip-covered sofa, her arms tucked inside a sweater. Her face was streaked with caked mascara and blush, but the colorful brooks they formed could not conceal the finger-shaped bruises budding beneath her jawline. Joe sat in a corner wingback chair, pretending to read a comic, a reluctant spectator to whatever was unfolding around him, both a foreigner and a native, a dual citizen.

Miriam was a crate of unstable dynamite, explosions manifesting themselves as a series of shudders. She grasped her elbows, holding herself down in place, and spoke in measured words. "I want him dead." She let the sentence hover, then lit a cigarette. The bookbinder perked despite himself, piqued by the flavor of the words.

"Sit," he ordered. He flicked his head and Joe stood, walking to the edge of the kitchen—his mother took the chair. The bookbinder collapsed beside Tess on the sofa, and she started, scooting a few inches farther back. "Tell me everything," he said to both of them, his voice a forced peace. Tess sniffed, running the back of her hand against her dripping nose and eyes. She pulled the sweater back tight over her shoulders.

Miriam's hands were balled on the pleats of her skirt. "*St. Pierre*. Sam St. Pierre did this to my daughter." Each word rang like a gunshot through Joe, Ghost Joe. A cinematic version of the attack flashed through his head—then over again, another punishing instant. He closed his eyes, trying to block everything out, but even then a shape kept forming in the ether: his namesake, in full uniform, recognizable from the picture his mother kept on the mantel and the face that was transforming in the mirror a little more each day. Joe opened his eyes and marched past the others, down the hallway to his room. He shut the door gently behind him. Tess put her fist to her nose and began to shake.

The bookbinder exhaled, all his worst fears now inevitabilities. It was as if he could feel the night unfastening itself from the moon, the button spoke holding the sky in place. The scaffolding was falling away, falling apart; he could smell the cold black river again, could smell how near it surged.

Miriam's jagged voice cut through. "She fought him off."

The bookbinder turned to Tess.

"I cut him," she mewed. And then, almost ashamed: "He bled on me."

"I made her change," Miriam interjected. "And she was freezing." She held on to her rational explanations, sandbags on her coast.

"Cut him with what?"

"A switchblade," the girl muttered. "I had a switchblade."

"Where did you get a switchblade?" Miriam snapped back.

She had no idea why she hadn't thought to ask before. Tess ignored the question and turned to the bookbinder. "I dropped it, when he—"

"Where?"

The girl pinched her face. "On the carpet, I think."

Miriam raised her hand, almost as if steadying herself. "Wait—you told me he attacked you on the street."

"I told you it happened on Tanager Way."

"Inside? Inside where? Where were you with *Sam St. Pierre?*" Miriam stared at Tess, and then the bookbinder. Back at Tess. "I don't understand any of this," she finally admitted.

"There's a house." Tess bit the inside of her cheek. "An abandoned house."

"Tess!"

The bookbinder held his hand up to Miriam. She fell back in the chair. "The Dyson house," he said. Tess's eyes widened. She nodded.

"Why in God's name did you go in *there?*" Miriam's hands sprang around her, her cigarette bouncing along for the ride, ash raining.

Tess cradled her elbows in her hands. She tried to imagine a way to answer the question within the bounds of words, to describe the wash of unnameable things that, unprompted, slammed into her where she sat—sometimes in a classroom, or at her dining room table, or on some desolate curb or other—and dragged her in its undertow, then back again, every single day. In a way that she could not explain, she knew what happened in that house—what was *still* happening in that house—somehow correlated to the torment surging through her own mangled spirit. There was an answer to a question she hadn't properly formed somewhere in the splash pattern of

Paul Dyson's blood. "I just wanted to see for myself." Her eyes shimmered, glinty as her mother's.

"With Sam St. Pierre?"

Tess remembered the awful noises he had thrown at her as she stumbled down the stairs, yaps and bays that scraped against the descending walls. She could hear the other voices wailing behind, echoes of each jumbled slur. She realized, once she had slowed the playback in her head and split them apart, that every single insult screamed was a thing that she had, at one time or another, said to herself. She shivered. "No."

"Why, Tess?"

Tess remembered her first sneaking expedition, how she'd spooked herself so badly that she tripped and busted her ankle. She'd had to hide the limp for weeks.

"Answer me!" Miriam blurted, and took a protracted drag from her cigarette to do something—anything—more than just sit there. Her daughter held her tongue, a fleeting flash of prudence trumping pride. She was itching to put a flashlight on her own mother's evenings with a bottle beneath the swinging chair on the porch, or her unexplained late nights with the very man now sitting on this couch. She focused on her shoes instead. "I just wanted to be alone." It was the opposite, of course—she was always alone. Even in a house full of people who loved her—a whole damn town—it didn't matter. *How could she explain that? How could she explain that if she just altered her chemistry to make* less *of her, she could belong* more *to something else?*

The bookbinder sank into the sofa and leaned his head against the back cushion, suddenly nauseated, as if he had swallowed a whole swarm of something vile.

"I just wanted to get in from the cold." Tess snapped her

jaw after the last word as if to make it more convincing and signal that this explanation was both definitive and objectively reasonable.

Miriam glared at her daughter, and then the bookbinder, and then back to her daughter. "Nothing you're saying makes any damn sense." She stood up, puffing furiously on her cigarette. She turned to the bookbinder and paled. "You're shaking," Miriam said. "You look like hell."

"I'm fine." He held his focus on Tess. "Tell me what happened."

The girl nodded and relayed her story. When she got to the part about Sam straddling her, Miriam stifled a howl and grabbed at the mantel.

"Then something—changed. He fell off me."

"Fell?"

She pinched her face, trying to get the details right. She shook her head. "I'm not sure. He kept saying that it didn't want me." She surprised herself at how easily she mimicked Sam's voice. "He said, 'Get out of here, you little bitch.'"

"That's enough." The flatness of Miriam's voice diverged from the shake of her hands. Tears ran, but she would not acknowledge them, nor blink them away. "I've heard enough." She rolled her shoulders back, remembering the perfect posture she had been taught all those years ago at finishing school, after the family sold the farm and trekked to this side of the bay. "You should never have been there in the first place."

The instant, practiced callousness, the hard pivot, lit the kindling stacked beside Tess's momentary prudence; it withered in a flash, and she sprang toward her mother, their noses almost touching. The last year, and the year before that, and before that—tipped dominoes—all came cascading down on her, through her girl-woman frame, her own black river that started on a beach somewhere on the edge of France and ended right here, right now. Tess scorched through the kindling first, and then the heavier wood. "Yes, Mother. I've been inside the Dyson house—*many* times. I wanted to see what all the whispers were about. For *myself.* I wanted to see what people like you dress up in bullshit. Paul Dyson blew his head off and, for some reason, the blood won't wash away. I wanted to see."

"Sit down."

Tess didn't budge. "I'd think you'd be more excited about a real-life miracle, Mother. *Let us pray.*"

Miriam glared at her daughter. She raised her hand, then caught sight again of the bruises snaking along the pounding vein that ran down Tess's skinny neck. She dropped her palm and slapped it against a table, a restless cocktail of maternal dread and exasperated pride rising within her. Had she tried to speak, it would not have been words that escaped her lips, but an animal shriek, both a condemnation and an assent.

"This town is *lousy* with bullshit," Tess continued. "Everybody covers for everybody else. Everything's always perfect, and it's always a lie."

"That's not true," Miriam mumbled, on her heels.

"Half this town is drunk more nights than not. Nobody practices what they preach. Chief Hillary is a walking dice game with a gun, and men up and down these streets are running scams, and scams on top of scams. Their pride and joys run around breaking shit just to try to get their attention, or get in on Daddy's action themselves. And the wives and daughters—my God, Mother, we don't even pay attention anymore." She pointed at her own swollen neck, holding back a sob. "We tell them they should never have been there in the first place."

The bookbinder feared Miriam might collapse; the mantel seemed the only thing holding her up. She held her face in her hand and began to weep.

Tess hardly noticed; she was running downhill, unshackled, a two-alarm fire heading for three. "And there was a whorehouse—just down the street! A *whorehouse*, Mother! Everybody knew it. Everybody pretended it wasn't there. Except, you know, Mrs. Dickerson—and *she's* the one they tossed in a nuthouse on the other side of the bay." Tess wiped her eyes, spying her mother's cigarettes. She walked across the room and plucked one. She lit it and took a deep drag while her mother cried. "This town is lousy with cowards," Tess pronounced from behind a gray-black plume.

Miriam plopped back in her chair. The three sat in silence for a long time, Tess smoking and catching her breath, Miriam and the bookbinder lost in their thoughts.

Miriam wiped her hand over her face. She looked to the bookbinder and then to Tess, back again; neither looked well beyond their bruises, their faces sallow. She strode across the room and put out her daughter's cigarette with a long, hitched sigh. "It's late. You should go lie down."

Tess, suddenly spent, pliable, nodded, but lingered for a moment after she stood. "I *am* sorry, Mother," she said, and searched for something more, but Miriam cut her off.

"I was built to love you, Tess," she said, her voice balancing itself, if barely. "And, whether you like it or not, you were built to be loved by me." She cleared her throat. "I'm sorry for that, and I'm sorry the world makes it all so goddamn hard." They considered each other for a long moment, mother and daughter, variations of a theme, until Tess nodded and turned down the hallway to her room.

The bookbinder listened to the ticking of the old grandfather clock beside him. Miriam fished out another cigarette but didn't light it. "What now?" she finally asked.

"I have to find him."

Miriam's eyes widened. "Oh my God. I'm so selfish—I was so wrapped up with Tess. Rebecca—"

"I have to go."

"I'm going with."

The bookbinder ran his palms over the fabric of the sofa, feeling the warmth where Tess had been. He took in the room, the ceramic photograph frames peppered throughout, the throws and needlepoint, the mixing of shapes and colors that somehow, a kind of magic in itself, made a home. He shook his head. "This is not your fight anymore, Miriam."

"Like hell it—"

"Tess made it out." His eyes met hers, and she could see the struggle in them, the pain. And something else, a pall just creeping in around the edges of each iris, a shroud taking hold of the blue. "You need to accept that victory."

Miriam started to argue but pulled back her own reins. She took a breath. "What is it? What in God's name is in that house?"

The bookbinder tried to find words strong enough to pin to that which haunted the Dyson house. Or if not *to*, then *around*, scratched abstractions that could serve as outposts to cage the hole that could not be christened. "Emptiness" was all he could conjure.

"What?"

He shook his head again. He ran his hands over his face, his whiskers. "I have to go, Miriam."

"Okay."

The bookbinder stood in the lamplight, and Miriam could see the creases in his face, at his temples, around his mouth, buried in his beard. She realized she could not guess how old he was, how ancient he might be.

"I don't think you understand."

Miriam straightened. "I think I do." She felt the beginnings of numbness, the ironic tingling sensation right before everything dulled. She felt how dry her mouth had become.

"I have one last thing to ask of you," the bookbinder said.

⌄

He stood to leave, and Miriam marched into his chest, hoisted the weight of all her fear and worry, crashed her skin and bone like a miles-journeyed wave against him; he wrapped his arms around her, held her up—held himself up against her.

"I can't do this without you," Miriam mumbled, and he sat her down softly.

"You already have."

The bookbinder leaned down and kissed her cheek, pressed his forehead against the side of hers, summoning her tears once again. She would remember so much of that night, moments big and small, memories that would wax and wane as memories always do, stretching or shortening themselves under the scrutiny of wisdom or distance, but the one thing that she would hold on to for the rest of her days with absolute clarity was the deathly chill of the bookbinder's own tears—only one drop, two, no more—as they fell along the meandering curve of her neck, pressed down and into her skin.

The bookbinder straightened and turned, and Miriam noticed between hitched breaths the slight tremble in his step, a stiltedness she knew had not been there before. She watched him out the front door, and then down her steps, lower, lower, sinking until out of her sight.

⌄

The rain came quick. The bookbinder pulled up his collar and struggled along the sidewalk. He got as far as Meadowlark before he saw flashing blue lights reflected in the yellow stop sign ahead. The cruiser pulled up behind him.

Chief Hillary stepped out. "Imagine my luck. Just the man I needed to see."

The bookbinder hooked a wet strand of hair behind his ear. "Is this your idea of leaving me be?"

"Seems to me our little arrangement is null and void, seeing as I apparently made a deal with a dead man."

The bookbinder stared back at the chief, rain bouncing off both their frames.

"You got nothing to say?"

"You wouldn't understand it if I did."

"Let's cut the horseshit, Private Keane. Yeah, I know who you are. I know you're listed as killed in action in Okinawa in 1945. I know your body was never recovered."

A dark grin slowly blossomed beneath the police chief's hat. "Imagine my surprise when I pulled a dead soldier's fingerprints off that picture book you tried to threaten me with." The grin grew broader. "Then imagine my surprise to learn that that dead private had a sister, one Charlotte Keane—known around here, of course, by her married name: *Dyson.*"

The bookbinder could no longer feel the rain pelting him, yet he felt every bead at once. Hillary unfastened his holster strap. "I've always wondered how a man could shoot himself in the head *twice*. That always stuck in my craw. Now I have an idea how it might have happened. I think maybe you and I should have a little chat, Keane—what d'ya say?" The grin widened to full-staff. "I think maybe you should come with me."

28

⌣

"Are these necessary?" The bookbinder, crammed into the back of the patrol car, rattled the cuffs. It reeked of boot camp. He had let the old policeman take him in, mostly because he was bone drained and needed the ride. He was bonded to the rhythms shaking loose around him, the currents and where they led. He would play the captive to ride the swell.

Hillary wheezed as he maneuvered his girth into the front bucket seat. Almost as if it were waiting for him to settle in, the cruiser's radio squawked, all crackle and hiss.

"Chief?"

Hillary muttered a curse under his breath, rolling his head as he hunched over to grab the receiver. "What?"

"Chief, are you busy?"

"I'm over in Brookshire. What do you want?"

There was a pause. *"Actually, that's just where this call came in from."*

Hillary shrugged his shoulders to the rain smacking against

the cruiser's windshield. It was pouring now, raining harder by the second. "So go. I'm busy," he barked.

Another long pause—the officer on the other end weighing his options. The urge to avoid the chief's ample bad side translated through the shortwave's static. *"Woman called in a kidnapping, Chief. She's pretty upset. She said her husband beat her up good and grabbed their kid. I think it might be that idiot girl that always runs off."*

Hillary's large, round skull seemed to sink under the brim of his hat. He growled and turned back to his cargo. "Do you know what the fuck is going on?"

The bookbinder didn't budge, his relief tempered. Rebecca was safe—or at least alive. *Sam had Ava, though.* A latent realization was taking shape, a truth shaking itself from its shallow grave. The board was setting its pieces.

Hillary clicked on the receiver. "Ten-four. Is there anybody else that can handle it?"

"That's just it, Chief. It's cats and dogs out there. I don't think anyone can make it over to Brookshire." And then: *"And you're already there, so—"*

"I know exactly where I am, officer."

"Yessir."

Hillary removed his Stetson, wiped his forehead, shook the hat at nothing in particular. "Fine. I'll go."

"Roger that."

The chief drove with his hands at two and ten, crouched, chin at the wheel, his windshield wipers flapping. The rain had grown fierce, local. Almost *personal.* His eyes darted to the rearview, then back to the curtains of rain ahead. They traveled five miles an hour, his foot heavy on the brake. "Can't see a fucking thing," Hillary complained.

He coughed and shook his head again. He was growing

more irritated with the conditions, and it loosened his tongue, as if he and the bookbinder were complicit in the wake of a bigger conspiracy. "You probably don't think much of me, do you?"

The chief could make out only the broadest brushstrokes of the bookbinder, electric light bent by rain playing against his static frame. He couldn't see the man's mouth move when he answered: "Not directly, no."

Hillary pinched his face but focused on his turn off Meadowlark and down Robin Road. He sucked in his breath. "Christ on a pike, it's like a river."

The bookbinder glanced through his side window. Water rushed alongside the patrol car, dancing maniacally in its race to lower ground.

"Maybe I'm not much of a husband," the chief admitted, starting a new thread, his voice a straight line. "Maybe I'm not even much of a swell fucking guy." He nodded to no one, trying to see past the downpour. "I've been the law a long time, though, and I know trouble when I see it. I *know* trouble." This time he looked in the mirror for a long beat. "And I saw you coming from a mile away. Bookmaker my ass."

The bookbinder was motionless, save for the bumps from the ride. Thunder rumbled.

"Okinawa is a long way away, ain't it, boy?"

"Sure. And not so much, too."

"Where'd you go after you 'died'? What did you do?"

Silence.

"Nothing?" The chief laughed. "You're a pretty tough one, huh?" Back into the mirror: "You know who else is pretty tough? You shouldn't have crossed Mr. Brooks like you did. All you accomplished was putting him on your scent. He was a pretty big deal during the war—big, *big* contracts. With the

government. You know, all those warehouses out by National?"
The chief leaned forward, making himself bigger in the rearview. The wind was howling, the thunder a steady baseline
beneath it. "Let's just say he did very well. He's a good friend
to have, Mr. Keane. And a bad enemy to make."

Hillary grinned, but his eyes were angry, his yellow teeth
flashing. "You fired him up, and he fired me up. Not that I
needed much pushing. Like I said, I'm a pretty damn good
cop. I swiped that fucking book for prints, not sure if I would
get anything. And then"—the chief turned, resting his elbow
on the seat back—"to find out my mystery man was nothing
more than some AWOL grunt—"

A loose whip of lightning flashed—a silhouette darted
across the path of the patrol car. The chief overcompensated,
forcing the car into a skid; it spun out and rammed tailfirst
into a parked Studebaker.

"Fucking cocksucker!" Hillary held his fingers to his temple; he had rapped his head against the driver's-side window,
leaving behind a spiderweb crack. "You okay?" he asked over
his shoulder, not all that concerned with the answer.

"Fine."

Hillary's door was wedged against the Studebaker, so he
climbed across the front seat and tried to exit through the
passenger side. He pushed opened the door, but it slammed
right back on him, the sky whistling. "Fuck me!" he yelled, and
heaved the door back open, bracing it steady. Rain burst in,
sideways, like sniper fire. Drops pelted him, bounced off the
leather seat. He cursed steadily as he maneuvered his ample
body out into the storm.

The chief limped around to the other side and shook his
head. The visibility was so bad he had to peer down, inches

close, to see the bent steel. He made his way back to the passenger side and opened the door for the bookbinder. "Come on."

The bookbinder struggled getting out with his hands behind his back. Rain shelled his face; he closed his eyes, long strings of hair soaked and flat against his cheek. He shook the cuffs again. "Now?" he yelled over the wind's wail.

"I can't take that chance, boy."

The bookbinder splayed his hands as much as he could. "Where am I going to go?"

"Somehow, according to the government of these here United States of America, you don't even fucking exist. You've already bribed and tried to blackmail me. Why in the holy fuck would I trust you?"

"You can shoot me if I run."

"I can shoot you even if you don't." A pause. "Don't forget that." Hillary flipped on his flashlight, the light struggling against the downpour. "Now, come on."

They staggered, side by side, down along Robin, then turned right onto Phoebe Street. It was slow moving, the storm's arms pummeling them. There was an incoherent yelp off to the side. It took shape on the second effort: "Officer!" a man slurred from his front lawn. "Officer!" he hollered again.

"Christ! I'm busy!" Hillary barked back. "What is it?"

The man was waving his arms for the attention they were already giving him. He stumbled about the sopping grass, little splashes popping with each footfall. "My whole basement is underwater! I mean, like four feet and rising. The place next door, too!"

Through the downpour, the bookbinder caught lights on inside several houses. He could imagine many a man at the bottom of these hills opening the door to his basement stairs to discover an unwelcome, but no longer surprising, occurrence: J. M. Brooks's cut corners taking on water, sinking their savings accounts. The bookbinder was sure their buyer's culpability was laid out in the fine print of the housing contracts, all reading very legal, all in meticulous order.

"Is anybody dead?" Hillary was back on the move. He grabbed the bookbinder by the elbow.

"What?" the man called back, confused.

"Is anybody in your house dead?"

"No."

"Dying?"

"No."

"Your neighbors, that you know of?"

"No . . . no."

"Then handle your own fucking business." He yanked at the soaked bookbinder. "Keep up."

They marched forward, grimy water rushing past. The bookbinder managed to raise his head long enough to catch sight of the streetlight across the road, the way the glow smeared itself in the storm, the way it ran and blurred.

Hillary paused in front of the St. Pierre house, unsure. "I don't like this," he grumbled to himself through the raging rain. "Not one bit." He turned. "Stay near, you hear?"

Rebecca St. Pierre swung open the door, her face fury, red and on the edge of collapsing in on itself. Blood had already begun to crust over part of her swollen lip; her left eye kept a purple crescent, bulging at its center. "Where the hell have you been?" she snarled into Hillary's face. Just past the chief, the bookbinder lurched under the porch light; Rebecca took a step back, touched her mouth, winced as if she had been hit again. It was to him that she spoke. "Oh, Christ—what have you done?"

"I've been stuck in the goddamned great flood, ma'am." The chief's voice carried just over the racket of the rain on the porch's tin roof, overtly professional, defensive. "Can we get out of it?" Rebecca nodded and stepped aside for the two men, who entered, dripping on her living room carpet. She studied the handcuffs behind the bookbinder's back, his spent eyes, and he held her gaze, a grave understanding forming between them.

Hillary took off his cap, vainly pushing his hair to the side. "Now what did you mean just then? About where I've been?"

"You. The police." Rebecca folded her arms, watching the wet spots spread into the fabric. "I called and no one came."

"The storm," Hillary said, as if that were the answer to everything. His eyes scanned the room. "And I did come. I'm here now."

Rebecca's attention had already moved back to the bookbinder in chains. She remembered her face, then caught herself starting to turn away. "Why are you—what happened to—"

"I'll ask the questions, ma'am," Hillary cut in, displeased that the woman didn't instinctively defer to his authority.

"He took her," she snapped.

"Who?"

Rebecca's eyes narrowed, annoyed. "My daughter."

"*Who* took her?"

"Sam St. Pierre." She uttered the name as if he were not her husband, the distressed prize not his own daughter.

"When?"

She began to fade a little, right there in the living room, sparse of furniture, though she had tried over the years to make it a home. The bookbinder had never actually stepped inside before. The walls themselves seemed worn, as if scrubbed repeatedly. Cheap area rugs, pieces cut from better things, covered scratches in the floorboards.

Rebecca found her voice. "I don't remember exactly." She pivoted to the bookbinder. "I blacked out." There was a noticeable click, the metal of the cuffs taut behind the man's back.

"He took her out in this shit?" Hillary was almost incredulous. "On *foot?*"

Rebecca took a deep breath to gather herself. She ran her hand over the puffy edge of her orbital bone and turned to the bookbinder. "Why are you in handcuffs? What's happened?"

The bookbinder's voice was itself worn, stained with and by the sundry answers to those very questions, things imperfectly scrubbed away, written on top of each other, scrawls of love and vengeance. "I know where they are."

Hillary spun on the bookbinder, his hackles up. "What?" His face reddened, splotches that quickly burst into a mask of crimson.

"And why. I see it now." The bookbinder stepped past the chief to Rebecca. She rested her hand on his chest, but only her hand; she let the rest of her shake and sob. It was not a weakness, but a strength, to release it, to snap and set her own heart.

Hillary scratched at his hot neck. "What are you talking about, boy?"

"Let me out of these."

"You're dumber than you look. You don't call the shots— I do."

The bookbinder turned to the chief, his jaw as set as his eyes, which flickered and closed; the cuffs fell to the ground, shattering into a hundred little silvery crumbs.

"Fuck!" Hillary jumped back. Rebecca, too, withdrew, but

never took her eyes off the bookbinder's scowl; she met his stare when he reopened his eyes.

"What the fuck *are* you?" Hillary fumbled at his holster. The bookbinder took a step forward and faltered; Rebecca lunged to catch him, to hold him up. His labored breath whistled over her.

"You'll have to get me there," he whispered.

"Where?"

"Stand back, Mrs. St. Pierre." Hillary had his gun out, but held it down, unsure how to play the hand.

Rebecca shook her head, the heavy bookbinder dripping on her. She craned to turn to the old chief, pleading. "Please . . . it's my daughter. He has my daughter." She shifted her weight, and her voice hardened into steel. "And you're still the law around here."

Hillary puffed out his chest. "Goddamn right I am."

"Then help us."

Hillary's shoulders folded forward. He expelled a pouty sigh, something of a defeated toddler about him, and squinted hard at the bookbinder. "Try anything and I'll blow your fucking head off," he promised, just loud enough for them both to hear.

Rebecca spun back into the bookbinder's face. "Where?"

"Tanager Way," the bookbinder murmured, the street name thick in his mouth, his voice all scrapes and scuffs. He balanced himself back onto his own weight and rubbed his wrists.

"What the hell is over there?" Hillary barked. "Exactly what are we talking about here, boy?"

Thick beads of sweat slid down the bookbinder's cheek, mixed with the remnants of the tempest; he pinched his face, pain blistering from behind his eyes. "It's using him," he said to Rebecca. "I've seen it before."

"Seen *what* before?" Hillary tugged at the brim of his hat.

"It's happening." He held his head against Rebecca's shoulder. "We have to go. You have to get me there."

"Seen *what* before?" Hillary's eyes danced.

The bookbinder didn't answer.

"I'm not going anywhere without probable cause." The chief stiffened, reaching for his official jargon as armor.

"Sam almost strangled Tess there earlier tonight," the bookbinder apprised. Rebecca gasped.

"Who?"

"Miriam Hollanger's daughter."

"Christ."

"She'll live." Rebecca shrank from the verb, its vagueness. The bookbinder studied her face, the marks that flared as they stood there; he touched her cheek. "Rebecca—"

She shook her head, vehement—then nodded, agreeing to everything he couldn't say. Fates sealed long ago, no easier to accept at the moment of their reckoning, require a faith harsher than any word or ritual can muster. The bookbinder's little prayer book taught her that, the truth always right there, hidden in the spaces between rites she couldn't read.

Hillary holstered his sidearm. "We'll need a car."

"We'll take mine," Rebecca declared. "I had hidden the key."

Outside, the rain lashed the porch from every direction, the wind erratic, panicked. Rebecca steered the bookbinder to the Oldsmobile. "She's calling us, isn't she?" she asked from his arm and into the storm.

"She's screaming," he answered, almost too quiet to be heard in its wake.

29

It wasn't just basements taking on water; the torrent rose everywhere, and the makeshift trinity splashed through a frigid, ankle-deep marsh to Rebecca's driveway.

Hillary demanded the key and the driver's seat. He turned back to Rebecca and the bookbinder, rain popping and hissing at their faces. "This is a goddamned police investigation. I am not going to just let abject lawlessness rule the fucking day, you hear me?"

The bookbinder collapsed into the back seat, Rebecca over him, trying to conjure ways to comfort him. He was cold to the touch in places, burning in others, a city under siege from head to toe—whole blocks on fire, others left dark to smolder. "We need to get you to a doctor," she said.

The shake of his head was feeble, though the eyes yet ardent. "Dyson," he croaked.

Hillary threw the car into gear. He pulled from the curb and navigated the squall, stronger now, denser, than it had ever been. The bookbinder shifted to watch the waterfall coursing down the window glass. The world itself was a threshold on this night; all the nights that came before, he knew, were just destiny working itself out, pushing him here into this damp bench seat with its locker room scent, attended to by a woman likewise conspired against. *Called upon.* They were going to lose the world as it was tonight, together or apart, one and the same. The bookbinder had assumed his hubris was to involve her in his tragedy; the hubris, though, was believing he had any hand in it at all. That any of it had ever been his.

Rebecca had been pressed somewhere between the end of one story and the beginning of another. There had been earnest promises kissed into her skin. There were absolutions, but the world, and the world beyond the world, made such things provisional. There was always a ledger—the first book, the book behind and beneath all the other books.

The ends of things were just variations of the middle. Nothing ever ended because everything had infinite culminations; time was an orbit. There was only one battlefield, made up of all the other battlefields, and countless, nameless men to rise and fall across them, spilling themselves red across their grasses and bushes, their makeshift canopies and abandoned constructions. The *Yatagarasu* would always arrive in their sacrificial wake, the murder a huge mass of a thing splitting itself off into tiny shards of hunger, preordained to eat the fields clean, prepare it for new life, the same old death.

Rebecca reached down and clutched for the bookbinder's hand. He squeezed and closed his eyes, burying his face into the seat. She listened to his haggard breathing, sensing the pulse through him, the effort to keep whatever he was holding in check for just a few minutes more. She thought she could see his lips moving against the leather, a secret mantra, but she couldn't make out the words.

Exactly what are we talking about here, boy? Hillary's voice boomed in Rebecca's brain—secrets, confirmations passed amid the bookbinder and this low-grade despot between the conversational, transmissions she couldn't get down, couldn't translate, more clandestine than even the cryptic poems cut into his skin, his kiss. There were miles and histories—blood both spilled and *taken*—and this slob of a policeman driving her husband's car through a tempest knew things about this man she held that she didn't. Rebecca saw the bookbinder's arc in that moment—his waning in the wake of the unescapable, his body that had finally collected enough dirt to blanket it. She could see that he was afraid, too—not of all that would come, but of what he had managed to build and all he would lose. The insight split her; she at once felt a surge, a powerful empathy, an *equality*, while the other her, a reflection, felt a hand grabbing at her ankle, pulling her into the inky pool of her own terror. She wanted to protect him, begin at the beginning, but she couldn't fathom how to nurse back this creature in her arms—there was nothing she could change. All she could do, she knew, was walk beside him for as long as she could muster, hand in calloused hand, cheek to busted cheek.

Chief Hillary peered back in the rearview mirror. They were close. "If he's there with the girl, you follow my lead, you hear?" He straightened against the seat. "I'm not letting this become amateur hour, got it?"

The bookbinder lifted his head. Rebecca could see the struggle in the streaks of perspiration across his face, as if he had never escaped the rain. "He's there. They're *all* there," he grunted through his clenched jaw.

Hillary pressed on the brake just after the turn onto Tanager Way, a hundred yards or so from the little white house in
which the Dysons once breathed, the spot where one of them
died and the other lost her life, for better and for worse. He
put the car in park and cut the lights.

30

To endure a battlefield is to persist in two places at once; a war started never ends. Not when flags are raised, or papers signed, or parades planned. Not when the last soldier is dead. Not when the last child of a soldier, the last grandchild or namesake, is dead. It ripples out to infinity, like a radio wave through space, sometimes silent, sometimes static, but always there, a constant.

For the soldier, it all plays out at once, the life of war and the life after, like two phonographs spinning different records at the same speed and the same volume. Tilt your head, one symphony comes to the forefront; close your eyes, and the other pulls ahead. War, the business of living and dying, distilled yet violent, cuts through the membranes of existence, the myriad versions of a man left to stare through the gaping wound at all the other carbon copies.

As the bookbinder was led through the deluge, head hanging, toward the Dyson house, he sensed that the edges were gone, any front lines left between the beast and him breached; his human suffering flowed into its concentrated cousin, like the mud and the rain, like the lawns and the unfinished streets washing into them, a nasty blur. It was October 25, 1952, the Dyson house was dark, a place full of broken things with their sharpest edges pointing out; it was Easter Sunday, 1944, sunny, and his sister was shivering, a heavy red shadow; it was March 1945, and there was a muck river that ran so deep into the heart of the earth it came out the other side.

Rebecca propped the bookbinder up as best as she could, their march slow until Hillary, cursing under his breath, pitched in and slid under the other heavy arm. The three trudged forward without a word, the rain almost shoving them down. The thunder was a constant rumble, the lightning popped like photography. The wind seemed to change direction every moment, doubling on itself to become something desperate, a blind fighter swinging haymakers to end the bout. The bookbinder fell to his knee, and Rebecca dropped beside him.

"This asshole is going to get us all killed!" Hillary yelled over the roar. "What the hell is wrong with him? Stage fright?"

Rebecca shot an irritated look at the chief but instantly saw in his expression how empty his insult was—he was at least as scared as anyone else. She helped the bookbinder back to his feet.

"Just get me in there," he muttered.

They broke over a small hill that put the little white house in sight; the bookbinder fell to his knee a second time. He lifted himself back up.

The house was completely still, yet somehow pulsed. A horde of hearts, dark ones and light, pounded behind its shutters. It was older than the other structures, almost organic, a poisonous white toadstool emerging from the hill, not built on top of it. The bookbinder watched black ivy slither along its face, its sides. He blinked and it was gone, the brick again smooth. "She's here!" Rebecca yelled into the men's sopping faces.

A flash of lightning lit Rebecca's high, battered cheekbones, her jawline, the jade flicker beneath her furrowed brow. Another flash and she was Charlotte shattered, the blood—the silent cry of a lost baby—trickling from her middle. She was Ava, all bright magic ricochets. Rebecca again, the rain washing her wounds away only to summon them back. The membranes of time were translucent here, worn to almost nothing.

"How are we going to do this?" Hillary yelled, suddenly passive, open to suggestion.

The bookbinder struggled to breathe but had straightened himself for one final charge. "It knows we're here," he rasped, his voice just barely carrying over the rain, like a song from a far shore. "It's expecting us."

"*It?*" Hillary made as if to brush the water away from him, but it was hopeless. He was soaked, and the rain that fell just flowed over him anyway, his boots already waterlogged, spitting out from their edges with each step. He stabbed a ruddy finger at Rebecca and the bookbinder, but said nothing more.

Rebecca filled the silence. "Then there's no reason not to just go through the front door."

The bookbinder nodded, but his eyes lingered on the chief. The cards were the cards, and they couldn't be changed; to survive, you needed to learn how to play from a position of weakness. You had to play from good enough.

The bookbinder moved first; he closed his eyes, focused on his own threadbare breath—the *in*, the *out*. When his mind began to wander, he gently pulled it back, a cloud on a string.

It wasn't a matter of being somewhere else, of making the rain and wind disappear, but being wholly here—this now among nows—feeling each drop, accepting each drop. Strength and weakness; the trick of the universe is that one is never more powerful than when they let go. In this way, the meek—the *wronged*—inherit the earth. Bring it back. *Inhale. Exhale.*

Rebecca clasped tight against him now, her hand on his arm, electric, rattling. He saw the house in the autumn of dark and rain; he saw it in the brilliant shine of a spring sun—flowers in full bloom, hard shadows, and Charlotte, her head cocked just so, just beyond the painted chain-link, aware of a shift in the air, tension ratcheting quickly until an equally quick release—the realization that the man in the distance was just her little brother.

The bookbinder took a deep breath, brought everything back to now. *Here.* The rain helped. The rain centered him.

"What is it?"

He shook his head.

"This place?"

He looked at Rebecca, his fists knots at his sides. "I was never going to make it out of here."

He didn't need to say anything else. She saw everything in the way he held himself against the elements. The details were trivial. She looked past the bookbinder at Hillary, leaning in so only the former could hear. "I don't trust him."

The flashing was frantic. The bookbinder read the sky. "It doesn't matter anymore. *He* doesn't."

They stopped just before the yard, facing a bare front porch where Charlotte Dyson had once kept her potted plants, her daisies, her geraniums. The bookbinder recalled the pops of color, how they had greeted him from the end of the street in 1944, a bright little wink. Beyond that, though—just a short sojourn inside the white walls—there proved an entirely different landscape, murky and cavernous, shadows infusing every crevice like broken black yolks. He remembered how his sister flinched, a twitch as constant as this lightning, behind her beaming smiles; anxieties hung like tightropes from wall to wall, a web from floor to ceiling. And sitting in his recliner, tethered to every snug string, pulling everything in, was Paul, his grin indistinguishable from a sneer.

Lightning flashed, close, the thunder quick and booming, and Rebecca was grasping his hand, calling him through the downpour. He tried to focus, but he was tired, so goddamned tired, memories scribbling on top of each other: Charlotte waving, the way her hand dropped abruptly, her fingers clutched over her heart. She held the pose as he approached, and when he was close enough, he could see tears spilling down her cheeks, her chin. They embraced, all skinny arms and shoulder blades, and he found himself surprised by how light she felt, how cool her skin.

She led him into the house. Paul wasn't home yet; it was Friday, "Good" or not, and though her husband had probably already knocked off from work, he surely had stopped at the new bar—Walter's? Willy's?—on the way home. She tried to cover her worry over what version of Paul would burst through the door—what he might say, what he might do. How would he treat a guest—her only brother, just turned eighteen—in his cloistered castle? The changes in Paul had started small enough, but were snowballing, becoming more obvious. More extreme. She could not bring herself to think of it as falling, because she could not conceive of any way to break it.

Charlotte offered her brother a cold drink. They spoke at the kitchen table in hushed tones, as if afraid talking too loudly would tip the universe, interfere with the reunion. They spoke generally of the war, its various fronts, his intention to enlist after the holiday. Where he might land. Every few minutes, Charlotte would lose herself outside the window, commenting on the sheets hanging from the clothesline in the yard, a little touchstone for her, a safe place. Out as far as she could go.

It was still light out when Paul arrived home. The kitchen exploded with the front door's swing, Paul in stark relief, a tall black spot in the blinding gold, and it was only when he closed the door behind him, flipped on a lamp, that the siblings at the table could see his expression. His face was austere, solemn around the mustache, but the eyes danced like a child's. Charlotte played with the edge of the tablecloth.

"Paul, dear—"

"Who the hell are *you*?" Paul threw his keys onto a small side table by the door.

"Paul." Charlotte cleared her throat, blushing. "Remember? We talked about this." She bit her lip. It had been a talk in only the loosest sense of the word. She had the cigarette burns as a reminder. "This is my brother, Michael. He's going to stay with us for the weekend."

Paul squinted—then burst into a giant, shit-eating grin, an expression too loud for the moment. "Holy hell!" he exclaimed, his voice booming, attacking the walls. He rushed to shake hands and gripped the teenager at the shoulders, squeezing them. "Welcome!" Paul pressed closer, his haircut as crisp as his eyes were blurry, his jaw the same, handsome with something furtive tucked into the margins. His breath was antiseptic, kept its own secrets. "Charlotte has been so excited about you coming. Can't stop talking about it." He did not let go for a long beat. "Isn't that right, darling?" he said, not paying her cautious nod any mind.

Paul released the boy's shoulders with a dramatic flair of his fingers and took a step back. For a moment the three of them held their positions, almost but not quite looking at each other, until Paul asked what was for dinner, Charlotte's cue to disappear into the kitchen.

The man of the house poured himself a stiff drink from a collection of bottles that rested in his den, shook out and lit a cigarette, and sized up his guest again. His wide smile was an aggressive thing, and he guided—goaded—his brother-in-law back to the table.

Paul finished his glass almost as soon as they sat down. He went back to the bottles and poured, returning now with two. "How old are you, kid?"

"Just turned eighteen, sir."

Paul gripped both glasses. "You a fucking dodger?"

Michael shook his head. "No, sir—I'm going to enlist next week. Straight up."

Paul pushed one of the tumblers across the face of the table. "Good deal. Well, drink up, pal." He winked. "Hell—I almost envy you."

"Sir?"

"To mow down those dirty yellow fuckers one more time. To watch it all burn."

"We're here." Rebecca's expression betrayed concern. The bookbinder blinked. He ran his hand over his dripping beard. The record had skipped once more; they were standing on the Dyson porch, and he had no recollection of how he got there.

Hillary popped the strap to his holster. "Step aside." He took a cursory look at the front door's lock and slammed the hard sole of his boot into it.

31

~

The door exploded inward just as lightning burst across the night, emblazing the front rooms for an instant, then pulling everything back into a total blackness punctuated by a churning, deep curl of thunder. The bookbinder crossed into the entryway and crashed to the ground; the beast could not contain its need, slamming itself against the bars of its man-shaped cage. Lightning flashed again and he—*they*—stared at a figure at the back of the house, child-size, in full relief.

Rebecca ran to the fallen bookbinder, Hillary hanging back, more tentative. She could not see anything, a kind of double-blindness—the lightning flared and imprinted itself on her vision just as its vanishing sucked everything into a deeper, truer blind. The effect was disorienting, and when a hand gripped her shoulder, followed by a gust of rancid breath near her ear, she swung wildly and missed. Something slammed her to the ground, then pinned her down. She knew it was Sam—could feel the fraying, stinking bandage scratch against her neck.

The bookbinder, curled over himself, could measure the

room only by ear and hoisted himself toward Sam's snarl, wrestled with whatever he could grab, thrashing arms or legs, tripping his assailant with a groan. He heard scampering, then a click—he had just enough time to remember Tess's missing knife before it sliced across and through his bicep.

The room exploded with a blast, a duet to the bookbinder's pained scream. Hillary switched on his flashlight, aiming it first on the crumpled vagabond, then to Rebecca clutching her throat. From its halo, they could make out the smoke trail rising off the police chief's gun, pointed at the ceiling.

He shifted the flashlight, and the beam landed on a purplish stain defacing the far wall. The bookbinder thought again of Charlotte, surely sleeping now among careful nuns in the as-yet undisturbed woods of the peninsula, far away from this place. He considered Chopin's nocturnes and the impossibility of escape. The beast shrieked in his head and from the cut along his arm.

The bookbinder crawled to Rebecca. She exhaled, an awkward whimper that twisted into a raw cough; she hadn't realized until that moment that she had been holding her breath. She relaxed into his embrace, then started, wiped smeared crimson from her skin. "You're bleeding," she said.

"It doesn't hurt."

"It's gushing." Rebecca moved to apply pressure to the wound, but the bookbinder waved her hand away. She sat back on her haunches, her eyes wide.

He closed his. "It's all right," he averred. The blood flowed, running down his arm, and dripped from his fingertips to the carpet. *Be the pain. Don't run from. Run to.* "This is the way." Rebecca gaped into his visage only to recognize a calm she had never before seen in all her examinations.

She shook her head as the bookbinder struggled to stand. She rose to meet him. "You're *hurt*."

He turned from her, tracking Hillary's light as it passed across a long rightward arc, through the living room and into the entrance to the den. Another stain. The beam doubled back, landing in the general vicinity of where the dining table over which Paul Dyson had held court once stood, the pulpit from where he'd told lie after lie until even he grew exhausted. In the end, the Emptiness revealed itself. It couldn't help but reveal itself.

Focus. Sam St. Pierre was in here somewhere, as was Ava. Rebecca stood behind his shoulder. He could place himself by placing them. *Something. Something else.*

"You'll die," Rebecca cried, the fire of her protests dampened by the dawning understanding that what was happening in these walls did not follow the rules as she had learned them. There was a crash; Hillary swept the light back, and the party stepped forward, almost in unison. They flared out in a wide arc until they faced the den and its giant purple smear head-on—and below it, Sam St. Pierre, smiling wide, a crescent cut at the corner of one eye. He hovered behind and over his own daughter, the open switchblade to her throat.

Rebecca's scream froze them for a moment, a roar so distressed it challenged the now unceasing tide of thunder that kept the house shaking. The beast pressed itself toward her lament; the bookbinder stumbled against the force.

Another flash of lightning washed out the flashlight's beam, then again. The strikes flared almost on top of each other now, a dizzying strobe, time skipping ahead in tiny increments, scratch by electrified scratch.

"Let her go!" Rebecca's primal maternal roar had molded

itself into coherent words. In the bedlam, the bookbinder caught the click of Hillary cocking his gun.

Sam caught it, too—his grin-sneer didn't shift, but the milky eyes did; they churned with fear and recognition, two small orbs in a disheveled sky. A black cloud, a smudge, made manifest, all bony angles. To the bookbinder, he resembled a lesser Paul Dyson, that Easter morning all those years ago, when he lurched out of his bedroom for the last time.

Sam's hand juddered, the knife tight against Ava's neck, a little bead of blood forming at its tip. The otherwise-silent, still girl released a tiny yelp between booms, a spur—Rebecca broke for her daughter, Hillary caught her by her dress with his free hand, yanking her back.

"Get off me!" Rebecca struggled, shrieked—tear streaked, bruises flaring.

"He'll slit her from ear to ear if you go at him like that," the chief replied, his words cool.

"He'll do it anyway," the bookbinder heard himself say. "It needs her dead."

Hillary arched an eyebrow. "*It?*"

"Ava was what it wanted all along," the bookbinder conceded. He regarded the ceiling, stumbled back. "*She* is the threat to it. Sam's fighting."

"Fighting what?"

"The thing inside him."

"And what in the holy hell might that be?"

The bookbinder lowered his head, his hands splayed. He could draw a picture like the ancients did. A circle head. Lines for arms and legs, sometimes even a member between them. But in the center of the figure—nothing. *Emptiness.* "There's nothing holy about it."

"Kill me!" Sam's scream was a nasally whine, as if filtered through a crack in the man. The Emptiness had been taking hold—taking *over*—a measure every day, for months, maybe years; it ran through his organs, pulling them tight, stringing everything inside him up. "*Shoot me!*" he frothed over strained, bleeding lips.

Ava stood out like a porcelain fence post, a shock of white against the black. Her eyes were either hollow or full, but all color, pinpoint pupils despite the dark. Outside, the storm continued to rage.

Sam's body loitered in stark contrast to his child's perfect symmetry—he was all gawk and whiskey sweat stains, an over-ripe teenager. The bookbinder stared through him, seeing him for what he had become—a husk in another ghost's lair: Sam St. Pierre was Paul Dyson, a tape of a tape. And more—deeper, farther back. A parade of lost soldiers, as if a portal were opened just in the corner of your eye, just out of reach, shadow pressed over shadow pressed over shadow. Blacker than black.

The bookbinder shuddered at the echoes. The storm un-settled time.

"Why?" he had finally asked over a glass of warm whiskey, all those years ago—*1944*. He stared at the strung teeth tossed on the kitchen table. The dried scalp. He had not yet seen war. He did not yet understand what urges it could shift.

Paul lit a cigarette, then regarded the tip, inhaling the trail of smoke from its end. "They were fucking slant-eyes," he slurred, dismissive. "Yellow, through and through."

"They were men, same as you." He recognized how young he must have sounded, how impotent.

Paul's eyes ignited. "Whose side are you on, sweet tits?" he snarled. "They were fucking *animals*."

Animals: beings of gristle and bone, sometimes feathers. The bookbinder blinked himself awake in 1952, focused on Sam St. Pierre's waxing grin, the glisten around his eyes, tears rung out by strain. It had him, he knew, the thing that Paul Dyson had brought back along with the blood-soaked flags and the rooted teeth, the Emptiness so dense it could fill up a certain kind of man, hide in his corners.

The lightning strobed, and with each burst, each small shift of Sam's head, his body, an impression was left behind, a trace, as if there were a halo of men scribbled on top of one another, Sam, first of all, but also Paul, others the bookbinder didn't recognize, but recognized all the same.

"I've got a shot," Hillary said. The bookbinder could hardly hear him for the thunder and the pulse of his own pumping blood, the squawking. He blinked as the chief asserted he was taking Sam out.

Sam cocked his head. The grin pulled even wider, the bookbinder able to make out deep red around the corners, where the skin was splitting. Sam's mouth a crimson sieve. What was left of his eyes rolled into the back of his head. The bookbinder felt Hillary shift beside him.

A lightning flash, a record skip: "*Wrong?*" Paul's laugh like thunder, thick and low. "Like there's a *right?* That's some simple shit, boy. That's black and white in a Technicolor world." Paul threw back the rest of his whiskey. His eyes were burning. "You sit here in my house and think you can judge me. Why are you here?"

"I came to see my sister. She wrote me."

"No, why are you *here!*" Paul screamed in his face, all spittle and sharp canines, slammed his fist on the table. He pointed vaguely at a wall, some direction or other. East. West. From far enough away, it was all the same. "And not out there—doing your fucking duty!"

"I'm fixing to enlist."

"Fixing to—you waiting for a personal invitation from Roosevelt himself?" Paul shook his head and sneered. "Are you a coward?" he demanded, his voice teetering, low as it was, clumsy. "Or just fucking slow?"

The teenager rubbed his temple. The whiskey was making him feel clumsy, too, confused. She was so thin in places, out of symmetry. Jumped at every little sound. And he could hear his own pulse resonating in his ears. He would not jump. He would not look away. "What have you done to Charlotte?" He considered another sip. Considered against it. "She an animal, too?"

Paul winked, almost proud. "She been talking? Crying on baby brother's shoulder?" He stood up. "Hell, that's fine. I don't mind. But you should know, you little shit, that I can't even imitate the noises that bitch makes—an animal?" He thrust his hips, a pantomime. "Nah. A harpy! A she-devil. *Yeehaw*." The sound cut, cracked against a thousand cigarettes, a thousand whiskey gulps.

Another flash; the bookbinder's own ragged voice seemed distant, out to sea. "Wait," he said. "No."

Hillary either didn't hear him or didn't care; he fired one shot. Sam's head popped back, a new splash of crimson wet smacking the stain that was already there. His body dropped limp, but a tangled, hissing blackness scrambled up the wall, all whipping, pulsating limbs, and along the ceiling.

Crack. There and not there. Stacked, in a way. It wasn't remembering, not exactly. "I've seen her bruises," he uttered, trying to sound as threatening as he could muster. The world was growing fuzzy quicker than he expected. He studied his hand gripping the glass, the skinny vine of an arm that extended from it. It was late, too late, Saturday night. Holy Saturday, and he was suddenly tired, so tired. "I know what you are," he slurred, desperately mistaken.

Paul chuckled. "You don't know anything about being a man, kid." He swallowed a long drink. "The worst was the mud," he admitted. "Smelled like shit. Couldn't even bury your buddies—there were too many, first of all, and the monsoons would just wash 'em up anyway. And the fucking maggots. We all went a little nuts there." He chugged another mouthful. "The enemy of my enemy is my enemy. *Christ.*" Paul belched, chuckled again, but it wasn't Paul's voice, not exactly, not *just* Paul's voice—something else lurked behind.

The Emptiness chuckled. They all heard it; it came from the rafters, from between the floorboards.

"Dear God," Hillary sighed.

Ava, standing alone now, shaking, her eyes pinched closed and her father dead behind her, opened her tight fists; two Baoding balls fell into the shag. She blinked her eyes open; they were white as orbs, a faint mist of sparks emanating from her sockets. Her body rose, her little bare toes hovering just above the carpet.

Once more, she conjured the rain. Changed it in her way.

It lashed inside the Dyson house, as furious as the tempest beyond, lightning cutting through the rooms. Water pounded against the carpet, the hand-me-down furniture Roy Dickerson used to stage the doomed house, the half-pints spilled in the corners, a dissonance of errant notes.

"I'm a goddamned war hero," Paul Dyson growled from 1944, forever and moments ago, rabid, as he stumbled out of his sunlit bedroom in his boxers, everything tousled, everything dank. Charlotte wept softly behind the door ajar.

The monster had lived a night too long.

Her brother jumped from the couch, from his blackout stupor, slamming shoulders with Paul as he burst past, into the bedroom. Charlotte hardly seemed to notice his scramble over the bed, her blood smearing across yesterday's clothes; he rifled through her husband's nightstand, got lucky, and pulled Paul's standard-issue sidearm from a wobbly drawer.

There was no standoff, no last words. Michael Keane, all of eighteen years old and a hundred fifty pounds, stormed into the den with its overflowing ashtrays and empty bottles, put the barrel to the self-ordained war hero's neck, and pulled the trigger. The blast shook the little room, and Paul Dyson struggled to scream, deep rose bubbles foaming from the hole in his neck; the men wrestled toward the rear of the house, upending a chair and side table until Paul's leaking body was pinned against the kitchen wall. Charlotte howled from her bedroom, awoken from one nightmare directly into another the moment her little brother pinched her husband's nose shut, shoved the pistol into his gasping mouth—chipping Paul's yellow teeth— and pulled the trigger a second time.

The past was the present, the timeline folding in on itself. The bookbinder could smell the smoke escaping Hillary's barrel, could smell it now pointed at him. He focused past the gun, landing on the spread-eagle grin just south of the darting, frightened eyes of the chief. They were just starting to blur; the Emptiness didn't have to go far to find another welcoming vessel, another vacancy.

Hillary held the gun on the bookbinder, rain slapping against its metal, tickled the trigger, and gawked past his target, against the farthest wall. Where the bookbinder's silhouette should have contrasted against the lightning flash, there emerged an unexpected black shape—a hooked beak, wings. Three drawn sets of talons.

The shadow the brightest light casts.

Hillary's face wrenched back, contorted into a grotesquerie beyond human expression, shiny with downpour. His pistol lurched from the bookbinder to Rebecca, a shot fired—but no flare erupted from the end of Hillary's outstretched arm, no lightning. Instead, the old police chief crumpled, his right temple opened into a crater of splintered skull and brains, hissing black tendrils scuttling out.

The bookbinder spun, unsteady, the torrent running into his eyes; the gunshot had come from behind. Another flash, a clap: Joe Hollanger shivered in the room's gale, two hands grasping Michael Keane's own standard-issue sidearm, resurrected this night from its paper grave on Kestrel Street, the first volume the bookbinder ever bound.

Rebecca screamed a warning; the Emptiness, all serpent arms and legs, hoofs, claws—locked in on Joe, spinning, spitting, both solid and ephemeral, all shapes becoming no shape, compressed desertion: a black hole. And from the hole surged veins, spindly threads that stretched and strove for Joe's frozen face to slide inside his mouth.

Rebecca ran for the boy without a second thought, straight for the foul ink spot hovering above Joe. He was not her child, but he was *somebody's* child, and the maternal instinct dutifully rose above humankind's weaker distinctions. The bookbinder tried to seize her as she passed, and they collapsed on each other, falling into the puddles now spreading into pools across the carpet. The bookbinder, dazed, grabbed at her scrambling over him, and pulled her face to his. He held her there, his long-frightened eyes telling her everything that words had always failed to convey, filling in the spaces between her prayers. He kissed her as hard as he could, quick like silver but with everything he had left, and when he pulled away, she tracked his gaze down to his arm, to the blood that continued to gush loose, torrents fed by Ava's rain. The blood spilled into dark rivers that branched off across the floor.

Something arrives. Then something else to answer. The bookbinder watched his own loosened blood, and Ava conducting her storm. The Emptiness takes a foothold, only for the Everything to counter. *Darkness, light, yin, yang*—and he her soldier, the Everything's special weapon, an instrument for the light and shadow to dance through, to change and be changed.

Rebecca watched the slick, feathered heads rise from blood rivers, cawing, the dusky beaks dripping as with oil, birthed, anointed; the wings spread next, and then the talons, each crow three-legged. A handful rose, and then hundreds, and instantly thousands, across the room—more than could reasonably fit in the space—all fluttering and screaming and gnashing. They scrambled between the bookbinder and Rebecca, and the woman felt herself being pushed away. She fought back toward him but was scratched, pecked, vanquished. As the crows closed over him, she saw in his face not just the etchings of their murderous screams, but again her own reflection, a near-perfect mirror, cropped in jagged ways. The union of the scavenger and the scavenged.

The crows molded themselves into a behemoth, each a screeching, gnashing feather of the *Yatagarasu* as it unfurled. Its eyes unsheathed as enormous opals; the beast's wingspan blacked out the lightning with a single stretch. Rebecca heard three deep flaps of its wings fashioned of blood-soaked beaks and claws, their foul wind knocking her on her back, and then suffered the deafening shriek as it reached its scuttling prey. In the chaos, she caught a glimpse of Joe flat against the opposite wall—something like safe, and anything but—his face ashen, mouth agape. The Emptiness whipped through the sheets of rain, but the *Yatagarasu* pinned it with one saber-like talon, slicing through its pitch mass with the others.

Its great head leaned forward, as if whispering a secret, its eyes unblinking, and Rebecca suffered the terrible, awesome sounds of tendrils snapping like wet worms; she heard her dead husband's choked squeal, and others behind him, whole armies of empty men. She covered her ears, folded over herself, and shut her face so tight she saw stars behind her eyelids.

She remained there for minutes or hours or days—she could not track time under the horrific opus's din, its dirge. It was as if the thunder and lightning had breached first from the sky into the Dyson house, and then from the Dyson house into her head.

Then it was over. Silence like a flat plain. The beast was gone, its belly full with the other beast, the nature of things. Rebecca shuddered as a cold hand clutched her shoulder; she opened her eyes to Ava dripping over her. She tried to say her daughter's name, but nothing escaped save a sandpaper pain— Rebecca had screamed her voice to shreds.

And the rain had broken.

32

⌣

The rooms of the little house hushed, save for the furniture's tears—heavy, round droplets falling from chipped and grated end tables, bookshelves, chairs. Rebecca collected her daughter in a panicked embrace. Ava said nothing, offering no expression as she traced her index finger along the edges of the fresh scratches crisscrossing her mother's arms. Lips against ear, white-ice strands of hair, Rebecca whispered a rasping confession, an apology, a celebration—all wrapped together in a string of words like hoarse incantations.

She caught a rustling in a far corner; she crawled to Hillary's body and the flashlight that shone on without him. She grabbed it, tacky with the chief's congealing blood, and aimed it at the noise. Joe stood in front of her, sopping, rubbing his head in a daze.

"Go back," the boy said.

Rebecca started. She wished she could. She wished for nothing else. "What?" The word came grated.

"Please," the boy asserted, softer. "Go back with the light."

She did as Joe asked, running the beam across the length of the room.

"They're gone."

"Who?" Rebecca asked over her shoulder.

"There were stains on the wall, just a minute ago. Big dark things. They're gone." Joe could see more clearly now, fresh moonlight peeking in from the windows. He stared at Ava staring at whatever it was Ava St. Pierre stared at. "*She* washed them away," he added, not sure whether the sounds made it past his tongue. He was here, after—but a part of him was, or wished to be, strained to be, still back there, before.

Rebecca heard him, though, heard the wonder and confusion in his voice, and walked to gently pluck the gun from his loose grip. She bent down and touched her hand to his cheek.

"I killed him," Joe said. "I killed the police chief."

Rebecca gripped his shoulder and shook her head. Her throat was still raw, but she spoke as clearly as she could manage. "No, you didn't."

"I *did.*"

"Joe, I know you won't understand this—but he was already gone." She squeezed, made sure Joe looked right at her, and bounced the gun in her hand. "Where did you get this?"

"I found it in a book. It's his." He blinked. "I found it snooping around the shop. I know I shouldn't have."

"It's okay, Joe."

"I never touched it until tonight. I swear. But your—" Joe's voice faltered. "My sister, he hurt my sister—"

"It's okay, Joe."

"No. It's not."

Rebecca squared herself in Joe's line of vision. "You saved

me. That is what you did. Whatever that was—" She thrust her head back toward Hillary's body. "All it wanted in that moment was to kill me. You *saved* me." She rose, straining a little to kiss the boy's forehead. "You're a hero, Joe Hollanger," she confirmed, sealing his fate.

Rebecca walked to where her dead husband lay, crouched down, and wiped the gun—a dime a dozen in towns like this—against the hem of her dress, then again, carefully crouching, placing it in Sam's hand to stage the scene, two dead men each other's killer, a closed circuit. She jerked at the sound of a flutter, only to realize it was her own pounding heart.

The woman rose again and turned to Joe. "It's good enough." A beat. "It will have to be." And though the boy didn't know exactly what she meant, he nodded, trusting her.

He scanned the room. "Where did he go?"

Rebecca held back a hitch, bit her lip. "He's gone."

"Is he coming back?"

"I don't think so," Rebecca admitted, suddenly unable to barricade the horror. She took a step back, dazed, her mind racing. She felt she might be sick.

Joe tried to hide his own shake like a man, like his father. Like the bookbinder. Rebecca cut through the pretense to hug him as hard as she could until they were both shivering, sobbing, each holding the other up.

Ava shuffled to them, watched their huddle for a long moment, these two perfect examples of imperfection, and reached out her little palms. It looked taciturn, but it was something else entirely, all the transmissions intermingled. She almost, but not quite, touched their heads.

"We have to go," Rebecca acknowledged after some time;

they took Hillary's flashlight, and Joe led them down through the basement and out the back door—the way he'd sneaked in, the way he'd watched Tess do it.

⌣

Rebecca decided it would be best if Joe were not seen with her and Ava. He broke off and crossed Brookshire through backyards and empty lots, the cool air slowly drying his clothes and hair. Thoughts flapped around the corners of his mind like frightened, exhausted birds with no place to land. Jumbled realities—the boy he was before this night, the one after—caught up to his body and tripped over themselves, Ghost Joe now a clumsy, bloated thing, in the way. A new kind of haunting. He was scared they would get nabbed, no matter what Mrs. St. Pierre had said. "They will only see what they want to see," she had promised when he left them. "You can't imagine how much of this won't have to be explained."

He was even more scared that they *wouldn't* get nabbed. He was not yet thirteen years old and he had killed a man, a police officer—a dirty police officer, a bad guy, he was sure—but a police officer. He felt the wind against his clothes and thought it would eventually wear him down, whittle him into nothing but his raw secret. He forced a deep breath and kept walking through the sleeping town anyway.

Joe watched his street, and then his house, come into focus, and he thought about the bookbinder, how he had let go of everything in the end to save them, how no one would ever know what was lost. He thought of his father, the stories that were already beginning to fade. The myths.

He thought about Mrs. St. Pierre, how she had run to him

when the thing took him and charged right at it, meaning to do whatever the heck she was going to try to do. He thought of his mother, his sister—he realized it was not some female madness that made these women do the things they did, but an urge deep and true inside, like a tiny blue flicker, a suffering at the center of a fire, the hottest part: their enormous, ridiculous capacity for bravery.

Joe stepped onto the pavement of Sparrow Lane, then made his way to his house, the only one still lit.

His mother flung the door open, a cigarette bouncing in her hand. "Joe!" she screamed, and there was more around the edges of his name, but she couldn't bring herself to say it, and he couldn't bring himself to need it.

"Hi, Ma," he said simply. He stepped past her into the living room. Tess was back out on the sofa, wrapped tight in her robe. Joe took a long look at her—his teacher, his mender, his protector, his accomplice—strode to her, and wrapped his arms over hers. The room around them reeked of smoke, all the anxiety their mother had been puffing out for hours.

A siren wailed in the distance, then another. Miriam swallowed air, picking at the shirt she still hadn't changed out of. "Joe," she said, trying to sound as steady—as *in charge*—as she could muster. The words came out slow, almost practiced. "I need to know where you've been. I need to know where you were tonight."

It was Tess who opened her eyes first and spoke from behind her brother's neck, her voice as steady as Miriam had tried to shape hers. "He was right here," she confirmed. "He was right here all night long."

Miriam stepped forward, a protest forming on her lips. Tess locked in, nipping it with narrowed eyes. "Mother," she declared, "I know one thing in this world, and that is that my little brother was in his room next to mine, sleeping soundly, all night long." It was both an order and a promise.

Miriam regarded her children, aware she was as much in their possession as they were in hers. She studied them together, recognized them for what they were, their inheritance since they were both tiny: warriors.

She turned to shut the front door and cut the porch light, and as she did, she thought she caught a figure across the street. She flipped the light back on—a flock of black birds scattered from under a lamppost. She watched them rush up the hill where Meadowlark Avenue met Sparrow Lane, her slope of a street where all the mud ran by, then cut the porch dark once again and pressed the door closed.

EPILOGUE

$\smile$

The flooding receded overnight, and first thing the next day, neighbors began to coagulate around the most wounded parts of Brookshire—the lowland homes, mostly, but also the scandalous house on Tanager Way. News of the deaths spread quickly; there was much hand-wringing, false nostalgia that the world wasn't what it used to be. The year 1952 had its good old days, the same as 1944 or any other span where a man or two could think back hard enough to make up a new past for himself, themselves.

There was a passing interest in the bookbinder's disappearance, but just as no one knew exactly when he had arrived, no one could pinpoint exactly when he'd left. The Appleton police questioned Rebecca, though they treated her somewhat carefully, not leaning too hard on the rumors of her adultery in the wake of all the ways she and her daughter had been victimized in the whole sordid affair. She looked the part with her bruises and cuts, and true to her prediction, they seemed none too interested in inventing loose threads they would ultimately be expected to tie up. Occam's razor—two dead bodies with guns in their hands equal a quickly closed case. Eventually the authorities even returned Ava's Baoding balls, found at the crime scene, no longer considering them evidence.

J. M. Brooks, as well, was far too busy with the crop of investigations into his more nefarious connections, as well as the lawsuits filed on account of the faulty Brookshire drainage and shoddy construction materials, to spend time or money digging deeper into the death of his subordinate lawman. Instead, he doubled down on the church and the goodwill he figured it would generate, riding contractors like horses to finish it by the Christmas Vigil. He couldn't help himself, though—old habits dying hard—and inflated costs all down the line, throwing Saint Anne's further in debt to pay his own legal fees, and Father Jim in more and more precarious straits. On one particular occasion, the priest collapsed in the chair opposite Miriam's rectory desk and confessed the extent of the trouble the parish was in; she responded with a startling coolness, only nodding and admonishing the pastor to have faith. He caught a steely glint that both troubled him and shored up his confidence in, if not necessarily a *higher* power, a *different* one.

In the end, Rebecca wasn't sure when she gravitated to the big house on Kestrel Street, or if it was ever actually her decision at all. She brought their possessions to the upper floors one at a time, piecemeal—a jacket one day, a doll, a pillow, a book, a ribbon. While her daughter slept, the bookbinder's scuffed meditation balls held tight, she walked the small square rooms at night, breathing in the sandalwood and pipe tobacco as long as they would last.

Nobody stopped her and Ava, or even questioned what was happening. Roy Dickerson alone had one long night of the soul—and half a bottle of scotch he saved for closings—up late in his office, staring and restaring at the name typed on the deed, as it had been all these months. It had been her maiden name that Roy didn't recognize. It didn't make sense back then, and made so much perfect sense now as to render his perception of "making sense" meaningless. The big bastard had known everything, all along. Or if not the whole road, at least where it ended. Where it had to go. Roy emptied his last glass and got all the paperwork for Doc Magruder's place in order for Rebecca St. Pierre, née Corbeau. After, he even helped her put her old house on Phoebe Street up for sale.

⌣

In the hours before the Christmas Vigil, Father Jim inspected the new Saint Anne's Church, the high ceilings devastating him, not just in their beauty but because he knew they represented the end of his time as a pastor. He didn't know how deeply in debt—how *in the pocket*—he was to Brooks; he had stopped looking at the paperwork weeks ago. It had become absurd, in the darkest way; only Miriam knew the full extent of the damage. He was completely powerless, a so-called man of God at the strained mercy of the dollar. If Brooks moved to collect, it would bankrupt the parish; the diocese would cover it, of course, but he would certainly be reassigned, and most likely demoted. The other possibility was perhaps worse: Brooks wouldn't cash out but would make Father Jim his personal sacred puppet. The priest decided then and there he would resign when that came to be, even if it meant going against the diocese and abandoning his holy orders.

He stood before the altar, perfect stillness on a raised marble floor. *My God, it is extraordinary*, he thought to himself, gripping the edge of a pew. And then he considered the fleetingness of extraordinary things, their short half-life, and shuddered.

The church's heavy front doors opened, then closed. Father Jim turned; Miriam, bundled up in a smart coat and hat, stood behind him, a large package in her arms. She marched down the center aisle toward the priest and altar, as if presenting the offertory.

"What's this?" he asked.

"A gift from a friend." She presented the paper package to him. "Be careful—it's heavy. Merry Christmas." She stood on her toes and kissed Father Jim on the cheek, then turned back the way she came. She promised in fleeting to be at Mass later that evening.

Father Jim lowered himself into the first pew and slowly peeled back the paper. Inside was the most magnificent Bible he had ever held, all gilded gold and carved detail around a thick stock frame, the raised feathers of the trumpeting angels so delicately engraved, they seemed to dance in the breeze of his own warm breath.

When he opened the good book, a thick manila package fell, with a pinned address: simply *Padre* scrawled on a piece of handmade stationery. He carefully set the hardback aside and tore open the folder; its contents were nothing less than a road map of the graft and corruption of one J. M. Brooks—the forged documents and fraudulent surveys, the double billing, the inflated prices, the shortcut materials, the years of bribery and payoffs—not just regarding Saint Anne's Catholic Church, but Brookshire, Maryland, at large, as well as some significant properties around National airfield and even the new interstate. Illicit payments to New York and New Orleans, shakedowns at shipping yards up and down the coast. Even a building inspector's body discovered in the soft ground next to the Potomac. A bulk of the evidence had been documented, copied, and organized by Miriam Hollanger herself; the rest—and some of the most salacious, it would later be revealed—had been lifted by a pretty young receptionist at Brooks Industries headquarters, a former friend of the owner's daughter and the occasional object of both Brooks's ire and lust, and to whom a certain kind church secretary at Saint Anne's had made a special effort to befriend in the last few months.

It was only when Father Jim's cough shook loose the tears that he realized he had been crying where he sat. Later that night, with the developer and his extended family sitting in that same first pew, the troubled pastor gave perhaps the most heartfelt homily of his career. "He sounded ten years younger," gushed one parishioner as the congregation exited. Miriam bit back a smile. She nodded politely to Father Jim and then, with Joe and Tess beside her, walked home, unbothered by the sharp Christmas chill.

⌣

As 1953 took hold, the newspapers were packed with slavering exposés on the exploits of Brookshire's namesake. The local scandal of Sam St. Pierre gave way to the bigger, more far-reaching one of J. M. Brooks, and the press, once they had a sense of the size of the larceny, dug in with all they had—the bigger they were, the harder they fell, and the more papers that would shake out in the stir. Lawyers from up and down the Eastern Seaboard converted motel rooms into makeshift offices to file suits as numerous as stars in the sky on behalf of the homeowners of Brookshire and points beyond.

One morning, after reading over the latest Brooks revelation set to newsprint, something nefarious to do with Nazi sympathizers going back as far as the 1930s, Rebecca folded the paper and peered out the side window, through the sheers. Thinking and not thinking, something about chickens and roosts. Paying for what one gets.

A knock rapped on the front door. *Her* front door. When she opened it, Stan Chandler was leaning against a railing on the stoop, a cigarette dangling from his cracked lips. "Ma'am," he said, tipping his cap.

"Morning, Stan."

The old cord of a man covered his mouth with one hand and coughed, his cigarette barely jostling. With his other hand, he offered a ring of keys.

"What's this?"

"Well," he said, scratching at the thin hair beneath his cap, "Your . . . friend . . . and me, we had an understanding, you see." He lowered his voice. "I knew him once." He winced at some harsh memory and shook his head. "What I mean is, I was privy to some things."

"Privy? I don't follow."

Stan stared out at the crisp blue of the sky, remembering the bookbinder as he once was, the thin young man waving to his sister in greeting from the street, lugging a suitcase in his other hand. Coming from somewhere. Headed somewhere else. And then Easter, all that violence condensed in that small cluster of rooms. How Stan could see the boy in the empty spaces between the splatter somehow, his handiwork. It was pretty clear what had happened—Stan had heard the hollering from the place for months. Infernal things. And the cries for mercy, or something like it.

He had never intervened, figuring it wasn't his business. But this kid had. This visitor already in the wind. And Charlotte, she was somehow even farther away, gone as gone. Stan read between the lines and did the only thing he could do to try to make it right—he bit the kid out of the story he told the police altogether. He nodded toward Rebecca. "The big fella—a long time ago. He was different then. Very different. But we had occasion to cross paths once, at least in a sense. I might even have helped him a little." The old store owner sighed, pulled from his cigarette. "I honestly don't know anymore."

He kicked his toe at the stoop's painted concrete and took a drag. "Anyway, this spring, he comes back around and I know right who he is." He snapped the fingers of his free hand. "I mean, right away. He looks completely different and all, with the shaggy stuff, the crazy tattoos—twice as big—but exactly the same. I know it. And he sees I know it." Stan chuckled a chuckle that collapsed into another hoarse cough. "I figure he could have killed me right then and there with those tree-trunk arms." The man's eyes danced. "But he didn't. He just talked to me a spell as if he were a stranger, just a regular customer, not quite showing his cards, but not quite hiding them, either. You know, that way he had about him." Rebecca smiled, tucking her own memories behind her lips.

Stan shrugged. "I helped him where I could." He sighed. "I didn't help much."

Rebecca stared at him, soaking in every muttered word. Stan coughed once more, then grimaced. He took a last drag, stubbed the cigarette out on the railing, and stuck the butt in his pocket. "I'm rambling."

"No, you're not."

"I am, but that's okay. The point is," he said, "we weren't friends, exactly. I won't say that. But I think he trusted me." He nodded. "And I couldn't help but trust him. He could sense things. He knew I was winding down."

Stan, still leaning against the rail, regarded the back of his own hands, his hoary fingernails. "I was worrying about the store and what would happen with it and all, so he said when I was ready, he would take it off my hands. He said he would sublease from me."

Rebecca caught the shake in the hand he was studying. She also realized she was out on the stoop with him; she did not remember coming outside. She placed her hand over his.

"He laid out the terms and they were unjust—to *him*, of course. He had me *making* money by just closing up shop, letting him have the space."

"For what?"

Stan regarded her with a hint of a smile.

It dawned on her. "For a proper bookstore."

He nodded. "And now I'm ready. I'm tired. It's getting harder and harder for these old bones to get up each morning."

"But he's not here. He's gone." Rebecca's voice sounded sparse to her own ear. She knew there was more. There was always more. "What was he like?" she asked gently. "When you knew him before?"

"Oh, that." Stan sighed, trying to find words. "He was *young*. Too damn young to be mixed up in what he got mixed up in. A boy sent to do a man's job, I reckon—just like the boys we sent across those two big oceans to save us from the worst version of ourselves." He turned to Rebecca. "He was probably something like Sam was, once upon a time." He rapped his palm against the railing. "But sometimes the world gets its claws in you and turns you into whatever it will."

Neither said anything for a long while.

"Thing is"—Stan finally lit another cigarette, pressed the match, and stuck it in his pocket, getting back on track—"your friend already paid me a two-year advance." He looked at her, and then away, down the street. "The more I thought about it, the more I figured he'd want you to have a go at it." He jiggled the keys in his hand for Rebecca. She hesitated before reaching for them—then dangled them from her fingers, enthralled by how they caught the sun.

"What happens in two years?"

Stan shrugged. "It turns into a pumpkin? Hell if I know. But you'll figure it out." His cough was ragged, and he grimaced at some unseen pain in his chest. He winked without smiling.

Rebecca thanked him, offered him coffee inside, but he waved her off and nodded his farewell. She shut the door and placed the keys softly in her pocket.

The young widow climbed the stairs to the top floor. Ava labored in her adopted bedroom, folding paper into intricate shapes no one could untangle, except to understand that they held more grace in their creases than almost anything human hands could fashion.

Rebecca stepped into her own room and wrapped a sweater around her shoulders. She slid open the window and perched on the roof to inhale the cold, the naked gamble of the bloom yet to come. She held herself, watching her exhale mingle with the sky and disappear. Sometimes she came out here to feel him, to sense his presence beside her. But now she understood the bookbinder had never been a fixed creature; he was a conduit, a transistor, a river—the space between a prayer that bent life, changing its very course. He was a harvest of nightmares, a scavenge of tragedies, the murder that cleaned and christened all the little battlefields on which a place like Brookshire was built.

The trees were bare, and Rebecca could see for miles. Spring would soon return, and, with it, new life. The world would keep healing itself, the wronged would hold their sway. One book ends; another—*theirs*—begins.

ACKNOWLEDGMENTS

TK

ACKNOWLEDGMENTS

© Dan Bettinger

RYAN BURRUSS has enjoyed fiction bylines in *Prairie Schooner, The Carolina Quarterly, Whiskey Island Magazine,* and *New Orleans Review,* among many others. A native of the East Coast, Burruss now resides on Colorado's Front Range. He is a participating member of the Lighthouse Writers Workshop.